Perfect Love

A Reviewer Top Pick! I absolutely loved The Perfect Union. It is one of my favorite reads now. The characters in the story pull you in right from the beginning. The story pulls on the heartstrings... The storyline flowed seamlessly through everything. ~ *Night Owl Reviews*

4.5 out of 5!... Ms. Lane is a new author in my library, but you can bet I will be reading more of her work in the future. Don't hold back on getting "The Perfect Balance" if you are looking for a hot ménage to read because this one will definitely curl your toes. ~ *Whipped Cream*

PERFECT LOVE
Volume Three

The Perfect Union

The Perfect Balance

TRINA LANE

Perfect Love Volume Three
ISBN # 978-0-85715-431-6
©Copyright Trina Lane 2011
Cover Art by Lyn Taylor ©Copyright 2011
Interior text design by Claire Siemaszkiewicz
Total-E-Bound Publishing

Published in 2011 by Total-E-Bound Publishing, Think Tank, Ruston Way, Lincoln, LN6 7FL, United Kingdom.

THE PERFECT UNION

Dedication

To everyone who celebrates the magical land of
Shannon & To Mary Ellen this fantasy's for you.

Prologue

November 2006

Calleigh Wells was so glad the sun came out from behind the clouds as she walked down the street. Boston had been in a dreadfully rainy pattern over the past week. It had been cold but not enough to turn to snow. She lifted her head to the sky to soak up the burgeoning rays. Now, the temperature was low, but at least, the sun was shining.

She opened the door to *Bean Town*, her favourite coffee place, and stepped inside. The warm air from the heat flowed over her cheeks that tingled from the crisp air. There were four people ahead of her in line as she tried to decide if she wanted her standby hazelnut latte or if she wanted to be adventurous and try the caramel macchiato.

She felt a vibration against her side and opened her purse to see an incoming call on her iPhone. She didn't recognise the number, but it was a long distance area code.

"Hello?"

"Is this Mrs Wells?"

"May I ask who's calling?" She moved forward a step, glancing to the board and decided to be adventurous on another day. The hazelnut sounded good right then.

"This is Sergeant Cooper. I'm trying to locate Calleigh Wells, wife of Sergeant Kevin Wells."

"Oh God. No." Her heart stuttered, and she couldn't breathe. There was only one reason someone from the Armed Forces would be calling her.

"Mrs Wells, I regret to inform you that your husband had been injured in the line of duty. He is being transferred to Ramstein Air Force base in Germany."

She blindly reached out to keep herself from falling down. When she looked up, she had hold of the man's shirt in front of her. He turned around with a questioning look, but it immediately changed to concern.

"What happened? Is Kevin okay? What—"

"I'm not at liberty to discuss the event. If you wish, I'll put you in contact with his unit liaison. They will be able to make arrangements for you to fly to Germany. Do you have a pen and paper handy?"

"No...wait...please." She looked at the two men standing side by side in front of her. "Do you have a pen and paper I can borrow?"

The man with black hair held out a pen while the man with auburn hair grabbed a napkin off the counter beside them. Taking the items, she put the phone back up to her ear. "Okay, I'm ready." She wrote down the information and ended the call.

She couldn't seem to move. Her feet were cemented to the floor. She looked around aimlessly, but nothing was in focus. The colours blurred, and her vision swam. She felt herself being guided over to the side and found herself sitting in one of the chairs scattered around the room.

The dark-haired man knelt down in front of her. "Are you okay?" He looked up at his auburn-haired friend who had pulled the chair out and was resting his hands on her shoulders. Taking her cold hands between his, the first man rubbed. "Miss? Do we need to get you help?"

His deep voice cut through the haze in her mind. She looked down into a pair of bright sapphire blue eyes. "I need to go home."

"Okay. Did you drive here?"

She shook her head no. She tried to dial the number to her house, but her hands shook too badly. She held out her phone to the man in front of her. "Can you call? I can't get it to work. My mom can come get me. She has my babies."

He took the phone from her shaking hands, and handed it to his friend. "Tell you what? Why don't we make things easier on your mom? Conor and I will take you home. I'm Rick." He stopped the woman's head from shaking back and forth by putting a hand to her cheek. "We are completely safe. I promise you. You can talk to your mom the entire way there if you want." He helped her to stand and turned her around so she could see Conor behind her.

"Miss. I think I got the number ye wanted," Conor said, holding out the phone.

She took the phone from the tall man. Her vision was still blurring and all she could decipher were images of red hair and blue-green eyes. She noticed that he had some kind of soft lyrical accent. "Thank you."

Putting the phone up to her ear she heard her mom's voice.

"Mom?" she interrupted. "They called. Kevin's hurt." Tears started slipping down her cheeks. "I'm at *Bean Town*... No, I walked...These two men said they'll drive me home." She listened for another minute then held out the phone to the man with the black hair and blue eyes. "She wants to talk to you."

Rick took the phone from her hand. "Hello? Yes, ma'am. My name is Richard Connor. My friend and I were here at the shop when your daughter got the call. We'll be happy to bring her home. She's in no condition to be out on the streets by herself right now. I assure you we mean her no harm. Can you give me an address?" He listened then continued, "Okay we should have her there in about twenty-five minutes." He ended the call and gave back the phone.

Conor walked around to stand next to Rick. "Can ye tell us yer name, miss?"

"It's Calleigh. Calleigh Wells."

"Calleigh, I'm Rick Connor and this is Conor McGuire. Let's get you home to your family." He escorted her to the door Conor held open for them.

They walked half a block down and stopped in front of a dark sedan of some kind. The auburn-haired man opened the front passenger and assisted her into the seat. She sat in silence as the door was secured, habitually reaching for the seatbelt. She thought they seemed nice, and she was desperate enough to trust two strangers.

Rick looked over the top of the car at his best friend. "What in the hell just happened?"

Conor shrugged. "It doesn't sound good. I think somethin' might have happened te her husband or brah'der or somebody. Feck man, she said she had babies at home. I hope to hell 'tis not her husband."

"Yeah, me too. Let's get out of here. The mother said she lives in Mission Hill."

The two men climbed into the car. She sat silently for several minutes before realising it was pretty rude not to talk to her two rescuers. She could worry in a little bit. The sergeant on the phone said injured not dead. Kevin wasn't dead. It would all be okay. She figured her mom must have given the men directions to the house because they seemed to know where to go.

What are their names again? Rich? Rick? And the other one is Connor? Wait, I heard the name Connor twice, I'm sure of it. So who's who?

She turned to face the man driving, the one with black hair. "Excuse me, but maybe I didn't hear you right. You're both named Connor?" She swivelled around as the auburn-haired one in the backseat laughed.

"That is going to plague us 'til our deaths, man. His last name is Connor. With two 'n's, my first name is Conor with one. It's how we met. We were on the soccer team at B.C. First day of practice, coach called out 'Connor', and we both answered at the same time. We've been friends ever since."

"I went to B.C. too. Class of 2003."

"We graduated in 2000," Rick said. "So you said you have children at home?"

She smiled at the thought of her precious little babies. "Yes, I have twin boys. They're two months old." She figured she owed these two some explanation of her erratic behaviour. "Their father, my husband, is in Iraq. Army Reserves. The phone call was from a sergeant informing me that my husband's been injured, but that was all he could tell me. I sure he's fine...right? I mean if it was serious they would tell me or send someone or something wouldn't they?"

Rick watched the beautiful woman next to him. She was looking at him like he had all the answers, and damn, if he wished he didn't. Her honey-blonde hair was pulled back in a ponytail and fringe fell over her forehead to end right above her eyebrows. She had bright brown eyes that looked like gemstones under black sooty lashes. She was a tiny thing, too, probably just over five feet. The pain and uncertainty in her eyes made all his protective instincts kick in.

"I don't know what military protocol is, but it stands to reason that if things were dire they would do something other than call you on a cell phone."

He looked at Conor in the rear-view mirror to see if he knew but saw the man shrug. Conor's dad had been Air Force, stationed in England, before retiring. He wanted to keep Calleigh's hopes alive and distract her mind for right now. "What are your little boys' names?"

"Michael and Brandon. I guess the good thing is that if Kevin is coming home he'll be able to meet the boys. He was deployed eight months ago, so he's only seen them in pictures and over the internet." She smiled "They look so much like him. Both have his green eyes and his mouth, but so far they have my blonde hair."

"They sound like *dathuil ógánach*. I love little kids. Always wanted brothers an' sisters, but not te be."

"Conor, those words, they were beautiful sounding, but I don't understand. What did you say?"

"I said they sound like handsome youth. 'Tis Irish Gaelic. I grew up in Ireland."

"I noticed your accent earlier but couldn't quite place it."

Rick laughed. "That's because Con's a real mutt. Born in Ireland and lived with his Mom then spent summers in England with his Dad. He transferred to the States when he started college, so he's picked up a little American in the past few years. Most people only understand half of what he's talking about. If you get lost, just smile and nod. I do it all the time."

Conor kicked the back of his seat. He laid on the Irish brogue nice and thick, "Ye bloody arse. Stop acting de maggot. Total ballsch ye donna understan' me."

Rick looked over at Calleigh and saw her first genuine smile. It lit up her entire face. He rolled his eyes. "See told you."

Seconds later, they pulled up in front of a quintessential Boston brick rowhouse. The stone base had wrought iron rails leading up the steps, and flower boxes graced the bow windows.

"Wow. Very Nice."

"Yeah, we rent the first and second floors. I have a neighbour in the basement apartment. We got a deal on the place because the owners are army friends of Kevin, stationed overseas." She turned so she could see both men. "Please come in. I'll introduce you to my mom, and you can meet the boys if they're awake."

Rick opened the door and walked around to get Calleigh's, but Conor beat him to it. He looked up, and a woman in her early fifties was standing on the front steps. He guessed she was Calleigh's mom, since they looked like carbon copies of each other. He tensed when he took a closer look at the woman's face. There were tear tracks down her face. When they walked up the steps, the older woman pulled Calleigh into her arms and held tight.

They all walked inside, but Calleigh stopped dead when a man in uniform stood from the sofa and turned to face her. His face was grim as he held his hat under his arm.

"I'm very sorry, Mrs Wells. I regret to inform you that your husband Sergeant Kevin Wells —"

"I already received the call of his injury, Captain. What do I do now?"

"Ma'am, there was a miscommunication. Your husband was not injured. He was killed in action."

Rick and Conor both caught Calleigh as she fell into a heap. Sobs echoed through the room. Her cries of denial ripped into Rick's soul. His arm wrapped around her, holding her head to his chest. Conor's wrapped around her waist as the heaving shudders racked her small body. They'd only known her for a short hour, but she'd already wormed her way into his heart. Her clear love of her husband and little boys was a testament to her character. He vowed then and there to protect this woman and her children from that day forward. Looking into Conor's eyes, he knew the man felt the same.

Chapter One

Conor walked into Rick's office and saw that he was on the phone. He settled himself into one of the padded leather chairs, turning the small box in his hand over and over. Inside was their present to Calleigh. Tonight, they would celebrate her twenty-seventh birthday. More importantly though, tonight they would begin their quest to make her theirs. It had been three years since the death of her husband. For the first two, they had lived up to their silent vows of that horrible day. They'd become good friends to Calleigh and her family.

Helping her through the grief had been difficult, but they'd made a little family of their own with small traditions that helped move the days forward. His favourite was movie night. Every week, one of them would choose a movie, and after the boys were put to bed, they would pile on the living room sofa and watch with all the lights out and a huge bowl of buttery popcorn in their laps. Usually, Calleigh ended up with her head in one of their laps, sound asleep. He loved to stroke her silky hair or give her foot massages to soothe her after spending all day at her job at the hospital.

Last week, they celebrated Mikey and Bran's third birthday. The boys had gotten to choose the movie, and *Finding Nemo* had swum into the living room in full colour. They had been so excited when he and Rick had carried out a giant cake with all the characters from the movie printed on it.

His head jerked up as Rick hung up the phone and he watched him walk over to sit in the chair opposite him.

"Did you get it?" Rick asked.

He held up the small box. Opening the lid, he showed him the necklace they had designed for Calleigh. It was a three-stoned pendant, a bastnäsite with blue sapphire and aquamarine gems on either side.

Rick picked up the box and turned it from side to side, watching the light reflect off the coloured gemstones. "Think she'll see the significance?"

"If she doesn't, I'll be happy te point it out te her." Conor smiled.

He looked at Rick and could tell the man was nervous about the taking this next step. Conor had initially questioned the decision but could no longer deny his feelings for Calleigh. Over the past year, the dependable friendship had turned into something much deeper. He wanted the woman, like no other. Every time he and Rick brought someone home, he saw the resemblance to the sexy siren who filled their thoughts and made their bodies burn.

Whether they shared a woman or he picked up one on his own, she always had blonde hair and brown eyes but they never sparkled like Calleigh. At the end of the evening, he generally felt hollow, physically satisfied for the moment but never complete.

"I know yer nervous about changing things between us, but I canny fight it any longer. She's been casually talking about getting back out there more and more. I willna do this without ye, but I love her. Ye love her. We both adore those little boys, like they're our own. It's time we stop bringing home substitutes. It's time we made her ours."

"I know, I know. I want her as bad as you do." Rick ran his hand through his hair. "Fuck, every time in the last year we've had some nameless pickup between us, I've pictured her in our bed. I've even had to hold back crying out her name when I came a time or two."

Conor knew exactly what his best friend was talking about. He'd almost done the same, and more than once when their eyes had locked in that crucial moment, he'd known they'd both been thinking the same thing. He looked over at Rick's desk as his phone rang again. Jumping up, the man went to answer the summons.

"Rick Connor... Hey, Calleigh. Happy birthday, angel." He spun around in his chair catching Conor's eye. "Of course, we'll be there for dinner tonight. Six o'clock right?" He laughed. "The boys did what? I can just imagine... Sure we can talk about it... Okay, see you then." He hung up the phone. "Calleigh said the boys, with grandma's help, made her a huge birthday sign with their handprints painted on it. Unfortunately, the paint didn't get put away, and they decided it needed just a few more decorations. Only it happened to be lying on the sofa at the time."

Conor was laughing so hard he had to clutch his stomach. "Go on otta that!"

"I'm not kidding. You know you have to watch them twenty-four-seven." Rick was laughing, too. After several minutes, he stood and walked over to look out the window of his office. "She said something about wanting our advice at the very end. It sounded serious."

That instantly sobered Conor's mirth. "Feck. I hope nathin' is wrong with the boys."

"No. I don't think so. It sounded more like a personal problem. I hope to hell nobody is haranguing her. If they are, I'll put a stop to that real damn quick." He looked over his shoulder and saw Conor stand then come over next to him. He held out the box in his hand with the lid still open then put his hand on Rick's shoulder.

"I willna let anything happen to *Ár Ghrá*."

* * * *

When Rick opened the front door to Calleigh's house, he saw the big sign the boys had made for her. The little blue handprints were accessorised with swipes of green.

"Hello?" he called out.

Two little voices yelled out then, it sounded as if a herd of buffalo were running down the hallway. He turned to towards the commotion and was tackled by a pair of leg-latching spider monkeys. "Why, if it isn't the deadly duo."

He scooped up a boy in each arm. He looked at Brandon and said, "Mikey, did you tell your mommy happy birthday?" Peals of laughter rang over his ears, and Brandon pointed at his brother, shaking his head.

"I not Mikey."

"Are you sure you're not Mikey? I think you two are trying to trick us again."

Conor came over and took the real Mikey from Rick. "I know how te tell them apart." He lifted his hand high in the air in the shape of a claw. Wiggling his fingers on the way down, he made like he was going to tickle the little boy.

Mikey started laughing and squirming in Conor's arms. Brandon kept pointing at his brother and merriment danced in his dark green eyes.

"See works every time. Mikey is ticklish," Conor said.

Rick looked at Brandon. "I'm still not convinced. We may have a couple of doppelgangers on our hands. Let me try." He swooped in and started tickling his stomach. Brandon began squirming and laughing the same as his brother. "Well, it looks like we have two Mikeys on our hands."

Calleigh walked into the room. "What's going on in here? It sounds like a bunch of monkeys live in my house."

Rick put Brandon down at the same time Conor put down Mike. The two boys ran back down the hall to their playroom.

"No running," all three adults yelled.

Rick walked over to Calleigh. Gathering her close, he kissed her the on the temple. "Happy birthday, angel."

He still had Calleigh in his arms when Conor came up behind her.

Conor placed his hands on Calleigh's waist above Rick's arms and leaned down to her ear, "*Breithlá shona duit, muirnín.*" Then he kissed her temple on the opposite side Rick had.

Rick watched Calleigh's eyes close and felt a shiver travel down her body. It appeared to be from arousal not nerves. This was the first time they had purposefully put her between them. He smiled inwardly at her reaction. When she opened her eyes, he nearly gasped at the desire he saw for a split second before they changed back to their normal glow.

She turned from Rick's arms and faced Conor. "I love it when you speak Gaelic. Of course, for all I know, you're insulting me, but it sounds so pretty."

He effectively switched holds with Rick. "Never. I said 'Happy Birthday, sweetheart'. We have a gift for ye. Would ye like it now or after dinner?"

She peered down the hall. "I don't hear any crashes or yelling. I put on a cartoon for them shortly before you arrived so they're probably content for the moment. We'd better do it now, while they're distracted. Come with me into the kitchen, I have to stir the sauce."

As they walked down the hall, Rick peeked into the playroom. Both boys' heads turned, and they smiled but remained seated on the floor. He winked at them, and like little mirrors, they blinked both eyes back, obviously trying to imitate him. He chuckled then followed Calleigh and Conor into the kitchen. After Calleigh stirred the spaghetti sauce, he lifted her to sit on the counter.

"Rick! What if the boys come in? This is hardly setting a good example."

"They're fine, but if you insist." He lifted her back into his arms and sat down in a chair at the table, keeping her on his lap. "How's this?"

"Ye just wanted te carry her around." Conor said, pulling out the necklace box they'd tied a white ribbon to.

He shrugged unapologetically and pulled Calleigh a little closer. She took the box from Conor and gently pulled the bow loose. The hinge on the box snapped when she opened it, and he held his breath until he heard her gasp of delight.

"Oh wow! You guys, this is so beautiful." She looked down at the three coloured stones then back up into the smiling faces of her best friends. "It's us, right? The blue, brown and aqua?"

"See, I told ye she would figure it out," Conor said. He undid the clasp and attached it behind Calleigh's neck. "There. Looks perfect against ye skin."

Calleigh was going nuts being held by Rick, while Conor attached their gift. His fingers caressed her skin as he traced the chain down to the pendant. He was so close she could feel his breath puff against her neck. Rick's arm was around her waist, and every once in a while, his fingers would caress her side. This was new behaviour. Never before had the two men surrounded her like tonight. Their body heat and scent wrapped around her like a cocoon. She so wanted to close her eyes and swim in the forgotten sensations but knew the boys would soon be chanting for dinner. She linked her fingers with Rick's and moved his arm so she could stand.

Stepping away, she caught a look between her two best friends. They both had little smiles on their faces and each slightly nodded his head. She bent down to grab a large bowl in the cabinet by her feet and could have sworn she heard one of the men groan. She flipped off the switch on the stove and lifted the heavy pot of boiling water to drain the noodles.

She'd told Rick on the phone earlier that she wanted to talk to them about something. She had intended to tell them she'd accepted her first date since Kevin's death and wanted some advice on getting back into the dating scene.

The first year after Kevin had been killed, she had pretty much been in a daze. She'd been able to function and take care of the boys, but it seemed as if the only emotion she could express outside of being a mother in love with her rapidly growing and developing babies was pain.

The day Brandon and Mikey had taken their first steps, Rick and Conor had been there. All three of them had cheered and encouraged the tentative steps towards independence. That was day she'd woken up and found that the two men who had rescued her on the blackest of days were still there. Not only were they there, but she'd become dependant on their support. So many nights she'd cried in their arms only to find peace once the tears passed. Now, she found herself wanting more. She wanted to feel the pleasure of being a woman again. She wanted to feel a man's desire, and on the darkest of nights in the silence of her bedroom, she'd dreamed of the tangled limbs and sweat-slicked bodies of three.

Ménage wasn't foreign to her. When she and Kevin were in college, they had invited a third to their bed on a number of occasions. They had a circle of friends who were trustworthy and treated the experience with respect and honour. Everyone in the circle knew that the third was only a participant in the sex. It was understood that they would not interfere in the relationship of whomever they slept with.

Looking over her shoulder, she saw Rick and Conor speaking softly to each other. She couldn't hear what they were saying though. Their behaviours suggested a familiarity with having a woman between them, but she'd never heard anything about them sharing before. She knew they dated, hell they were both stunning specimens. Both men had kept the athletic bodies of their college soccer days. Neither bulged with muscle, but their bodies were hard, trim and defined.

It was a few months ago when she realised she was attracted to her two best friends bodies that she'd decided it was time to start dating again. She figured she would start out slow and see what happened. As much as she'd recognised her desire for Rick and Conor, she didn't want to risk losing them over her awakening hormones. Also, there was no way she would want to choose one over the other.

They were fixtures in the house on a weekly basis. The boys looked upon them as father figures, even if they didn't quite understand that yet. They always obeyed Rick and Conor as much as they did her. As much as three year olds obeyed anyone. Brandon and Mikey were always eager to show the men a prize drawing they had done that day, told them stories of their adventures together, recently they even started asking for an occasional bedtime story. Rick and Conor had been there for every milestone. They were even helping out with the potty training, as much as they could. They were parents in all ways except having an intimate relationship with her.

Now, she'd accepted the date with Miles from the hospital, where she was a nurse anaesthetist, because Rick and Conor were out of her league and off-limits in her mind. But what if they weren't? What if they wanted to take their relationship to the next level, and what if they wanted to do it together? Her pulse raced at the possibility, and she felt dampness between her legs that hadn't been there since before the boys were born.

* * * *

After dinner, Rick and Conor took the boys upstairs for baths and bed while she cleaned the kitchen. It was so nice on the nights they came over. The four extra hands made things run a lot smoother. She saw them come down the stairs about forty-five minutes later.

"They tucked in?" she asked.

Rick nodded. "Yeah, go on up and give them a kiss goodnight."

She did, and when she came back down, they were both sprawled on the sofa watching news. Taking her customary place between them she sighed and relaxed into the deep cushions. There was still a little damp spot from cleaning the paint earlier, but she didn't let it bother her. She was absently playing with her new necklace when Conor put his arm around her shoulder and Rick placed his large hand on her thigh. She absorbed the heat from their touch, and her muscles relaxed even further.

"So, is either of you working on any cool new games?"

They both worked in the sports division for a major video game company. Rick was a game designer, and Conor a software engineer. Frequently, they told her about new games they were working on, and she'd even gotten pre-releases for the Xbox they'd bought last year. She had laughed so hard when they said it was for the boys with such innocent expressions on their faces. At the time, Mike and Bran were only two. They had promptly set up the system and played for hours that night.

Rick turned to look at Calleigh. "I just got the proposal for a new game. It's going to feature famous Olympic athletes and their sports. It'll be released at the same time the Vancouver games begin." He picked up the remote and turned off the television. "Calleigh, you said you needed to talk to us about something tonight. What's going on?"

She worried her bottom lip between her teeth for a moment. She figured she couldn't blow off this conversation, but it might be interesting to see their reaction to her announcement after the chemistry she'd sensed earlier. She stood and turned so both men were in her line of vision then sat on the large ottoman in front of the sofa.

"Well, the thing is, I have a date." She waited to see their reactions. Both men's eyes darkened, but their outward expression didn't change.

Conor's hands fisted into the sofa but he said, "I'm glad yer getting back out there. Is it someone we know?"

She shook her head. "His name is Miles, and he works at the hospital with me. He's a radiology technician. I met him in the cafeteria a few weeks back. We've eaten together a few times. He's a nice enough guy."

Rick sat up straight and rested his elbows on his knees as he leant in closer to Calleigh. "Angel, I'm glad you feel you're ready to start seeing people again, but what do you know about this guy? Have you talked to any other staff who know him? What if he's a complete jerk? What if he only wants to get in your pants?"

"*Muirnín.* I donna want ye doin' a line with some paddy who just wants te shag ye."

Calleigh could tell despite their calm faces that they were upset. Conor's accent always got a little thicker and his colloquialisms more frequent when he was riled up. Rick generally got stoic, and right now his face appeared as if it were a wooden mask.

She knelt on the floor and took hold of a hand from each man. "I appreciate your concern. I even love you for it. But it's time for me to try this again. Don't worry so much. The two of you have spoiled me so rotten over the past three years that I have impossibly high standards. I'm sure we'll just go to dinner, and I'll be home before eleven o'clock."

She leant in and kissed each one of them on the cheek, letting the little caress linger a tad longer than usual. "I know this is a lot to ask, especially given your misgivings, but would you be willing to watch Mike and Brandon that night?"

"Of course, we will. I plan on being here when he drops you off to make sure he behaves like a gentleman," Rick said, looking over to see Conor nodding in agreement.

Chapter Two

Rick paced the living room waiting for Calleigh to get home from her date. He was too keyed up to watch the late night news. Thinking about that other man touching her, holding her hand, or God forbid, kissing her was driving him nuts. He heard Conor come down the stairs after checking on the boys, again. He could tell the man was just as much of a wreck. As Rick turned to face the front windows, he saw a car pull into the open spot in front of the house. Conor must have caught the direction of his gaze because he sprinted past him to peer out the curtain.

"Conor get away from there!" Rick said, walking that same direction.

"Go an' shoite." He pulled the curtain back just enough to peak around the corner. "*Damnú ort Bualadh craicinn Bastún!*"

Rick stomped over to the window to stand behind Conor. "I have no idea what you just said, but it didn't sound pleasant. Let me see."

"The fecking gobshite is practically ridin' her!"

"Move, Con!" he hissed, looking out the window. "Goddamn fucking bastard is practically giving her a tonsillectomy!"

"That's what I said," Conor murmured.

"Yeah but nobody can ever understand you when you get riled up."

He pulled Conor away from the window before Calleigh caught sight of them. Moments later, he heard the key turn in the lock at the front door. He hoped like hell she wasn't going to bring what's his name inside. He might have a hard time restraining himself from punching the man.

"Conor, get your ass over here."

He flipped on the news and pretended to watch. Conor flopped down on the sofa just before the latched opened. Rick heard Calleigh say goodnight and released the breath he'd been holding. A few seconds later, she was sitting between then where she belonged, but she definitely did not have the look of a woman who'd been blissfully kissed. He did a little happy dance inside.

"How was the date?" Conor asked.

Calleigh heaved out a breath. "It was okay. He was polite. Made all the right conversation. Even kissed me, but it felt like his tongue was a tentacle. No spark. Nothing. Maybe, I'm not ready after all."

She looked disillusioned. Rick knew there was fire in her. It just needed the right kind of spark to ignite. He looked at Conor and saw him nod. He turned Calleigh's head towards him. His hand tunnelled in the silky mass of her honey-blonde hair. Her amber-brown eyes darkened as he leaned his head forward. He touched their lips together for the first time. She tasted vaguely of cherry as he flicked his tongue out to taste. Her mouth opened, and he slipped inside, moaning at his first real taste of Calleigh.

Her mouth was sweet and welcoming. He turned his head to get a better angle and sealed them together tighter. His mouth moved on hers in a slow rhythm. Her tongue came out to play with his, and slipped into his mouth as his retreated from hers. He was instantly hard and aching. His hand moved lower to caress her breast only to find Conor's already there. He pulled back and looked into her passion-dazed eyes. Conor's hand cupped her cheek and turned her head towards him.

Rick watched their lips meet and fuse. Their mouths moved together in perfect synchronicity. Rick cupped her breast in his hand and moulded the full mound. Her nipple was erect and stabbing his palm. He slid his other hand up underneath the hem of her dress, touching and caressing the soft skin of her inner thigh. Her legs opened a little, and he angled his fingers up to touch the edge of her panties. He skimmed the fabric, but didn't reach underneath. Little moans and cries were swallowed by Conor's mouth as he continued to lick and devour Calleigh's plush lips.

It always made him hot to see Conor pleasuring the woman they'd chosen to bring home, but knowing that this was Calleigh, their Calleigh, made the experience ten times more erotic. Conor loved to kiss. It was one of his favourite things to do to a woman. He would kiss them all over for hours, while Rick was more of a touch person. He loved the feel of a woman between them, touching her skin and slipping his fingers inside her body. His cock inside the snug, wet heat of a pussy or hot, velvet clasp of an ass could melt his brains with pleasure. Add Conor into the mix, filling the woman's mouth or other available opening, and the melt actually exploded. Hearing the screams of her pleasure echo in the room, feeling the rake of her nails down his back was the best feeling in the world. They would have that with Calleigh, and they would have that soon.

Calleigh pulled back from Conor and looked over at Rick on the other side of her. "Holy shit," she whispered. "Umm, guys? What was that all about?"

"Did ye get yer fireworks, *Ár Ghra*?" Conor asked

"More like a nuclear explosion. But I don't understand. Since when…"

"Since when have we wanted you, angel, or since when have we shared our women?"

Calleigh couldn't decide which question she wanted answered more. She was still in shock that not only did she now have proof they wanted her, but that they did in fact intend to share her. The lust coursing through her system made thinking clearly difficult. She had sensed they could be powerfully addictive as individuals, but when they combined their powers of seduction, there was no equation in her past.

"Why don't we start with since when have you wanted me?"

Rick looked at Conor. "You want to take this one?"

Conor took Calleigh's hand between his. "The desire te make ye mine began a little over a year ago. 'Til then I was happy being yer friend, yer confidant, yer shoulder te cry on. I canny mind a specific day it changed. I started lookin' forward te yer smiles. The little touches ye gave made me shiver. I started dreaming of ye at night. Since Rick and I live together, he called me on it. When I admitted the truth, he told me he felt the same." He looked over at Rick, "Yer turn."

"We started sharing women back in college. We were roommates for four years. The first time was junior year. I had a girl over and Conor came back to the room after studying at the library. He didn't realise I had company and walked in on us. The girl at the time was rather…we'll say…free with her affections. She invited Conor to join us. It was then that we recognised the power of giving a woman pleasure together. Working together to provide a woman with pleasure unequalled to her previous experience not only enhances her satisfaction but ours as well."

"Do you always share?" Calleigh wanted to know if they were convenient thirds for the other or if this was a lifestyle they intended to adopt permanently.

"Not every time. We do date on our own, but more often than not, we're together. Five years ago, we decided that ultimately we are happier this way. There is something about giving a woman such incredible pleasure that she screams with need. Watching her eyes wild and desperate for the release only the two of us can give. I enjoy watching Conor fuck with his drive and determination to bring a woman the most intense orgasm possible. I enjoy sinking myself deep inside a tight pussy or ass, knowing that he is there stimulating her body in ways I couldn't do in that moment of time." Rick laced his fingers together with Calleigh's. "We want to live as a triad with one special woman permanently. We want a marriage of three. As friends, Conor and I balance each other out. I can't imagine living my life without his presence surrounding me every day. I need him. I love him. The only problem is we're both men and not gay or even bisexual. We need to complete the triangle. We need a woman to love, to cherish, to protect." He cupped her cheek and placed a soft kiss on her lips. "We need you, angel. You and the boys have become our world. We want to marry you, be fathers to Mike and Brandon and have future children with you. We also want to see you fly from passion, see you burn from our touch, feel your soft skin between us and know the ecstasy of being inside your body."

Rick's dark description of their passion for ménages had her lightheaded. She wanted to feel them surround her as he'd described. The two men she thought she knew inside and out had hidden depths. She knew they each had a tremendous capacity to love, and they worked seamlessly as a team, but seeing them in this new light was a revelation. They wanted to build a life with one woman as their wife. As the mother of their children. While she had experience of three in the bedroom, she didn't know how a marriage of three would work. How would they interact on a daily basis? How would relationships between the individuals grow? When they fought would sides be drawn?

"I can see that we've thrown lashing of information at ye the-nite, *muirnín*. The necklace we gave ye was our way of telling ye our desires te build a new relationship between the three of us. We want ye te take the next few days te think about it. We know ye have te think of the boys, not only yer wants an' needs. I think ye know that we already love Mike an' Brandon as our own. We don't want to replace their owl lad, but we do want te fill the hole his death left in all ye lives."

Calleigh stood and walked them to the front door. She stopped before opening it and leaned into Conor. Reaching up on her toes, she wrapped her arms around his neck and lifted her head for another kiss. His hands dropped to her waist to steady her as his mouth descended. His lips were warm and firm, his tongue soft as it entered her mouth. Instantly, her skin heated and her blood rushed through her veins. The man certainly knew how to kiss. Little flicks kept her searching for deeper contact. His lips pulled away only to tease and torment before capturing hers again. His hands practically spanned her waist. She imagined being lifted by his strong arms and wrapping her legs around his lean waist as he thrust inside her. His hard body against hers felt so good. It felt right. His erection pushed against her stomach. The hard column of flesh was long and thick. He wrapped his arms around her back and pulled her into his body so no space separated them.

Another pair of hands lifted her hair away from her neck and lips touched her neck. The delicate caress countered Conor's now deeply thrusting tongue. Rick's tongue traced her pulse and nipped behind her ear.

They surrounded her with their heat. The intensity of their touches was overpowering. Rick's deep voice whispered seductive words in her ear and planted images of the three of them entwined on her bed, arms and legs touching, lips meeting, bodies sliding and thrusting together until they were consumed by their passions. His hands came around and cupped her breasts, his thumbs and fingers pulled on her elongated nipples. The stiff peaks were aching and needy. She tilted her head away from Conor's and leant back on Rick's chest.

His head descended and their lips met in a backwards kiss, softly melting together. Conor kissed her bare shoulders and down the neckline of her dress. His tongue flicked out to catch the inner swell of her breasts, and she moaned into Rick's mouth. Conor's deep voice now seductively murmured in her ear. His lyrical accent thick with passion. She didn't understand the Gaelic, but if his reverent tone was any indication, the words were filled with desire and longing. Finally, the three separated, each of them breathing hard. The two men couldn't hide the arousal that matched hers. She wanted them to finish what they started, but her brain knew there were things to consider before that irrevocable step was taken.

She turned and placed her hand on Rick's cheek stretching up for one last chaste kiss. "Goodnight, Rick."

He pulled her into a tight hug. "Goodnight, angel."

She did the same to Conor. "Goodnight, Conor."

He pulled Calleigh into his arms, "*Oíche mhaith, muirnín.* Goodnight, sweetheart."

As she closed the door, she thought if they did continue in this relationship, she was definitely going to have to learn some Gaelic. She walked up the stairs and peeked in on the boys. She smiled at the way their limbs were flayed out all over their twin-sized beds. She, Rick and Conor had made a big production of going to the 'big boy' bed store on the boys' third birthday. Mike and Brandon had picked out their own bedding. They were going through a space phase right now, so their room was filled with glow in the dark stars and the bed set they picked out had stitched rockets, comets, planets and stars. They'd also picked out their own potty seats, and so far things seemed to be working out well for the most part. She leaned over and gave each of her sons a kiss on the forehead and smelled the baby shampoo from their baths Rick and Conor had given them earlier.

Closing the door, she made her way into her bedroom. Stripping off her dress, she decided a warm bath would soothe her before going to bed. She padded her way next door to the bathroom in her robe. Drawing the bath, she added salts and oil beads. The hot water surrounding her was luxuriant. The moisture washed away the stress of the day. Her muscles went lax, and she closed her eyes.

Immediately, images of aroused Rick and Conor floated behind her eyelids. Rick's eyes darkened from their normal bright sapphire blue to navy. With his lighter colouring, slashes of colour popped up on Conor's cheekbones. She had felt the press of both men's erections against her body, the pressure of the thick bulges against her stomach melting her core. She still felt their hands on her breasts and their fingers pulling at her nipples.

Lifting her hands out of the water, she cupped her swollen mounds and milked the turgid peaks. Spikes of pleasure streamed down her body to her clit, and she moaned. Reaching down, she slipped the fingers of one hand between the plump folds of her pussy. Using her first finger, she circled her clit. She rolled the little bundle of nerves a few times before flicking it with her nail. Sliding down, she gathered some moisture from her channel to bring it back up. The water lapping around her body made her feel as if she were suspended in a bubble of pleasure. Her finger continued to circle her clit, while her other hand started to pinch the nipple she been previously playing with. The slight sting quickly morphed from pain to pleasure. She dipped her fingers inside her cunt. Wetness coated her fingers and the soft plush tissues gripped tight around her. It had been a long time since she had anything more than a couple of fingers inside her.

How would it feel to be stretched around Rick's or Conor's thick cocks? The burn as they entered her unused muscles, the long columns of flesh reaching deep inside her? Her fingers pumped but were too small to reach the depths she really needed. Pulling out she concentrated on her clit. It was Rick's head between her legs. His tongue lashing at the protrusion, sucking it between his lips and occasionally scraping his teeth across it. Her fingers tried to mimic the sensations by circling around and pushing down, flicking her nail on the underside. She felt her orgasm closing in.

Sticking the first finger of her other hand back inside her pussy, she coated it with moisture then reached below to circle the small rosette of her back opening. She imagined it was Conor stimulating the tight opening and moaned his name. She slipped it inside up to the second knuckle then placed a thumb at the dripping centre of her core. Any second now she was going to come. She pushed both fingers as deep as they would go and pinched them together to rub on the thin membrane separating the two spaces.

Her body erupted as she cried out their names.

Chapter Three

It had been three days since they informed Calleigh of their desires. Rick was anxious to get to the house after work to see how she was processing things. He was sure she would have some questions for them. After shutting down his laptop, he locked up his office to meet Conor in the lobby of their building. When he got there, the man was already pacing.

"What took ye so long?"

"Con, it's only five after. Settle down, okay. I'm sure things are fine. You saw how she responded to us the other night. If she has any misgiving, I'm sure it'll be about the boys, and I don't see that as insurmountable."

"You're right. I'm sorry. Let's just go." He walked out the lobby doors and turned towards the T station nearby.

Twenty minutes later, they were at Calleigh's front door. Rick opened the portal and stuck his head inside. "Hello?"

He heard Calleigh's voice from the kitchen, telling them to come back. He and Conor walked through the living room and into the bright, friendly space. Calleigh was lifting freshly-baked chocolate chip cookies off a baking sheet. They were his favourites, and he was determined to steal one.

"Angel, you didn't have to bake me cookies." He reached over and tried to snag one but got his hand slapped with the spatula.

"Hands off, cookie monster." She looked over her shoulder with a smile.

He looked over his shoulder to see Conor snickering. "What are you laughing at, you mick?"

"Ye, pouting like a babby because ye canny have a cookie. Fer bleedin' sake the boys are better behaved than ye."

With a saucy smile, Calleigh picked up an oatmeal raisin, Conor's favourite, and sauntered over, holding it out to him.

"Are you hungry, Conor?"

He smiled. "I've a mouth on me." He accepted the treat and moaned at the first bite.

"Hey! Why does he get one, and I don't?"

"Because you get this…"

Calleigh wrapped her hand around his neck. She lifted up on her toes, and he met her head halfway. Their lips met, and his insides soared.

She was theirs!

Cupping his hands underneath her ass, he lifted her and swung around the kitchen in circles. Calleigh's legs wrapped around his waist, and he held her close to him, not wanting to break their connection. She felt so good. Her small body held in his arms, her soft curves pressed against his chest.

He opened his eyes to see Conor's riveted on the sight of them. Their blue-green colour was bright and the telltale slashes of colour across his cheeks gave away his desire. Rick set her down on Conor's lap at the kitchen table, so he could get his acceptance kiss. Their mouths met, Conor's hand holding the back of Calleigh's neck to keep her close. Calleigh's arms coiled around Conor's neck, holding him tight. Watching them kiss, Rick's cock hardened even more. Their heads finally lifted.

"Does this mean what I hope it does?" Rick asked.

"Yes, I want to be yours. I know there are some logistical things to work out, and I don't know exactly how a marriage of three works. My only experience with ménage was when Kevin would invite a third to our bed on occasion, but I've never tried to have a full relationship with more than two."

Rick swallowed at Calleigh's confession. He had no idea that she'd experienced ménage before. "You and Kevin used to…"

She adjusted her position on Conor's lap, turning so she could lean against his chest and face Rick. "Sometimes. Back when we were in college. For the most part, I know what I'm getting into, and I can honestly say, I can't think of two men I want more."

Rick looked over Calleigh's head at Conor who seemed just as shocked as he was, but then a huge smile lit up his face and Rick found himself mirroring it. Their woman was full of wonderful surprises. He had to admit a slight disappointment at not being the ones to introduce her to the intensity of a ménage, but on the other hand, having experience meant that she would know whatever explosive feelings occurred were a product of the three of them, not the newness of the situation.

He stalked her from across the room. Her words setting him on fire. He was harder than a spike and wanted nothing more than sink inside her hot body. "God almighty, Calleigh. I need you. I want to feel you between us. I want to hear your screams of pleasure. I want to sink so deep inside we can't tell where I stop and you begin. When are the boys being dropped off?"

She was breathing rapidly and wiggled against Conor's crotch. "Not enough time tonight for the full five courses, but I think we can do an appetiser."

"*Muirnín*, yer gonna kill me with that sweet mouth." Conor held her tight and kissed her deeply.

Rick knelt in front of Calleigh and Conor. He undid the drawstring of her scrubs from the hospital. Conor lifted her by the waist while Rick pulled down the pants and her underwear, revealing the smooth silky skin of her mound. She had a small strip of hair, but most of the area was bare. He saw moisture slick and dewy coating the lips, and his mouth watered for a taste. Conor lifted her shirt to bare her breasts. His fingers rasped and pulled at her nipples. Rick leant in and flicked his tongue around and across the peaks. They were large and plush, the areolas encompassing several inches of her full breasts. Calleigh's head leant back against Conor's chest, but her eyes opened to watch Rick. Her eyes were dazed. Rick knew they were limited on time but had every intention of Calleigh experiencing the full amount of pleasure due.

He separated her legs, and Conor reached down to hold them open. Rick circled her navel with his tongue several times. His teeth nipped at the sensitive flesh then soothed with slow licks. He put his nose to her belly and breathed warm moist air on the skin as he dragged it down to the top of her pussy. He placed little kisses all along the outer edges. His hands glided up from her knees until they reached the top.

"You're wet, Calleigh. I'm going to taste this lovely cream."

He used his thumbs to spread open her swollen lips. He stroked through the moist folds, and her taste exploded over his tongue. The sweet musky flavour was nectar in his mouth. He alternated long and firm upward strokes with dips inside the clasping heat of her core.

"Oh God, Rick. It's been so long. Please don't stop." She started to pant.

He felt the muscles clench around his tongue and knew she was close. He looked up to see Conor's eyes burning at the sight of Rick's mouth fastened to Calleigh. His hands had released her legs and were pinching and rolling her nipples again, stimulating the sensitive peaks. Calleigh's sweet little cries for more echoed in the kitchen. She bucked her hips up, searching for greater connection.

"Don't worry, angel. I won't stop until you're screaming for us."

Rick slid two fingers inside her in one smooth thrust. The fiery heat scorched his skin, and the tight muscles clenched around the digits. She spasmed around his fingers, every ripple of her cunt embracing him. She was overwhelming tight. He wondered if she's had anything inside her since before her husband had passed.

Gasping cries poured from her throat as she arched, legs tightening, back bowing against Conor's chest. The cream of her response soaked Rick's fingers. He leant down, closed his lips over her clit and sucked hard while thrusting deep inside and massaging the hypersensitive nerves. He heard her gasp, felt her muscles lock down and a surge of warmth spilled into his hand as she climaxed.

Calleigh's eyes slowly opened as Conor eased her down from the explosive orgasm. She wanted to be fucked. She needed it now. Rick and Conor had awakened her body, and now, it demanded the feel of a hard cock pushing deep. The orgasm Rick had given her had been fantastic, best in a long time, but she wanted to be filled. Rick, on his knees at her feet, had opened his trousers and was slowly stroking his cock. The long thick stalk was red and dripping with desire. She wanted a taste. She wanted to feel the thickness slide deep down her throat.

She slid out of Conor's lap and landed on her hands and knees in front of him. Her head hung limp poised over the crown of his cock, her long hair falling around to create a curtain. She panted over the top as Rick continued drag his fist up and down. One of his hands came up to rest on top of her head, and he guided her down in obvious invitation. Her tongue came out and licked across the top, catching the drop of pre-cum oozing from his wide slit.

"Oh angel. I'll give you one hundred years to stop that."

She opened her mouth to take the first several inches inside. Her tongue swirled around the crown as she pulled up, working the head with her lips. Rick's hands threaded through her hair and pulled gently at the strands. She heard the sound of a chair being forcibly pushed across the hardwood floor and the heat of Conor's body was behind her.

Seconds later, she felt a pressure at her opening. He seemed huge and hot. Conor slowly pushed his way inside her channel. The head of his cock stretching the narrow space. It burned a little but felt so damn good. Exciting.

She pushed back, demanding more. She wanted all of him. He was hot and hard, and she could barely stand the teasing. He stopped when the first couple of inches were inside her, and they both paused.

Her head was imprisoned in Rick's hands. What were they waiting for? She needed them. She needed to be taken. She was desperate feel both their bodies fill hers. She tried to look up, but Rick kept her head imprisoned between his large hands. She couldn't use her hands on him because they were holding her up. Trying to incite them to move she whipped her tongue all around the head of his cock. It filled her mouth completely. She didn't know if she would be able to take the whole thing but would damn well try her best.

Suddenly, as if on a timer, they both moved forward and filled her body at the same time. Her scream and their moans of pleasure mingled together. Rick's cock was deep and thick in her mouth, and Conor's length was deep inside her.

"*Naofa damnú air! Go mboga mé!*"

"English, Conor. You want us to understand you, speak English. That's it, baby. Take me deep. All the way to your throat." He hissed as she moved further down and swallowed.

"Holy shite! I have te move!" Conor pulled back and thrust inside in one long smooth stroke. "Goddamn, Rick, you've never felt anythin' like this. Her cream is so hot an' wet, it feels like movin' through liquid silk."

They moved in practiced rhythm. At first, one would pull out of her as the other pushed in. Then they both filled her at the same time. Over and over. She shook with arousal. Rick was driving his cock deep into her mouth. She tried to swallow whenever it reached the back, wanting to give him the most stimulation possible. Conor was fucking her in long, deep thrusts. A smooth slide into her body, followed by the rough retreat. The pace increased. Her brain shut down, and she was along for the mind-bending ride on a wave a pleasure. She vaguely remembered similar sensations from a time long ago, but nothing compared to the feel of Rick and Conor inside her.

Her body countered their rhythm, moving down on Rick's cock as Conor pulled back and pushing into

Conor's thrusts as she sucked up Rick's length. She heard moans and cries and realised they came from her.

Her body was on the brink of combustion. Her blood was on fire as it raced through her veins. She clenched around Conor and heard him cry out behind her. Rick was thrusting fast and deep into her throat. They were taking her. Her men were claiming their mate, and it was the most incredible thing she had ever experienced. God help her when one of them filled her ass and the other her pussy. She might not survive.

"*Chan fhad'thuige*! I'm gonna come. *Tá mé chomh mór sin i ngrá leat.* Ye burn me alive ye feel so perfect surroundin' me."

"I'm almost there, angel. I'm going to come deep in your throat. Conor's going to shoot, too. I can tell he's close. He only starts speaking Gaelic when his brain has been melted."

Her orgasm was building deep in her womb. The contractions spread outward to consume her entire body. Both men thrust faster, and a few moments later, she felt the first shots of Rick's cum hit her tongue. She let the salty taste linger before swallowing everything he had. The feel of him releasing inside her triggered a second more explosive climax in her. She screamed around him as her body convulsed. Conor thrust hard then held still deep inside her. She felt him swell even thicker, and his cock pulsed. His fingers gripped her hips as he yelled out her name.

Rick pulled out of her mouth, and her arms collapsed. She ended up in a heap on the floor with Conor still buried deep inside, his arms braced out so he didn't crush her. He rolled to his side and slowly pulled free from her body. Rick promptly scooped her up into his arms and

Conor scooted into her back and held her tight between them.

"I think that was the single best moment of my life," Rick whispered.

Her body still trembled with aftershocks. As much as she wanted to curl up with her men, she knew the boys would be home soon.

"We have to get up."

Twin groans echoed above her head.

"I know I don't want to either, but Bran and Mikey will be home soon."

They helped her to stand and slip her scrub bottoms back on. Both men righted their trousers.

She went upstairs to change into jeans and a soft sweater. The material sliding over her still sensitive skin caused goose bumps to rise on her arms. As she left her bedroom, she heard the front door open and twin exclamations of excitement. She smiled at the joyful sound of her boys. They really did love Rick and Conor.

* * * *

Two days later, the three of them went out on their first official date. Conor and Rick took Calleigh to dinner at nice restaurant then they wanted to take her somewhere exciting and fun. It had been a long time since the three of them had gone out to play. A popular piano bar in Back Bay seemed like the perfect idea. They were seated at the table, and immediately, the duelling pianos kicked up. Playing classic rock songs as the whole place sang along. An electric fiddle player even got on stage and played an amazing rendition of *Devil Went Down to Georgia*. Strobe lights flashed as he stood on top of the pianos and wailed on the strings. After an hour or so, Conor brought drinks back from the bar for all three of them. He leaned over to Rick and spoke directly into his ear the noise was so loud. "I have gotta little surprise for our girl."

Rick looked over and saw a very self-satisfied look on Conor's face. "What did you do?"

"Don't worry ye will love it. Ye mind senior year when we went te that place in Allston?"

"Yeah...oh shit...you didn't!" He started laughing so hard Calleigh looked over at them.

A few minutes later, they had finished their drinks, and the players announced into the microphone for Calleigh Wells to come up on stage. She looked over at Conor with wide shocked eyes. He stood and taking her hand in his led her up to the dais. He lifted her by the waist so she stood front and centre. Her cheeks were bright pink, and she kept looking around at the audience who were cheering and clapping. She looked over to the man at the piano.

The piano player winked at Calleigh. "Ladies and gentlemen. We have a very special request this evening. Normally, we would not allow this, but Conor here was very persuasive." He held up the fan of cash in his hand. "It seems that Calleigh here is on a date with these two men." He pointed to Rick and Conor.

Conor took a bow as the crowd yelled and wolf whistles floated through the air.

"They would like to serenade their sweetheart."

He accepted a microphone for both him and Rick as they got up on stage. The pianos began to play *Stay the Night* by Benjamin Orr. He had the better voice of the two so he sang most of the lyrics and Rick joined in during the chorus. They circled Calleigh and took turns dancing with her. At the end of the song, they were all flushed from excitement. The entire crowd was on their feet and cheering and yelling for Calleigh to kiss them. Conor saw her eyes flash the moment she decided to go for it. He handed his microphone to Rick and swooped Calleigh into a dip then kissing her deeply. The place erupted in thunderous applause. After only a few moments, he lifted her up and Rick swung her around to plant one firmly. Calleigh gave him no quarter and speared her fingers though his hair to deepen the lip lock. Whistles and cheers rang in Conor's ears. Figuring they'd given everyone enough of a show, he swung Calleigh into his arms and headed for the exit.

They raced out into the street, and he led them between two buildings. He leant back against the brick and pulled Calleigh into his arms, kissing her with everything in him. Their tongues duelled, and his hands grasped her ass to pull their hips together. Rick lifted his hands and pressed against her back, adding more pressure as their bodies rubbed together. Ricks hands were at Calleigh's hips, and every time, he ground against her ass, Calleigh was pushed into his erection. The sensation set Conor on fire.

Calleigh burned with excitement. Conor's lips devoured hers. One hand massaged her breast while the other tunnelled in her hair, pulling on the strands just enough to create extra stimulation. Conor separated their mouths and dropped little kisses down one side of her neck. Rick's hands were at her hips, and his mouth latched onto the other side her neck. His teeth lightly scraped down the column and his tongue soothed the sting away. He nibbled on her ear.

"When we get home, we're going to fuck you all night long. I can't wait to drive my cock deep inside you. Conor has felt the sweet clasp of your pussy, but now it's my turn. I bet you're dripping for us, aren't you, angel? You can't wait to feel both of us filling you front and back, can you? Conor deep inside your ass, while I fill that creamy tight cunt."

She panted as she tried to clench her legs together to ease some of the tension radiating through her.

"I canny wait te feel yer delectable little arse grip me, *muirnín*. You're gonna feel like hot velvet as I fill ye."

She was desperate to get her men inside her as soon as possible. "Home... Now, before I take you both right here," she growled.

Conor pushed away from the wall. Both men took one of her hands, and they raced to Rick's car.

Twenty minutes later, they pulled in front of her house. They walked upstairs into her bedroom. Rick lit the candles she kept scattered around to give a little light without turning on the bright overhead. They stripped her slowly, each of them removing an article of clothing, one after the other. Conor picked her up and placed her in the centre of the bed then stepped back. He and Rick began to strip. Each unbuttoned their shirts, chests and firm stomachs showing through the separated edges of fabric. When they removed the material, their muscles flexed, and she caught herself licking her lips. They flicked off their shoes and removed their socks. Hands reached for belts and the closures of their trousers. They were teasing her with the slow strip show. Buttons flicked open, and zippers slowly lowered. They stood there without moving. Her eyes were locked on their groins, wanting to see those bulges that pressed against the fabric. Her chest heaved, and her eyes burned, but she refused to look away. Finally, they dropped their pants and boxer-briefs and stood in all their nude glory. She moaned. Both were amazingly hard. She raised her eyes to theirs and saw the mirroring burn in bright sapphire and aquamarine.

Rick sat on the bed and slid over to lie on his side in front of her. When their naked bodies touched for the first time twin groans left their throats. Rick lifted one of her legs over his hip. Conor walked to the other side of the bed and reclined behind her. His hand trailed down her back, and his fingers slide inside her pussy. His lips landed on her shoulder. His long fingers reached up inside her with devastating effects. She felt moisture seeping onto her thighs, and her clit pulsed. His fingers rasped through her folds and rubbed on the swollen tissues. They separated to loosen her for Rick's invasion. The stretch sent fiery impulses through her entire body.

"Conor, yes." She closed her eyes and leaned her head back against him.

"Open your eyes, angel. I want to see that pretty amber darken."

Rick leant forward and captured her lips, intensely thrusting his tongue into the depths, claiming her. He worked his way down her neck. Sucking and licking across her collar bone. He reached the well of her throat and took a tiny nip. Moving further down, he finally reached her breasts. They were swollen and heavy, aching for his touch or his mouth. He placed little kisses around the edges, moving closer to the tight tips. She kept trying to guide his mouth to her nipples, but Conor wrapped an arm around her middle and held her still.

She cried out in complaint when his fingers left her body. A second later, she felt the thick coolness of lubrication touch the skin on her backside. Conor's fingers massaged it into the skin around her hole. He pushed at the opening, and she felt the tip of one finger enter. Rick had finally reached the centre of her breast, and as though they timed the event, he pulled her nipple into his hot mouth at the same time Conor pushed his finger deep into her ass. She cried out and pushed back against Conor. His other hand reached around her and pinched the nipple not being worked over by his friend. Rick had moved his hand down and thrust two fingers inside her pussy. Their hands and lips were everywhere. There wasn't a part of her untouched, and it sent her soaring for the skies.

Rick's fingers were working in and out of her pussy, as Conor added a second finger behind her. She felt a pinch and burn but revelled in the both the pressure and fullness. Rick raised his head to once again latch their lips together. His tongue thrust deep, mimicking his fingers below. She felt an orgasm closing in, the edge of the cliff only moments away.

"'Tis gran' *muirnín*. Let go. We'll catch ye."

Suddenly, she jumped, tumbling head over heels into rapturous oblivion. When she landed, Rick had rolled onto his back and lifted her over on top of him. He had her poised over the head of his cock and slowly lowered her down the length. He was a bit wider than Conor, and the pressure was incredible. Even with the foreplay, she felt stretched tight around him.

"Oh God, wait. Too much. I don't—"

"It's okay, angel. We're going to do this slow. I know you can do this. Just breathe for a few seconds. You are so damn tight. Conor was right. I've never felt anything like you surrounding me." He didn't move any further until her channel softened around him. "There you go, baby. I can feel you loosening up, good girl."

He started to thrust in and out. His hands were on her hips moving her up and down his cock. He filled her to overflowing, but it felt so damn good. He felt different inside her than Conor had. Wider, fuller. His crown was fatter, and it pushed through her burning muscles with tenderness but determination. She felt herself getting slicker, and Rick was moving easier inside her. She cried out.

Conor pressed a hand to Calleigh's back to lower her down against Rick's chest. Rick reached back and held her lush round cheeks open for him. Conor placed little kisses along her neck and back. Holding on the base of his erection he fit the head of his cock against her back entrance. He slowly worked his way in. He could tell she was trying to relax her muscles.

"*Tá sin ar fheabhas.*"

Was that his voice so deep and throaty? The only words he could use to express how exquisite Calleigh felt were from his homeland. He finally made it all the way in, and the welcoming heat surrounded him. They paused for a moment to let her get used to the sensation. His brain had officially left the building as he was reduced to a being of pure sensation, demanding more of the incredible pressure and heat of Calleigh's body. He gave a little nod of his head, and Rick pulled back. Conor groaned at the feel of Rick's cock rubbing against his, separated only by the thin barrier. After a few strokes, he began to move, he and Rick counterthrusting into Calleigh's body. Her cries echoed around them as they loved her together. He loved this woman so much. He cherished her. He burned for her.

Calleigh felt so full. She was bombarded by sensations. Rick and Conor slid in and out of her body in perfect rhythm. Nothing in her prior experiences prepared her for this. Rick kissed her for long minutes as Conor leant forward to suck on her neck. All three of them panted. Their breathing was laboured and various moans filled the room as they sped towards completion. The intensity of the emotions being thrown around the room was overwhelming. Both Rick and Conor gasped and whispered love words in her ear. Rick was the first to cry out. His hips bucked up in rapid fire, his hands clenching her hips, and his head thrown back. Conor sped up immediately, fucking her deeper and harder. All of a sudden, all three of them stiffened. Multiple screams rent the air. She felt their cocks pulse as they filled her with their release, and pure mind-blowing pleasure washed over her. Lights exploded behind her eyes, and she felt as if she were floating.

Calleigh was awakened by the feel of a wash cloth wiping between her legs and across her bottom. She was lying on her side between the two men. Rick threw the cloth on the floor and lay back down on the bed. Conor rubbed his hands up and down her arms and across her back. He kept placing little kisses on her neck and shoulders. Rick searched her face.

"Are you okay, angel?"

She nodded her head. "It's never been like that before. Thank you."

"For us either, *Ár Ghrá*. Let us rest now, an' we can love some more later."

Chapter Four

Calleigh rolled over in bed as the sun slanted through the sheers on the windows. As she stretched she felt a wonderful ache in muscles that hadn't been used in a long time. Her arms encountered a large hard body, and she turned her head to see Conor still asleep next to her. Rolling to her side she watched him in slumber. His auburn hair looked more red in the sunlight. His fair skin showed traces of morning beard, and she wondered what it would feel like rubbing against her skin. She reached up to trace the slash of his eyebrows and ran a fingertip across his lips. She gasped as he opened his mouth and sucked her finger inside. The pull made her womb flutter, and she looked up to see those blue-green eyes twinkling in amusement. Pulling her finger out of his mouth, she leant forward to kiss him.

"Good morning."

"Mornin' *muirnín*." He reached out and pulled Calleigh into his body.

Since Kevin had died, waking up with a man in her bed had become unfamiliar, but with Conor it felt right. The only person missing was Rick. She had missed the closeness and lethargy of waking with a lover after a night of passion. She burrowed deeper in the blankets and snuggled in closer to the warmth of Conor's body, tangling their legs beneath the sheets. His eyes had closed again, and he caressed her hair as she laid her head on his chest.

"Conor?"

"Hmm?"

"What are you saying when you speak Gaelic? Not everything, but I'd like to know a couple of the words."

He rolled to his back and took Calleigh with him to lie on top of him. She propped her chin on her hands and looked up at him. "*Muirnín* means sweetheart or beloved." He kissed her forehead. "*Mo ghrá* means my love." He tucked a loose strand of hair behind her ear. "*Ár ghrá* means *our* love." He frowned. "Does it bother you when I speak the language of Shannon? That ye canny understand? I'll stop. Sometimes 'tis not something I do on purpose, it just comes out."

"No. It doesn't bother me. It's a beautiful language and sounds so damn sexy when your deep voice whispers in my ear. I was just curious."

"Usually the unconscious stuff only happens if I'm troilled, really full aff, or when you've melted me brain with pleasure." He reached under her arms and lifted her up so he could kiss her.

Conor's lips were soft with morning sleepiness. His tongue slipped inside and lazily rubbed against hers. The soft licks were just as devastating as the more demanding intense kisses. Her insides were turning to liquid as she floated in dreamy desire. Suddenly, her world spun as

Conor rolled. She landed on her back, and he levered himself over her. Her legs automatically separated to cradle his hips. The kiss deepened. Conor's hands threaded through her hair and held their lips together. His pelvis thrust against her centre, and she tilted her hips. She felt the moisture gathering between her legs and raised her legs to wrap around his back. One push and Conor was inside her. The invasion was heavenly. She cried out into his mouth. There was no pausing this time. He plunged deep in rhythmic strokes, hips canting forward and back as she lifted into the thrusts.

Conor separated from Calleigh's sweet lips. The feel of her warm wet channel gripping him so snugly was heaven. She was laid out for him like a feast, and he wanted to gorge himself on every delectable inch of her skin. He braced himself on his forearms and dipped his head to her round full, soft breasts. He traced his tongue over the thin line of a blue vein. He circled the areola and slipped the turgid plush nipple between his lips and suckled.

The boys had nursed here. Someday, his child would nurse here. He wanted to see that. A small head nestled to her chest, the scent of baby powder in the air. A child created in love by the three of them. It wouldn't matter if he or Rick were the biological father. They had known and fully accepted that when they'd decided they wanted to embrace this lifestyle permanently.

He slowly increased the pace of his thrusts. Calleigh's muscles were rippling down the length of his cock. He was so damn hard he knew this wouldn't last long but was determined to give her the best orgasm possible. Her legs were gripped tight around his back and her heels dug into his arse. Her hips lifted into each one of his thrusts. He reached up and snatched a pillow from the top of the bed and rising to his knees, lifted her to place it beneath her. The change in angle allowed him to reach the deepest parts of her. Calleigh's high cry signalled that she enjoyed the new feeling.

"I love being inside ye, *muirnín*. Yer made fer Rick and I te love. Yer body an' heart belong te us now." He groaned above her. "I have held back fer the past year, but no more. I canny keep me hands aff ye any longer."

"I want you, Conor. I want to feel you touch me. I want to feel Rick touch me. I need you both so much. I'd forgotten how it feels to be loved, but I've never been loved as I have by the two of you... Harder Conor... Please... Please... I need all of you. Don't hold back."

He looked down to see Calleigh's eyes wide open. The black of her pupils nearly occluding the bright amber colour. Her words sent fire screaming through his body. Lust and love were boiling inside him, totally uncontrollable. He lifted her legs over his shoulders and braced one arm beside her head. He fucked her unmercifully as she asked. Stroking faster, harder and deeper into her welcoming body. She panted, little cries and moans escaping from her throat in time to his thrusts. Their eyes locked, her entire body trembled and her cry echoed around the room. Sharp contractions squeezed around him — oh God! He came and came and came from the very depths of his soul as she milked him dry.

Conor rolled to his side. They were both breathing hard and her pulse was racing. This was the first time she had been with just one of her men. They were a devastating pair, but this morning felt special between her and Conor. As if they'd cemented their bond as a couple outside what the three of them had shared the night before. She heard footsteps at the door and looked up to see Rick enter the room. He stepped up to the side of the bed and bent over to kiss her.

"Good morning, angel. Conor gives good wake up calls, doesn't he?"

It occurred to her that Rick might be jealous about her having sex with Conor while he wasn't there. She frowned. "Are you upset we did that without you?"

"No, baby. I'm incredibly turned on, but never upset. You'll have private time with Conor, just as the two of us will have time together." He sat down next to her and smoothed back her hair that had flown all over the place with their exertions. "We love sharing you, but more importantly we love you individually. It's only natural for you to want to spend time with Conor apart from me and spend time with me apart from him. That's one of the things that will naturally develop between the three of us. Now, how about we all go downstairs and get some breakfast. You lazy bones have slept the morning away."

She smiled, feeling much better. Rick stood and reached a hand down to help her out of bed. When she placed her hand in his, he pulled hard and, dipping his shoulder into her stomach, lifted her over his shoulder. She squealed, and he slapped her on the ass. She heard Conor laughing behind them.

"Put me down, you Neanderthal," she said, laughing.

"Never. I've hunted and gathered all morning to provide food for my woman. Now, I will carry you to my cave."

"But I'm naked!" she yelled as Rick walked out the door and headed for the stairs.

Conor heard Rick ask why that was a problem as his footsteps descended the staircase. He looked over to the seat by the window and saw that Rick had brought up his jeans from the car. They had packed a change of clothes anticipating a sleepover. He slipped them on, foregoing a shirt for the moment. He picked up Calleigh's robe from the same chair and followed the pair down into the kitchen.

* * * *

Rick carried Calleigh into the kitchen and perched her on the counter top. She wrapped her legs around his hips and locked her arms around his back. He couldn't look away from the bright amber of her eyes. He'd never been privileged to see her all flushed and rumpled in the morning and wanted to enjoy the view. Her hair was a cloud of honey blonde around her shoulders, her lips swollen and moist from Conor's kisses. Her nipples, already tight, begged for his touch, and he saw evidence of her and Conor's loving on her pussy lips and thighs.

"You are so beautiful," he said reverently.

He craved another taste of her and reached around the back of her neck to pull her into a kiss. The first touch of their lips was soft, but not hesitant. He opened his lips and flicked his tongue out, a fleeting touch to her upper lip. The edges of their lips barely touched for several counts, breathing softly into each other's mouths. He prolonged the anticipation letting it build inside them. Waiting for that moment when they felt as if they'd explode if they didn't get the touch they craved. Finally, he couldn't take it any longer, and he bent to her and locked their lips together. His tongue plunged into her mouth, no longer soft and teasing. He wanted to consume Calleigh's essence. Her kiss grabbed something inside him, and he dragged her closer, his hands threaded through that soft halo of hair holding her in place. He groaned as her tongue twisted with his. When they finally lifted their heads, he looked over to the doorway and saw Conor watching them. He was holding out Calleigh's robe. Rick lifted her off the countertop so she could walk over, and Conor assisted her into the thin, silky covering, which to his satisfaction conformed to each of her lush curves.

They were sitting down to the table when the front door opened, and the thundering of little feet echoed through the house and two little voices called out for mommy in stereo. Rick looked up at Conor and Calleigh. He hadn't been expecting the boys to see them in morning dishevel. Conor had a slight deer in headlight look about him, but Calleigh seemed calm as a cucumber. He decided to go with the flow.

A little body was barrelling towards him when he snaked out an arm, caught the energised bundle and lifted it onto his lap. He looked and figured out that he had Brandon.

"What's up, speedy?"

"Hi, Wick. Why you hewa?"

"We stayed with your mommy last night. Did you munchkins have breakfast at grandma's?"

"Uh-huh. We have teareos."

Brandon was playing with his bare chest. The little boy had probably never seen a grown man without his shirt. His little fingers twisted in Rick's chest hair. Granted he didn't have much, but it still stung. He lifted the little hands, blew a raspberry on the palms and was rewarded with childish giggles.

"Where you shoot? Why you have hair?" Brandon was pointing at his chest.

"My shirt is upstairs, and I have hair because I'm an adult. When you grow up you'll look like me."

He looked up to see Mikey in Conor's arms, having a similar conversation. Calleigh was eating her breakfast with a smile on her face. Brandon wiggled wanting off his lap, so Rick set him down and he ran over to Calleigh to give her a hug. Mikey did the same then came over to him.

He lifted Mikey up onto his lap. "Did you have fun at grandma's last night?"

"Uh-huh. We play game."

"You did? What game did you play?"

"Hide and seek. We win."

Mikey had a huge smile on his face and bounced on his lap in excitement. Rick raised his hand to give Mikey a high-five. They had taught the boys that little game not too long ago, and they got a kick out of it.

"They most certainly did. Mikey and Brandon are very good hiders. You better watch out, Calleigh. They might be better than you were at their age."

Rick turned his head when Calleigh's mom entered the kitchen. "Good morning, Lilly."

She raised an eyebrow at the state of undress present in the kitchen. "Good morning Rick, Conor. Did the three of you have fun last night?"

"Yes, thank you for watching the boys. We wanted to treat Calleigh to a night out on the town."

"Then I'm glad you all had fun. Calleigh, dear, can I speak to you for a moment." She turned and walked out to the living room.

Calleigh knew that look from her mother. She asked Rick and Conor to entertain the boys for a few minutes then stood to follow her mother. When she entered the living room, her mom was sitting in the large chair by the bow windows.

"Yes?"

"Calleigh, is there something you want to tell me?"

She saw her mom's eyes twinkle and a little smug smile on her lips. Calleigh huffed and rolled her eyes back at her. "Don't act so obtuse. I think it's fairly obvious. Are you going to give us any trouble?"

She frowned. "Honey, don't get defensive. I just want you and the boys to be happy and healthy. The three of you have had enough heartache for this lifetime. If this is what you all want then your father and I will support you. Plus, I've seen the sparks flying around this house for the past year from all sides. Yours may have been a little more subtle, but still there. I know those men love you, and God knows, they adore Michael and Brandon. I'm glad you're ready for a new relationship. Should I bother asking if it's only one of them or both?" She smiled.

Calleigh threw her hands up in the air. "Oh for Pete's sake, mom. Fine." She started pacing around the living room. "Conor, Rick and I have decided to take our relationship to the next level. You can call us a unit or triad or whatever. We want to eventually have a marriage of three." She stopped and looked over at her mother who sat calmly in the chair. "Their words, not mine."

"Are you sure you know what you're getting yourself into?"

"Does anyone when they start a new relationship? If you're asking whether or not I'm comfortable being with both of them, the answer is yes. I love them. They have been my best friends, and now, they're my lovers. And since you are being so nosy, you may as well know that not all aspects of this relationship are foreign to me." She let that sink in and saw the moment her mom comprehended her meaning. "I can see you understand."

Lilly leant forward in the chair. "You and Kevin?"

Calleigh sat on the sofa, making sure her robe stayed closed. "Yes, on occasion. Back in college. So you see, I know this type of situation would not shock or disgust him were he still here."

Lilly stood and joined her daughter on the sofa. She turned her body to face Calleigh. "Have you thought about how Kevin's mom will react when she finds out? It may be more of a shock to her than to me and your father. We're neither naïve nor averse to alternative lifestyles, but she is much more conservative."

"I know that, but she really only sees the boys once or twice a year. It may take some getting used to, but I don't think she would let it affect her relationship with Kevin's children." She reached over and gave her mom a hug. "Thanks, mom. I love you."

"I love you, too, sweetie. Now why don't I go gather up the boys and get some toys out, and you and your men can go upstairs and finishing dressing. Although I must say, I greatly appreciated the view when I walked into the kitchen earlier."

"Mother!"

She patted Calleigh's cheek. "I'm happily married dear, not dead."

Chapter Five

Calleigh was bone tired. She'd taken a double shift at the hospital because one of the other nurses had called in sick. One of the major advantages of having Rick and Conor at home now was having them available for the boys should a situation like this come up. Before she'd have had to call her mom, and she hated disrupting her parents' evenings together even though they claimed they never minded.

She reached into her locker to grab her purse and coat. A nor'easter had arrived yesterday, and the temperatures were near record lows and predicted to stay that way for the next several days. It was November again. Hard to believe but true. She sat on the bench beside the lockers as tears pooled in her eyes. The anniversary of Kevin's death was coming up, and it was always a tough day for her. Kevin's mom was coming up once again. They always went and visited Kevin as a family. He was laid to rest in Massachusetts National Cemetery. She would like it if

Rick and Conor came with them this year but had yet to ask them.

Rick and Conor were subletting their condo and had moved in a month ago. The boys loved having them around and so far didn't even seem to question their presence in the house every day. They questioned everything else around them but seem to accept Rick and Conor's presence with no problem. All her men had formed a boys' only club, which she found hilarious. Every night, Rick or Conor would take them upstairs for baths then both men would go in to read a story before bedtime. When club time was over, she would come in and say goodnight. Rick and Conor's willingness to immerse themselves in fatherhood was amazing. Not to mention a perk on her end.

She and Kevin had been married for three years, and he had been sent on his first deployment to Iraq after only six months. He was gone a year. When he'd returned she got pregnant with the boys, and he was recalled when she was five months pregnant. She fully supported her husband's choice to join the service, but she would be lying if she said she hadn't been lonely while he was gone. Having Rick and Conor come home every night was a new and still exciting experience. Sleeping in their arms was heavenly, and the sex was beyond anything she could have imagined. Whether the three of them were together or she was spending time with them individually, it was always intense, always hot, and always better than the time before.

"Calleigh? You okay, hon?"

She jumped at the voice. "Jeez, Carla, you scared me. Sorry, I was drifting. Just finished a double, and my mind started to wander."

Carla smiled. "I know that feeling. Do you need a lift home? You usually take the T, don't you?"

"Normally, yes, but Rick is going to pick me up this morning."

"Good, I'm glad you won't be by yourself, walking around half asleep. Well, I'm off. Gotta get the kids off to school."

Calleigh waved goodbye as Carla ran out of the locker room. She had introduced Conor and Rick to Carla and her husband a couple of weeks ago. They both had been surprised but had accepted their relationship with little trouble. This so far seemed to be the consensus of all their friends. Carla was her only close friend, and all of Rick and Conor's had known of their lifestyle beforehand. They had gotten a few looks when they'd gone out, but for the most part, people didn't say much.

She looked at the clock and saw that it was 7:15 a.m. Rick would be there soon, so she closed up her locker and headed for the entry doors.

She groaned as she stood inside the doors and saw Miles walking towards her from the parking lot. The man had been making a nuisance of himself since that one date they'd had almost two months ago. It seemed as if he were always the person she had to talk to in radiology no matter what time of day, and he always tried to drag out their conversation. Every time they passed in the hall he would touch her. Nothing threatening but always annoying. A hand on a shoulder or he would even grab her hand and hold it tightly when she tried to pull back. He left little notes on her locker, and he frequently would be standing at the employee's entrance and walk with her to the T, even though he lived on the other side of town. She'd started eating lunch at a different time so they wouldn't cross paths any longer.

She hadn't said anything to Conor or Rick because she knew how protective they were, and they really, really hated Miles. It was almost funny. If his name was ever mentioned, they would get scowls on their faces, and she would hear the words 'wanker' and 'gobshite' under their breaths.

He was almost to the doors now, and Calleigh turned her back trying to be less noticeable. Unfortunately, it didn't work.

"Hey, Cal! I thought you were off today."

She reluctantly turned around to face him. "I am. I just came off a double."

"Oh wow, you must be beat. Can I give you a lift? I'm a little early. I don't start for another half hour. I was just planning on getting a cup of coffee. Do you want to grab one with me?"

She saw Rick's car pull into the parking lot and breathed a sigh of relief. "No, thank you, Miles. My boyfriend just pulled in. He's taking me home."

She wasn't prepared when Miles moved so quickly. Grabbing her upper arm and squeezing, he pushed her back against the wall.

"What the hell do you think you're doing? Let go of me!"

"What do you mean 'boyfriend'? What about us?"

"Let go, you're hurting me, Miles." She tried to wrench her arm away from his grasp, but he held tighter, and she winced. "There *is* no us, Miles. We went on one date two months ago."

"We had chemistry, Cal. You can't deny it. I know you felt it when I kissed you." He loosened his grip on her arm and reached up to caress the side of her face.

Calleigh turned her head away from his touch, but his fingers clasped her chin, and he turned it back.

"All I remember feeling was apathy."

"Apathy, huh? Well, maybe I ought to remind how good it was between us."

Miles was holding her head in a tight grip, and she watched him angle for another kiss, but when his lips were about to touch, a large arm wrapped around his neck.

"I wouldn't do that if I were you. Let go of her. Now!"

She looked up to see Rick. He was furious, the sapphires of his eyes practically glowing. Miles' hand released her head and she angled away from the wall to stand beside Rick.

Rick let go of Miles and gave him a little push so his back was to the wall. "Just what in the hell did you think you were doing? Is that the way you treat women?"

"Who the hell are you? This is none of your business. I was trying to have a private moment with my girl here."

Rick snorted. "I know for a fact that she is in no way, shape or form *your girl*. In fact, I can guarantee that she's *my girl*. I know this because I live with her."

Miles looked over at Calleigh. "You slut! You go from being the ice queen of the hospital to shacking up with some guy in two months?"

Calleigh was pissed. How dare this little twerp first accost her and then turn belligerent when she turned him down? She was so glad in retrospect that she hadn't continued to date Miles. She had no need for a Jekyll and Hyde character in her or the boys' lives.

"Actually I'm living with two men. Rick here and Conor whom I'm sure would love the honour of meeting you. The two of them are worth more to me than any number of you. Stay away from me, Miles. Stop calling my department, stop leaving notes on my locker and stop hanging around the doors when I leave. I have no problem alerting the administration if you harass me any further after today."

"You try it and I'll call Social Services. I bet they would love to know that a single woman is fucking two different men in the same house as her young impressionable sons. You never know, if they're both fucking you maybe they're even fucking each other. I'm a conscientious citizen. It would only be right for me to alert them that young children are living with sexual deviants."

A couple of people, either coming on shift or leaving, were standing there watching the scene. She didn't want to perpetuate anything further so she turned her back and walked out to Rick's waiting car.

They sat in silence as Rick drove down Commonwealth Avenue. Calleigh saw that his knuckles were white, he was gripping the steering wheel so hard. She couldn't tell if he was mad at her or the situation, so she figured it would be best to wait until he started the inevitable conversation. Nothing had been said as they pulled up to the house. Rick turned off the ignition but remained in the driver's seat.

He took a deep breath and let it out. "Let's go inside. Conor called Lilly and she's coming to pick up Mike and Brandon so you can get some sleep. Before you argue, she volunteered to pick them up last night, but we told her the boys would stay with us overnight and she could have them today. Then you, me and Conor can sit down and talk. I didn't want to start any discussion of this nature without him."

She nodded her head and climbed out of the car. She reached the front door and was surprised to see that her hand shook a little when she reached for the handle. Rick must have seen it too because he put his hand on top of hers and gave it a little squeeze. The trembling stopped. It was amazing what one of their little touches could do.

She opened the door and walked inside.

* * * *

Rick was beyond incensed. He'd seen red when he'd spotted that Miles character holding Calleigh to the wall and trying to force himself on her. The sliding glass doors almost hadn't open fast enough as he'd raced towards them. When his arm had locked around that son-of-a-bitch's throat, he'd wanted to squeeze the life out of him. These intense reactions were not normal for him, and it made him feel very off balanced.

From what Calleigh had mentioned, it sounded as if this guy had been bothering her since their date months ago. Rick didn't understand why she would keep something like that from him and Conor. It was their job to protect her. He had taken a vow. And those things Miles had said at the end just made it worse. But to threaten Calleigh like that was inexcusable.

Rick had used the drive home to try to calm his emotions a little so he wouldn't fly off the handle when they sat down as a family to talk about it. Seeing Calleigh's hand shake as she'd reached for the knob had sent a knife through his heart. He was mad, wanted to be mad but he did not want Calleigh to fear that he would take his anger out on her. After they had their talk, he would feed her some breakfast then put her to bed. He knew she had to be exhausted, and having to deal with this crap after working a double shift was not good for her.

He stepped into the kitchen and picked up the phone to call work. He told them that both he and Conor would not be in today, citing a family emergency. His boss knew their living situation and didn't question why both he and Conor would be absent. When he walked back into the living room, Conor was walking down the hallway tying his necktie. He looked up and stopped in the middle of the treads.

"What's wrong?"

"I called the office. We're not going in today. We need to have a family discussion."

He stopped in front of Rick. "Where's Calleigh? What happened?"

"That SOB Miles has been hassling her at the hospital. When I pulled up, he had her fucking pinned to the wall and was trying to kiss her." He spun around and started pacing in the living room. "The little fucker even threatened to call Social Services on her for living with us."

"I'm gonna kill that feckin' little gobshite!" He ripped off his tie and threw it over the back of the sofa. "Where's *Ár ghrá*? Is she gran'?"

"She's fine. She's saying good morning to the boys before Lilly comes to pick them up." He smiled when he remembered how Calleigh had stood up to the little fucker before they'd left.

"What are ye smilin' fer?"

"Calleigh gave no quarter. Once I got her free of his clutches, she lit into him. Our sweetheart has gumption if not the physical strength to defend herself."

"Bleedin' mess. If he had hurt her…"

"I know… I know."

Rick heard footsteps on the stairs and saw Calleigh come down with Mike and Brandon in tow. Both boys had rather hangdog expressions on their faces. He schooled his features so the boys wouldn't see any distress. Conor walked over and squatted at eye level.

"Are ye *gasurs* ready for a day with *mamó*?"

They both shook their heads.

"We want mommy," Brandon said.

"I know, *mo greine*. Your ma had te work all night, and she's real knackered. She's goin' te take a nap, and when ye get home later, ye can play."

"Will you be here, Conna?" Mike asked

"Yes, *mo gealachí*. Rick and I will be here when you get home."

The boys still didn't quite understand that the men lived there now, even though they saw them all the time. They'd yet to come into their bedroom at night or see either Rick or Conor kissing their mom. He heard the doorbell ring and went to let in Lilly.

She scooped up the boys and gave Calleigh a kiss on the cheek. "Good morning." She saw that neither man was fully dressed for work. "Aren't you two going in to the office?"

"Not just yet, Lilly. We need te have a family discussion first," Conor said.

"Is that what they call it these days?" She looked at her daughter and saw the dark circles under her eyes. "Calleigh, as your mother, I'm ordering you after your family discussion to go to bed, for *sleeping* purposes only."

Calleigh laughed. "I promise, mom. I don't think anything else is even possible at this point." She gave each boy one last kiss and saw them out the door. She turned to face Rick and Conor. "Okay. Let's get this done. Then you can go to work, and I can go to bed." She walked over and flopped down on the sofa.

Rick and Conor walked over and sat on the large ottoman in front of the sofa. Calleigh looked so tired. Her normally bright complexion was dull, her hair was tied up in a messy knot and her limbs looked disjointed. Rick hated to cause her further stress, but this was important.

"Calleigh, why didn't you tell us that Miles has been hassling you?" Rick asked.

"He wasn't doing anything threatening. He was being an annoyance, but nothing I couldn't handle. He'd never done anything aggressive like this morning. If he had, I promise I would have told you."

"Well thank God for that, but I still wish you would have said something. I know you're used to doing things for yourself, but you're not alone anymore. We're here for you, angel. We were your best friends long before we became your lovers. I don't want you to think that part of our relationship has changed."

Conor moved over to the sofa and placed his hand on Calleigh's cheek. "*Murinín*, if he's been blaggardin' ye in any way I want ye to tell me. I want te stop it before ye get hurt. The thought of that fecking gobshite's hands on ye is twisting me up inside. We love ye."

"I love you both, too. I'm sorry. I really didn't consciously keep it from you. Miles is all bluster. It's become widely known in the last month that he has a severe inferiority complex. I had no idea what he was really like when I accepted that date."

Rick joined them on the sofa on Calleigh's other side. "Angel, what about the threats he made before we left. Do you have any concerns?"

"No. I know I'm in the right at work, and the Social Services stuff is just ridiculous. We all know that there is nothing detrimental to the boys occurring in this house. Worst case scenario, he calls and someone comes out for an interview. We explain the situation and let them see with their own eyes."

He stood and held out his hand. When Calleigh placed hers on his palm, he lifted her up and gave her a soft chaste kiss. He rested his forehead against hers for a moment. "I love you, angel. Let's not do this again. My nerves can't take it." He smiled down at her.

Conor stood and pulled Calleigh into the circle of his arms. He gave her soft kiss. "Let's get ye upstairs and in bed. How does a nice warm bath sound?"

"Heavenly. I'll draw one after you leave."

"No, *murinín*. We're on the hop today." He took her hand and led her upstairs.

Chapter Six

While Conor was drawing Calleigh a bath, Rick went into the bedroom and pulled the blankets back. He found some scented oil in the nightstand and drew the curtains over the windows to dampen the light in the room. They had a small stereo tucked onto a bookshelf in the corner, and he put on one of Conor's Moya Brennan CDs. The soothing instrumentals and harmonies of Celtic music always relaxed Rick. It was funny that he'd never really appreciated his Irish heritage until Conor had come along. Now, he embraced it more than anyone else in the family. He looked up as Conor stepped into the room.

"Very nice. Yer thinking massage?" He stepped over and turned the volume down a little on the stereo.

Rick arranged the pillows on the bed to suit their needs. "Yeah. Thought it would be nice after the bath you drew. She's so exhausted she might fall asleep, but that's okay."

"I'll go see if she's ready te get out of the bath."

While Conor went to get Calleigh, Rick changed from work clothes into some comfortable lounging pants. He sat on the bed and waited for them to return. Conor carried Calleigh into the room and set her next to him. She was wrapped in a towel.

She looked around the room. "What's all this?"

Rick lifted the edge of the towel away. "We're going to give you a massage then let you get some sleep." He slid her down so she was lying flat and rolled her onto her stomach. "Close your eyes, and let us take care of you."

He put some oil on his hands and rubbed them together. He handed the bottle over to Conor, who'd also changed. He started on the upper part of her back, while Conor focused on her feet. It must have felt good because she let out a low groan.

Rick's and Conor's hands were magic. They smoothed the oil into her skin, and the scent of vanilla filled the air. Fingers dug into tense muscles, and the last of the tension from her double shift and encounter with Miles floated away. Rick slowly moved down her back while Conor stayed on her feet, his thumbs digging into her arches.

"That feels so good."

Rick's lips brushed against the back of her neck. The soft caress caused a tingle between her legs. She always went nuts when they kissed her neck. Conor's hands had moved up her calves and now massaged the top of her legs. His thumbs slid between her thighs. She spread her legs to give him more room. Time after time, his fingers grazed over her folds but did not advance. He placed kisses all over her bottom and dipped his tongue into her crease.

"Oh please."

"Please what, *muirnín*?"

Calleigh squirmed trying to get Conor's fingers to enter her. "Please touch me."

"We are touching you, angel," Rick whispered into her ear. One of his hands slid down her back and joined Conor's between her legs. He parted the folds, allowing only the very tip of his finger between them.

"I need more. I need all of you."

She wanted her men inside her. Their heat surrounding her, their hard bodies securing her between them. She cried out when two fingers entered her and realised that both men had a finger inside her. Together, they pushed forward and rubbed against her inner walls. Soon, it wasn't enough. She was pushing back against them. A hand landed on her back, stilling her movements. Then she was turned onto her side.

Conor was in front of her, his aquamarine eyes bright and his cheeks slashed with colour. He lifted one of her legs over his hip and pushed his cock in deep. It felt so good, and she tilted her hips forward to allow better penetration. His slow rhythmic thrusts filled her body and grasped his shoulders for balance. She wanted his kiss and leant forward to connect their mouths. His tongue slid inside her mouth. Hers wrapped around it and played. She heard him groan, and he drove his hips in with a hard thrust.

Warmth pressed against her back, and she felt Rick's fingers, slick with lubrication, brush over her anus. He placed warm soft kisses on her neck, and she sighed into Conor's mouth. One of Rick's large fingers entered her and was quickly followed by a second. They turned and pressed against the membrane separating them from Conor's cock, still slowly moving in and out of her, causing both her and Conor to cry out. Conor drove deep inside her and stilled.

Rick's fingers pulled out, and the slicked head of his cock pushed against her asshole. The brief sting was followed by pressure as he slid deep inside her. Low moans from all three of them echoed in the darkened room. Calleigh turned her head to look over her shoulder at Rick and received his kiss.

"So perfect," he whispered hoarsely. "So beautiful the way you open yourself for our love, angel."

Calleigh moaned and leaned into Conor's chest. Rick took a few slow plunges, and she started to pant.

"God, Calleigh," Rick gasped, His hands tightened on her hips as he slowly filled her over and over. "So tight. So hot."

His thickness sliding all the way inside her and adding to the fullness of Conor filling her in front brought unspeakable pleasure. Rick reached around her and stroked her open pussy gently, teasing her enflamed clit until she moaned and her inner muscles trembled.

"Ghawd all feckin' mighty!" Conor cried.

Conor's cock retreated almost all the way out, so that only the head remained inside her then shoved inwards again hard. She cried out as his shaft hit the top of her wet channel. She closed her eyes as four arms enclosed her. She felt such a deep connection to them both when they were like this. Rick withdrew, and both men paused at her entrances. She gasped and bit her lower lip as both thick cocks, in identical tempos, moved upward in a slow, smooth slide.

No space could be seen between their hips as both men claimed the deepest parts of her body she had to offer. Breathy little pants escaped as she lay between them. She heard soft words but couldn't understand their meanings. All her brain could process was the feel of two thick cocks pulling out and pushing into her body at the same time. Shocks of pleasure shot through her.

"Oh God... Oh please..." Calleigh moaned.

Rick's hands gripped her hips as he ground into her ass, and Conor's fingers played with her nipples as he thrust hard and deep. The slow wave built inside her. Pushing her higher and higher. She made soft, helpless sounds and couldn't stop them. At last, Calleigh felt their rhythm speeding up.

"*Muirnín*," Conor murmured in her ear, thrusting inside her. "*Tá ar chroís istigh ionat.*"

"God, Calleigh," Rick whispered, slamming into her back passage. "Conor is right. Our hearts are within you."

Calleigh nearly sobbed. She reached up to cup Conor's cheek then back to stroke Rick's. "Love you both so much."

She felt Rick's hot breath on the back of her neck as they moved in rapid accord, driving deep inside her. The wave reached a crest, and she tumbled over the edge, crying out as her orgasm rolled over her and tumbled her within its intensity. She felt both men push deep one last time, and their cocks pulsed as they released inside her.

Both men stayed buried deep for a minute. Her eyes were getting heavy. She felt soft lips touch hers and the sheet being pulled over her before sleep finally claimed her.

* * * *

Calleigh ran the vacuum across the area rug in the living room. It was the last thing she had to do before Susan, Kevin's mom, arrived. A set of arms wrapped around her, and she identified the scent belonging to Rick.

"You doing okay, angel?"

She leant back into his embrace. The last few days leading up to the anniversary of Kevin's death had been difficult. She'd been seeking comfort from Rick and Conor more, holding them tightly at night. She was sure if her motives were examined, it would indicate that she subconsciously was afraid of them dying so she clung to them more.

"I'm okay. Thank you for agreeing to visit Kevin with us. I plan on telling Susan tonight at dinner."

"You asked. Of course, we'd go." He placed a kiss on her temple and turned her around to give her another one on her lips.

"I hope you and Conor have fun at the game tonight."

"I'll have a good soccer game, a pint of Guinness and my best friend. The only thing missing is my girl. "

Conor walked in at that moment and wrapped his arms around Calleigh's back, "Our girl." He kissed the back of her neck. "It's cold enough to freeze the balls off a brass monkey, but we promise not te come home all gee-eyed." He looked at Rick. "We'd better be goin'."

They bundled up in coats and scarves. Calleigh gave them one last kiss and sent her big boys out to play.

* * * *

Calleigh, Susan, Mikey and Brandon were sitting in the restaurant. Conversation had consisted of Susan's trip and the boys filling her in on their most recent adventures.

Susan looked over at her daughter-in-law. "Calleigh, I can't believe how much they've grown. And they're talking so much."

Calleigh was sitting between her sons and ruffled their blond heads. "I know. It seems like their vocabulary has tripled in the last six months. For the most part, you can have simple conversations with them and understand most of what they say. Their daycare is fantastic. They really nurture social skills."

Susan set her glass of wine down on the table and twirled the stem. "So tell me. How are you doing?"

Calleigh finished cutting Mikey's chicken tenders so they could cool. "I'm doing really well actually. These few days are always going to be tough, but for the most part, we're just living our lives the best way we can."

They continued to discuss the boys and other national and world matters until their plates were taken away. Calleigh enjoyed herself but knew she had to broach the subject of Rick and Conor accompanying them to the cemetery tomorrow. Maybe if she ducked out to the ladies room for a moment, she could gather her courage. She took Mikey and Brandon's colouring books and crayons out of her ever-present bag and placed them in front of each boy.

"Susan, would you mind watching the boys for a moment. I need to step out to the ladies room."

"Of course. I was wondering, Calleigh, are you dating again?"

She stopped as she was about to leave the table and took a deep breath. "Actually yes. I started dating a couple of months ago and have something I wish speak to you about, but first, I really do need to use the ladies room. Will you excuse me?"

"Of course. Take your time."

Susan watched as Calleigh practically ran from the table. Turning, she saw the boys were both watching her.

"Hi *mamó*."

"Mikey, what did you call me?"

"*Mamó*," Brandon responded

"But sweeties, I'm grandma." She looked at both boys as they nodded. "Have you met your mommy's new friend?" More nods. "Is he nice to you?"

Brandon looked back down at the picture he was colouring. "Ah-huh. Conna read stories good."

Mike picked up a new crayon. "Wick plays cars with us."

Susan was confused. Michael had said one name and Brandon another, but maybe, they were just confused.

"What would you boys like for breakfast before we go visit your father tomorrow?"

"Wick make smiley takes," they said simultaneously.

Susan saw Calleigh heading back to the table and told the boys to gather their pictures. She was putting their coats on when Calleigh reached the table.

"Did the boys want to go?" She looked at Susan with confusion.

"I think it's time we got them home. We can have that discussion there."

"Well, okay." Calleigh knelt in front of her sons. "Do either of you need to use the potty?" Twin heads shook. "Are you sure?" They nodded. "Okay, we'll go when we get home."

"They're potty training already?"

Calleigh stood and faced Susan. "We started just after they turned three. It's still a little hit or miss, but they're getting better at telling me. I always ask before we leave anywhere so they get the idea."

When they arrived at the house, Calleigh got both boys out of the car seats and hurried them inside. The night air was frigid. She hoped Rick and Conor were okay. She was sure if they thought it was too cold, they would head to a pub close to campus.

"Okay, boys. Coats in the closet and go upstairs for PJ time. Meet me in the bathroom to go potty and brush your teeth." She looked over at her mother-in-law. "Susan, make yourself comfortable. I'll be down in a few minutes."

She was very proud of her boys when they went to the bathroom. Both of them were dry, and they each got a gold star on the potty chart. They were saving their stars for a Hot Wheels race track. Mike and Brandon tugged on their Spiderman pyjamas, and they all went back downstairs. She settled them in their playroom off the kitchen, and she started some coffee. Once finished, she carried the two cups into the living room. The first sip made Calleigh wince, and she decided to set the cup down to cool for a moment.

"So, Susan, is there anything in particular you'd like to do tomorrow after we visit Kevin?"

"Actually, I wanted to talk to you about something else first. I was talking with Michael and Brandon at the restaurant, and they said two different names for your new friend. What is his name?"

Calleigh was a little shocked that Susan would discuss something like that with her three-year-old sons. "You asked Mikey and Brandon about my boyfriends?"

"All I asked was if they had met him and was he nice to them. What do you mean 'boyfriends'? Are you dating more than one? Wouldn't that be confusing to the boys to introduce a new man all the time?"

"Susan, I appreciate your concern, but I think I understand the boys and their limitations better than you. I know you love them, but they are extremely bright and generally ahead of the curve when it comes to age-appropriate behaviour. I'm glad you brought this up because I wanted to speak to you about tomorrow. I've invited both Conor and Rick to go with us to the cemetery.

Both men are invaluable friends and have been there for both the boys and me over the past three years."

"I'm glad you had friends to help you through this. So this Conor and Rick, they're the ones Michael and Brandon were speaking of?"

"Yes. They're my best friends, and the boys look to them as father figures." She took a deep breath because this was going to be the hardest part. "They are also my lovers."

For several heartbeats, the room was silent. Susan's face was a stone mask. Calleigh tried to put herself in that position. Here she had come to visit on the anniversary of her son's death and her former daughter-in-law had told her she not only had moved on and was dating again, but was part of a ménage á trois.

"I don't understand, Calleigh."

"Conor, Rick and I are a unit. The three of us have a special relationship where we are all equal partners. I am not dating only Rick or only Conor. I am dating them both, and they are both dating me. In fact, they live here. Our intention is to blend the three of us, Michael, Brandon, and any future children into a complete family."

More silence filled the space. Calleigh heard the sounds of the boys playing in the other room. Plastic trucks were crashing against each other, and they were making screeching and crashing noises.

"I know this must seem like a shock, but please understand, we are happy. The boys have two surrogate fathers who love them as their own. I'm happy in this relationship. It's not better than what Kevin and I shared. It's just different. Rick and Conor will be a part of this family from now on, and I hope you can accept their roles in the boys' lives. They are not going to wipe Kevin's memory from this house. They are enriching our lives in the space he left behind."

Calleigh watched as Susan's face turned red, her fists clenched and her eyes took on a shockingly bright fever.

"You filthy whore! You Satan's mistress. You disgust me! I will not allow your deviant behaviour to taint my son's children."

Her ears rang from Susan's high-pitched voice, screaming in the small room. "Stop right there, Susan! I understand this being a shock to you, but do not for one single second think you have any say in how I raise my children. My behaviour is not deviant or immoral in any way. It's a lifestyle choice—one you may not understand or agree with. Regardless, I make the decisions when it comes to how *my* children are raised, and I choose to raise them in a loving and nurturing home with three adults."

By now, she was raising her voice and made an effort to restrain from getting any louder. She did not want to alarm the boys. "Another thing. Kevin would accept this relationship and be grateful that our children have the love and support they need and deserve. I know this because a marriage of three was not a foreign concept to him…or us."

Calleigh's head snapped around at the force of the slap from Susan's open palm. Her ears rang, and little lights danced in front of her eyes for a moment.

"Don't you ever speak such filth about my son! He was a God-fearing man. A national hero. He died for this country in a squalid desert, and you repay him by whoring yourself and exposing his children to disgusting perverts!"

The front door slammed open. Conor and Rick came running in and stopped in the entryway to the living room. Their eyes locked, and Calleigh was thankful for the low light. They wouldn't be able to see her face, but she was sure a bright red handprint glowed on her cheek.

"I will not stand for this. I am going to collect my grandchildren and take them away from you people. You've made a huge mistake, Calleigh. I'll have you declared an unfit mother by the courts and gain custody so fast it'll make your head spin." She turned around and spied two men standing in doorway. "And you perverts...keep your filthy hands off my grandchildren. God only knows what horrors you've already made them witness or even participate in."

Susan started walking towards the back playroom. Calleigh moved to stop her, but Rick beat her to it. He reached out and grasped Susan by the upper arm and spun her around.

"You will leave this house immediately. I will not stand for you treating Calleigh in such a manner. You have no idea what our relationship is like. Not one of us would ever do anything to hurt those precious little boys. They are the light of our world. It's bigoted spiteful bitches like you who propagate such lies. There are thousands of loving and committed alternate lifestyle relationships raising families in this country. Hell, most of those children end up being more stable than ones who are raised in what you would consider a normal home."

Susan jerked her arm out of the man's grip. "You'll be hearing from my lawyer." As she walked by the other man she heard him muttering in some foreign language.

Calleigh watched the woman she had, if not loved, always respected as Kevin's mother. She had no idea the woman was so narrow minded. Calleigh couldn't believe Susan actually thought they would hurt the boys or molest them. Just the thought made Calleigh sick. Then she realised she really was going to be sick. She sprinted past Conor and Rick for the powder room off the kitchen. Opening the door, she stumbled to her knees and barely got the toilet seat up before heaving the contents of her supper into the porcelain bowl. Her stomach continued to cramp even after nothing more came up as dry heaves racked her body.

Conor dampened a soft cloth and knelt behind Calleigh. His hand rubbed in slow circles as he placed the cloth on the back of her neck. "*Muirnín*. Please donna do this te yerself. We willna let anything happen te our family. I swear te ye."

When Calleigh's body stopped jerking, he wiped her mouth with the damp cloth. He handed her a glass of water so she could wash out her mouth. Sitting back on his heels, he gathered her into his arms.

He felt the coolness of her skin and wrapped his arms around her tighter to transfer as much heat as possible. Trembles took over her body, and she clutched his shirt as he rubbed her back and whispered soothing words in her ear.

Finally, she pulled back, and he got a good look at her face in the light of the sconces on the bathroom wall. A livid mark in the shape of a hand ran across her left cheek. Seeing evidence of violence on Calleigh made him see red. That vile woman had hurt his sweetheart. He reached up and touched the mark softly, and his heart twisted when he saw Calleigh wince. Leaning down, he placed a soft kiss on her cheek.

"I'm sorry she hurt ye, *mo ghrá*. Let's get ye some ice for that and check on the rest of our family. Rick went to check on Mikey and Bran. I'm sure they want a nice hug from ye."

They stood and walked into the living room. Rick sat in the club chair and had both boys in his lap, encased in his arms. Their heads rested on his chest, and Conor saw tear tracks on their cheeks.

"Come give yer ma a hug, little ones."

They looked up simultaneously and scampered off Rick's lap to run into their mother's arms. Calleigh gathered both boys to her and held them tight. She smoothed their hair and kissed their foreheads. His little lights were distraught, and it was all that *cailleach's* fault. The witch poisoned this house of love with her evil brew.

He didn't think either boy wanted to be put to bed away from their ma right now, but he could tell the little ones were about to fall asleep in her arms. "I don't know about ye, but I'm knackered. Why don't we have a camp out here in the livin' room the-night. The whole family."

"That's a great idea, Conor." Calleigh smiled up at him. "We can get the air mattresses and have a slumber party."

"She's right. Just what our family needs tonight. Mikey and Bran, why don't you come with me to get the blankets and pillows." Rick gave Conor's shoulder a squeeze as they left the room.

Not long after that, they were all lying on the pillows of air. He and Rick were on the outside edges, next came the boys, and Calleigh was in the middle of everyone. The boys were sound asleep, and Conor opened his eyes one last time to see Calleigh looking at him.

Thank you, she mouthed.

I love ye, muirnín, he mouthed back.

Chapter Seven

Mike opened his eyes as the sun came through the window. He looked around the room and saw Brandon next to him on the mattress. They often ended up sleeping together when scared. Last night had been scary. Grandma and mommy were yelling, and Rick and Conor didn't look happy, but he didn't understand what had happened. At first, he'd thought Grandma had been mad at him. She kept yelling his and Brandon's names. When the yelling had stopped he went to find mommy, but she was gone. He was scared she had left. Rick had gathered up him and Brandon and sat in the chair. He told them the grown-ups were having a disagreement, but they weren't mad at them. Mike liked it when Rick held him in his lap. He was so big and always warm to cuddle with.

He looked next to him and saw Brandon's eyes open and watching him. He knew Brandon had been scared last night, too. They didn't need to talk to understand what the other was thinking or feeling. Somehow, they always knew. He sat up and crawled to the edge of the mattress carefully. He didn't want to wake up mommy, Rick or Conor. Brandon was right behind him. They walked into the playroom. He picked up their trucks and held them out to his brother.

"You want to play?"

Brandon shook his head no. Mike looked around and pointed to the box of blocks. Again Brandon wasn't interested. Mike saw him grab the front of his pants and pull. He knew what that meant. Taking his brother's hand, he led him to the bathroom. He stared at the potty. They didn't have their step stools or seats down here. Brandon was dancing around. Mike was trying to figure out how to make this work when Brandon pushed him. He watched as his brother pushed his pants off, climbed up to his knees on the seat, put his hands on the back of the potty and started peeing. He didn't know you could do that. When Brandon was done, he did the same and felt much better afterwards.

"Where you 'earn that?"

"Conna show me. I see him do it. He was on his feet."

"I hungy. Let's get mommy."

They walked into the living room, and he giggled at all the grown-ups. They were in a pile on the floor. Conor and Rick had mommy squished between them. He pointed and Brandon giggled, too. Rick started to move and gave mommy a hug. He turned his head and kissed her. Mike had never seen Rick kiss mommy before. He looked over at Brandon and saw that he was watching, too. When he looked back, he saw Conor talking softly to mommy then he kissed her, too.

"Why you kiss mommy?"

Rick froze. He'd forgotten they weren't in their bedroom. He'd woken up to feel Calleigh's soft body next to him and reacted as he did every morning. Hearing one of the boys' voices catapulted him into wakefulness. He sat up on the mattress to see them standing next to each other at the archway between the kitchen and living room. Calleigh and Conor were sitting up as well, and they all looked at each other with questions on how to handle this one on their faces. He thought maybe it was time to explain everything to the boys.

"Come here, boys." He patted the mattress next to him.

They walked over and crawled across the mattress. Mike sat next to him and Brandon sat on the other side of Calleigh between her and Conor.

"I kissed your mommy because I love her and so does Conor." He saw the confusion on the boys' faces. "Do you know what it means for a man and woman to be married?" Both boys nodded their heads. "Well Conor and I want to marry your mom. You know we've been around a lot more lately, but what Conor and I both really want is to be a family. The two of you, your mom, me and Conor."

The boys didn't say anything, but he could see they were processing what he'd said. Especially Mike. He was the thinker of the two, always plotting out what he wanted to do before acting. Brandon tended to act first and deal with effects afterward. But they surprised him this time.

"Will you be our daddy?" Brandon asked.

Rick's heart flipped around in his chest at such a simple question. He and Conor already loved the boys as their own, but to hear them call him 'daddy' stirred him deep inside.

"Would you like that? Do you want to call us daddy?" His voice sounded hoarse to his ears.

The two boys looked at each other for a minute, doing that silent twin communication thing they did so often. He held his breath but refused to rush them. Then they both turned to look at him and nodded their heads in unison. Tears gathered in his eyes and he held out his arms. "Come here, sons. Can you give your new daddy a hug?"

He gathered their small bodies in his arms and pulled them onto his lap. Little hearts were beating in their chests and small fingers dug into his shirt. He looked up to see Calleigh smiling with bright happy eyes. Tears ran down her cheeks. He looked at Conor and saw the man's desire to hold his sons as well.

"Why don't you go over and give your other dad a hug, too. I'm sure he would love that."

They jumped and bounced across the mattress to launch themselves into Conor's arms. After a hard hug, Conor leant back. Mike and Brandon were each straddling one of his legs, and he was supporting them behind their backs.

Conor looked at both boys. "Ye *gasurs* are the lights of me life. I love ye so much. Brandon ye are like sunlight. Always bright and happy, filling our days with your energy. That's why I call you *mo grian*, which means my sun and Michael you are like moonlight. Reflective and beautiful, ever changing and guiding our lives. That's why I call you *mo gealachí*, which means my moon. I would love for ye te call me Da. That 'tis how we say dad in Ireland. Can ye do that for me?"

Both boys nodded and started jumping up and down on the mattress and cheering. Calleigh's face turned grey, and she put a hand up to her mouth. She leapt over Rick and raced towards the bathroom. He followed and found her bent over the toilet. After cleaning her up, he lifted her in his arms and carried her into the kitchen, where Conor was making the boys breakfast. He caught their gazes with the question plain in his eyes.

Rick set her down on one of the chairs at the table and pulled up another beside her. "That's the second time in two days, Calleigh." He put a hand to her forehead but didn't feel anything except cool clammy skin.

"I'm fine, Rick. Last night was just from anxiety and stress. I'm sure this morning was just lingering effects."

"Is there any chance it could be something else? We never did ask you about protection. From Conor's and my perspective, it wasn't important, but I realise that was selfish of us. So I apologise."

He leaned over and kissed her softly then heard giggles from the other side of the table and realised it would take the boys a little while before they got used to seeing displays of affection between them.

She placed her hand on his cheek. "I would love to have another child. I can't think of anything better than to know we created a life out of the love I share with you and Conor, but I know that's not the case. I take the Depo-Provera shot to regulate my cycles. Have since Mike and Brandon were born. The last one was administered a week before we got together, so I know I'm protected for another month."

"Okay, angel, I guess a small part of me was hoping that could be it. Promise me if you feel any worse you'll see one of the doctors at the hospital. I couldn't bear it if this was something more, and we didn't do anything to help you. This family needs you."

"I promise. Now, let's have a nice family breakfast because I'm sure this is only the calm before the storm."

* * * *

A beam of moonlight shone through the bow windows in their bedroom. Calleigh watched the sheer curtain flutter as the heat kicked on. She couldn't sleep. In fact, she felt smothered lying between Conor and Rick. She moved to climb over Conor. She was poised above him when he snaked his arms around her and pulled down so their bodies were flush. She could tell he was still asleep by the deep, even breaths softly escaping his mouth. She was stuck straddling his hips as he thrust them against her. He mumbled something incoherent, and she dropped a small kiss to his lips. A moment later, his arms fell back to his sides, and she climbed off the side of the bed.

Picking up her robe, she slipped her arms through the soft material and tiptoed out the bedroom door. She checked on the boys then crept downstairs. Sitting in the club chair by the bow windows in living room, she stared out into the night. The cars shimmered with a layer of frost in the streetlamps.

She was exhausted but couldn't seem to get her mind to shut down. For the past week, she'd felt like someone with bipolar disorder. She had floated the entire day the first morning Mike and Brandon had spontaneously called Rick and Conor dad. The next day, she got a call from her supervisor at the hospital saying Miles had filed a complaint of sexual harassment against her. Rick and Conor had nearly blown a gasket over that one. The boys were making real progress in the potty training. The other day she had gone to get them out of bed and found them already in the bathroom pulling down their pyjama pants.

Rick and Conor had lectured her at dinner tonight because she hadn't had much of an appetite. It didn't help that she was still randomly throwing up. Sometimes, she just ended up dry heaving because of the lack of food in her system. She hadn't told Rick and Conor because she knew they would worry. She knew it was from the stress. When she looked in the mirror before getting to bed, she saw dark circles under her puffy eyes and her hair looked limp. No wonder they hadn't wanted to make love to her all week. Daily harassing calls from Susan put a pall over the household. They'd stopped picking up the phone for the most part.

The last message she'd left said that she'd gotten a lawyer and going to sue for custody. She'd even mentioned making contact with a representative from the Department of Children and Families to file a report of abuse. Calleigh prayed every day that they couldn't take her precious babies away. She knew there was no evidence of physical or emotional neglect, but one never knew how government services could twist things to suit their needs. Could Susan really take her children? Didn't the courts always side with mother, except in extreme cases? Not for one second did Calleigh question her choice of staying with Rick and Conor. She needed them like air and was determined to find a way to make this work. She heard a creak and looked up to see Conor descending the stairs.

"*Muirnín*? Why are ye down here instead of in bed with us?"

"Couldn't sleep. Didn't want to wake either of you."

He picked up a throw blanket on the back of the sofa and walked over to the chair. Lifting Calleigh up, he sat then settled her on his lap and tucked the blanket around them. "Ye wanna talk?"

She shook her head. "Too much jumbled in there to sort out right now. Will you just hold me for a little while?"

"I'll always hold ye, *mo ghrá*. Put yer head down and try te get some sleep."

As Calleigh's eyes started to drift, he softly hummed one of his favourite Irish lullabies. He frequently did so for the boys when they had trouble going down, and it seemed to work on their mom as well. Calleigh had thought he was asleep when he'd tried to keep her in bed earlier, but he knew the moment she started to crawl over him that she was trying to escape. She hadn't slept through a night this week and it showed. He knew she was still getting sick, too. She had tried to keep it from them, but her friend Carla had called one evening to ask if Calleigh was feeling better since she'd gotten sick earlier at work. Once or twice, he could understand from stress, but this had moved beyond that.

He looked down and realised she was finally out. Her breathing was even, and her head was limp against his chest. Slowly standing, he carried her back upstairs. When he reached the side of the bed, Rick was awake.

"She get sick again?" Rick whispered

"No, just sitting down by the windy staring out into the night," he whispered back.

Rick helped him get her robe off, and he carefully laid her down on the bed. He climbed in next to her and rolled to his back. Pulling up the covers, he tucked them around her. He put his arms behind his head and he stared up at the decorative ceiling medallion. "We need te do something. She canny keep goin' like this. The boys are startin' te notice, too."

"I know. Let me think on it some. Try and get some sleep. It'll be another long day tomorrow."

Chapter Eight

Rick picked up the phone in his office and dialled the number he'd found online. He hoped a call to one of their good friends from B.C would provide some answers. As he waited for the line to connect, he fiddled with the screen shot suggestions for that new Olympic game they were working on. The art department was currently working on background effects before adding in the code for play. This one was a half-pipe competition, and he noticed that one of the spectators held up an Irish flag, but the colours were in the wrong order. He smiled because he knew Conor would have a fit if he saw that. He was about to give up when the line connected.

"United States Attorney's office. How can I help you?"

"This is Richard Connor. May I please speak with Ethan Harrison?" He leant back in his chair as the assistant connected him. A few moments later, the cheerful voice of his friend transmitted through the line.

"Rick? How the hell are you?"

"I'm good. How've you been? I know we haven't talked in a couple of months, sorry. What's new?"

"Same old, same old. How's my favourite gingernut?"

"He'd kick your scrawny ass if he heard you call him that," Rick said, smiling.

"I know, I know, ''Tis not red, ye arse'."

He laughed at Ethan's spot-on imitation. "As much as I wish this were a purely social call, we have a situation I wanted to get your take on."

"That never sounds good. Shoot. Then we can get back to the fun stuff."

"Well it's like this. Conor and I have finally found our third. She's a military widow, who has two little boys. I know I've told you about her. Her name is Calleigh Wells. Anyway, her mother-in-law flipped when she found out about our relationship and is threatening to sue for custody and get DFC involved. It's turned Calleigh into a wreck. What I was wondering is can the mother-in-law succeed based solely on our relationship?"

"It's about time you and Conor finally got your acts together. It's been so obvious for the past year that you're both in goo-goo love with the woman. She and her boys were all the two of you talked about." Ethan chuckled. "On a more serious note, no judge would take away children from a parent based solely on a moral objection from the third party. As long as you can prove the children are being provided for and living in a healthy home, you shouldn't have any problems."

"Thank God. I really didn't think it was possible, but you never know. So how's your love life? Seeing anyone?"

"Unfortunately my quest for love has hit a dead end. The last couple dates I went on were disastrous. I swear you'd think I could find one good man in the city of

Boston. Is tall, hot, built, smart and desperately in love with me really too much to ask for?"

Rick laughed. "No, my friend. I'm sure you'll find him. I'll keep my eye out for you. You know it's been way too long since we really hung out. Why don't I give you call when this all calms down, and you can meet the family?"

"Sounds good, buddy. My assistant just poked her head in and told me my next client is waiting so I got to run. Give my best to Conor. Tell that crazy mick he still owes me a margarita since I drank that nasty brew he calls beer on St. Paddy's."

"Will do. See ya, Ethan."

After he hung up, he felt much better. In fact, he felt as if a huge weight had been lifted off his shoulders. He picked up the phone to call Conor and share the news, but then looked at the clock. It was almost five o'clock. He could tell him on the way home.

He caught the elevator down to the lobby, and Conor was waiting in their usual spot.

"You ready to head home?"

"Actually I need te run a few errands. Phil called and said he finished the setting today. So I thought I'd stop by on the way 'ome and pick it up. I'll snag dinner so we don't have te worry about cookin'."

"Excellent. Then I'll meet Calleigh at the hospital when she gets off shift. I have some good news to share with the family tonight also, so don't be too late. Lilly should have the boys home by seven o'clock."

* * * *

Rick stood outside the door to the hospital when Calleigh walked through. When she saw him, a huge smile lit up her face, and she ran into his arms. Gathering her close, he buried his head in her neck and inhaled her scent. It was still detectible beneath the hospital smells covering her scrubs. Pulling back, he leaned in for a kiss.

He'd intended for it to be brief, but once his lips touched hers, he couldn't hold back. They were soft and felt so perfect against him. His tongue licked across the seam, and she opened to let him inside. He loved the sweet taste of his angel. His tongue slipped between her lips again and again. His arms slid around her waist, pulling her in tight. Calleigh's arms were latched around his neck, holding him to her.

He pressed his erection against her soft belly. It had been days since he'd been inside her warmth, and the fires that had been banked due to the stress surround them erupted. He needed her. Now. Spirals of heat streaked through his bloodstream. Calleigh's tongue dipped into his mouth and flicked over his teeth. The tangling of their flesh stoked the molten desire racing through him. He loosened his grip on her, and she moaned.

Separating their lips, he breathed heavily, "I need you angel. It's been too long. Where can we go?"

She looked around for a moment then grabbed his hand. Pulling him inside the hospital, they walked through an 'employees only' door and slipped inside a private bathroom. He flipped the lock on the door and pushed Calleigh against the painted wall across from the sink.

"I'm sorry angel, but this won't be wine and romance."

She pushed down her scrubs as he ripped open his belt and dress pants. They fell to his ankles. Their mouths latched together once again, and he reached around to grab her ass. Lifting her up her legs wrapped around his waist, he balanced her against the wall and reached down to see if she was wet enough to accept him. The evidence of her desire coated his fingers, and he groaned into her mouth. Slipping two digits inside her snug heat made her gasp.

"Please, Rick. I need."

"I know what you need, angel. Don't worry, I'll take care of you."

He held his cock and fit it to her entrance. In a single thrust, he slid home and captured Calleigh's cry with his lips. The hot, tight, wet channel gripping him was too much, and he started fucking her immediately. Calleigh's nails dug into his shoulders. His eyes bored into hers. Her hot breath panted against his lips. He started hammering into her, driving himself deeper into the heaven of her body. Whimpers escaped even though she tried to hold them back. His hips jack-knifed, and the pull of her muscles against his cock sent unspeakable pleasure racing down his spine. Suddenly, her body tensed and the ripples of her orgasm locked him deep inside. He cried out as his climax was ripped from the marrow of his bones. Pulsing, shaking, shuddering, the explosion went on forever.

When he regained his faculties, he realised he still had her pinned to the wall. He heard her hiss as he separated their flesh. His lingering pleasure was immediately replaced with concern.

"Angel, are you all right? Was I too rough?"

"No, love. That was exactly what I needed."

He leant in and kissed her again. He never got enough of her sweet lips. After several lingering soft kisses, he pulled back. Bending down, he helped her get back into her scrubs and tided himself.

"Let's go home."

* * * *

They just beat Conor back to the house, and Lilly dropped off the boys. Citing the need to get to her book club meeting, she left quickly. Conor's hello kiss lasted a bit longer than normal. When he and Calleigh finally separated, their gazes locked, and Rick knew the other man had caught the scent of their lovemaking on Calleigh's body.

"Did ye two just get home?"

"Yes, we had a bit of a delay at the hospital."

Conor chuckled. "I'll bet." He looked back down at his love. "*Muirnín*, you look much better tonight. Your eyes have their glow back and your cheeks have colour in them again." He leaned over to whisper in her ear. "I can smell Rick on ye, *mo ghrá*. Knowing the two of ye made love is gonna leave me gummin'. I canny wait to get ye in bed the-night. I'm goin' te lick every inch of this beautiful body then slide deep inside ye until ye shudder all around me."

Rick smiled when he saw Calleigh blush at Conor's whispered promise. He inhaled deeply as he opened the bags Conor had brought home. The scents of chicken modiga from their favourite restaurant wafted up, and his mouth watered. He set the table and managed to get the boys corralled into their booster chairs. He set their sippy cups filled with milk in front of them while Calleigh cut up their chicken fingers to cool.

"I even brought home some afters for us te enjoy lay-ra."

Calleigh leaned over and gave Conor a kiss on the cheek. "I love dessert, thank you. What did you bring home?"

"It's a surprise, *mo ghrá*. After Mike an' Bran are asleep the three of us can relax an' enjoy the treat."

Rick figured this was a good time to tell Conor and Calleigh about his conversation with Ethan earlier. He took a sip of his wine and looked up to get their attention.

"I placed a call today to an old friend of Conor's and mine from B.C. He specialises in securities law, but is familiar enough with family law that I trust what he says."

Conor rolled his eyes. "Why dinna I think of callin' grapenuts?"

"Who?" Calleigh asked.

"Never mind him, angel. Our buddy's name is Ethan Harrison. He's an assistant attorney for the U.S. Attorney's office here in Boston. Anyway, he said we really should have nothing to worry about from Susan. He assured me that a judge would in all probability not remove a child from a home strictly based on a moral disagreement between parties. There would have to be evidence of neglect."

He looked at Calleigh and saw the relief on her face at his announcement. He had been worried she would be upset he'd gone behind her back, but it appeared she appreciated his initiative.

She stood and went over to hug Rick, holding him tight for a moment. "Thank you. I can't tell you how much better I feel. It's nice to have someone with actual legal experience confirm my suspicions."

"Good on ye. I haven't talked to Ethan in donkey's years! How is the rossie?"

"He says you still owe him a frozen margarita for making him drink that pint of Arthur's last Paddy's."

He laughed at the memory of Ethan's face when he'd downed the Guinness. "The man never could stand the black stuff."

They finished their dinner, and he and Conor took Mike and Brandon upstairs for baths and story time. When all was settled for the night, Rick stopped Conor in the upstairs hallway. "Did you get it?"

Conor held out the small box and lifted the lid. The light from the hallway reflected off the diamond engagement ring they had picked out for Calleigh. Conor had explained to the jeweller what design he wanted for the setting and he had chosen the stone. The platinum band had a series of trinity knots, a classic Celtic design, along the shoulders and at the centre, a princess cut diamond. It had a matching wedding band with trinity knots inset into the band.

"It's perfect, Con."

"Are ye sure? It's not too Irish for ye? I dinna want ye te feel like—"

"Conor, stop. You may have thicker Irish blood running through your veins, but I come from Shannon, too. Those trinity knots are three interlaced triangles that represent unending love. I can't think of a better symbol for our lives with Calleigh than what you have in your hand."

He hugged his best friend. Their lives were united not only through their friendship, but through their mutual love for Calleigh and commitment to their chosen lifestyle. When he pulled back, he saw a glimmer of moisture in Conor's eyes and felt some in his own. He might not feel desire for Conor, but he always had and always would love the man.

* * * *

Calleigh put the last dish away in the cabinet and turned on the coffeemaker. The rich aromatic scent of hazelnut shortly filled the kitchen. Walking into the living room she knelt beside the hearth and lit the kindling in the fireplace. The crackle of the dried wood and the warmth of the flame were soothing. She turned her head as she heard footsteps on the stairs and saw Rick and Conor enter the room.

"Are they ready for me?"

"Yes, angel, go say goodnight then come back down so we can enjoy that dessert Conor brought home."

She rose from her knees and gave each man a soft kiss before heading upstairs to give her babies a final tuck in. Opening the door to their bedroom, she sound they were both already asleep. She leaned over and tucked the blankets tighter around Brandon—he tended to thrash around at night—and placed a kiss on his forehead. Slipping over to the other side of the room, she picked up Mikey's stuffed dog and slipped it under his arm, giving him a kiss. Stepping back to the door, she took one last look and whispered, "Goodnight, my little loves."

She stepped into her bedroom and stripped off her scrubs. Feeling the need for something special, she slipped a green silk negligee over her head and let the short skirt float around her thighs. The matching bikini panties rode low on her hips. She fluffed her hair as best she could, pinched her cheeks to add some colour and dabbed on a little lip gloss.

She stopped at the top of the stairs and listened a moment to detect any sounds from the living room. Not hearing anything, she slowly walked down and turned into the living room. She gasped at the sight of the champagne, strawberries and cannoli laid out picnic style. Strong arms surrounded her waist, and she was pulled back into Conor's hard chest.

"Ye look stunning, *ár ghrá*. The green of Shannon suits you. Come sit, and let us ply ye with sweets."

She turned around and looked up into Conor's beautiful aquamarine eyes. The flickering light from the fireplace created highlights and shadows on his cheekbones. She reached up on her tiptoes and wrapped her arms around his neck to kiss him. Flicking her tongue across the seam of his lips, he opened and she slipped inside. She found he'd already had nibbled on at least one of the strawberries. A large warmth moulded to her back, and Rick's lips caressed her shoulder. He slid the thin strap of her nightgown to the side, and his lips travelled up her shoulder and neck as he moved her hair aside. Separating from Conor's lips, she let them lead her over to the pillows they had set up in front of the fire.

"This is beautiful. I can't believe you two went to the trouble."

Conor propped against the sofa, and she nestled between his legs, leaning back against him. He lifted a flute of champagne and handed it to her. She took a small sip, and fruity bubbles danced across her taste buds. She'd never had such good tasting champagne before. The light taste was delicious. She could easily see herself imbibing too much and losing her head.

"It's never trouble to make you feel special, angel. We know things have been stressful lately, and we wanted to pamper you. Close your eyes." He reached down and picked up a strawberry. "Open those luscious lips for us."

Calleigh opened, and the tip of a strawberry rolled against her lower lip. She took a bite out of the succulent fruit. The combination of flavours made her moan. Conor's hands were around her waist and slowly rubbing circles on her belly. His lips occasionally landed on her neck. She started to open her eyes when his deep voice spoke softly in her ear.

"Keep them closed, *muirnín*."

She felt the edge of the flute at her lips and let them slip more of the cool drink in her mouth, letting the bubbles linger on her tongue before swallowing. Next, she felt something else at her lips. It wasn't a strawberry, so it must be one of the cannolis. Slipping her tongue out, she took a little lick at the end of the roll and heard twin groans. Opening her mouth, she let Rick feed her a bite of the dessert. The crisp dough and sweet filling filled her mouth. She leaned her head back on Conor's chest and enjoyed the delicacy.

Moments later, another strawberry was placed at her lips, and after she took a bite, she felt Conor's tongue flick across her lips to taste the lingering juice. Her eyes were still closed when his hand slid up from her belly to hold her chest against him. Rick must have scooted closer because her legs were spread and wrapped around a lean waist and hips. Hands slowly slid up her legs to rest on her thighs. Expecting him to go higher, she let out a little whimper when they stopped their travels.

Her hands were lifted and her fingers linked on one side with Conor and on the other with Rick. She felt Conor's lips next to her ear, his warm breath caressing her cheek. Her heart beat faster as Conor spoke softly in Gaelic while Rick translated for her.

"*Ár teaghlach churthaigh sibh.*"

"We created our family."

"*Luchtaíonn sibh grá, bríoghas, agus greann ár laethanta.*"

"Love, passion, and humour fill our days."

"*Coinníonn tú i gcónaí ár croi.*"

"You hold our hearts forever."

"*Slánaigh tú ár anam.*"

"You complete our souls."

"*An mbeidh tú mar chéile agam?*"

"Will you be our wife?"

Her eyes flew open with the last phrase, and she looked down. Conor slid a ring on her left ring finger. Tears gathered in her eyes as she stared at the artistry of the jewellery, the symbol of their love a solid weight on her hand. She turned her hand back and forth and side to side, watching the firelight dance across the silver band and clear stone.

"Angel?"

She realised she hadn't answered them. "Of course, I'll marry you. But how…"

"We took the liberty of discussing logistics. If you're agreeable, we decided you would legally marry Conor. He's both an American and Irish citizen so any future children we have would be eligible for dual status. The boys are a little trickier, but it wouldn't be any hardship to get them passports and such for when we want to visit Conor's mom and dad. We were thinking we'd have a private ceremony on Cape Cod with close friends and family shortly after, uniting the three of us."

She held her arms out for Rick. He moved in, braced his hands on the sofa and leaned to kiss her. Their lips met to seal their intentions. When Rick pulled away, she tilted her head back and raised her chin to accept Conor's kiss. His erection pushed into her lower back, and she wanted to feel him inside her again.

She pulled back from his lips and managed to wiggle out of the sandwich. Standing with the fire to her back she reached down and pulled the nightgown over her head, baring her body to her loves. Rick came forward and slid the silky underwear down her hips. She lifted her feet to step out of the material and accepted Rick's hand to help her kneel back on the nest they'd built on the floor. Rick knelt in front of her and slid a hand down the centre of her body to between her legs. Conor moved behind her and reached a hand around to caress one of her nipples. Her breasts swelled in response. She closed her eyes and revelled in the sensations of their hands moving across her body. It no longer matter which hand belonged to whom.

Lips nuzzled her neck and breasts. Conor gathered her into his chest when Rick leant back to undress. When his magnificent body was on display, he knelt back down in front of her and captured her so Conor could do the same. He kissed her deeply as his hands travelled down the length of her spine to cup her ass. His erection was hot and hard against her skin. They guided her back so she was lying amongst the pillows. They lowered their heads and both mouths latched onto a nipple, tugging and licking in different rhythms. Rick drew hard as Conor gave a soft lick. The dichotomy sent spirals of pleasure racing through her body. Her clit was swollen and begging for a touch.

"Oh my God…" she whimpered into the fire-lit room. Her hips surged upwards to let them know what she needed.

Rick and Conor slid a hand down her torso. One stopped at her clit and rubbed on the pulsing nerves, while the other dipped his broad finger inside. Calleigh spread her legs to give them more room as she pushed against their hands. Their long fingers alternated. One sliding deep, while the other tormented her bud. She felt her orgasm climbing. Writhing on the blankets, she reached for her climax but became frustrated as it seemed elusive.

"Don't fight for it, angel. Trust us to take care of you."

She tried to clear her mind of all but the feel of them inside her body. Their lips at her breasts, their fingers probing deep inside to massage her swollen damp tissues. Their tongues flicking across her skin and their teeth nibbling on tender flesh. The wave started to crest again, and this time she allowed them to carry her over. The pulsing climax rolled through her body. When she surfaced, Conor was between her legs. He gently spread her open and licked across her wet folds.

"Hmmm...it's been too long since I tasted ye. Yer a drug te me senses."

His nimble tongue was good for more than just whispered wicked words and lyrical seductions. Long licks up and down the folds had her arching her hips to get closer. The tip of his tongue tormented the opening of her pussy but never entered. He swirled around her clit, before his lips latched on and sucked. She cried out and surged forward, desperately needing something inside her.

She opened her eyes to see Rick holding his cock like an offering. Angling her head, she licked at the weeping head and relished his hiss. Trying to take him inside her mouth, she couldn't get around him at her current angle. He must have sensed her frustration because he quickly moved to kneel over her head and slowly fed his length down her throat as Conor simultaneously pushed two fingers inside her. Her cries vibrated around Rick's flesh. Rick was bent over her body and leaned down to flatten his tongue on her clit, while Conor thrust deep inside her pussy. Their heads were so close they could have kissed each other. It would only take a slip of someone's tongue. She redoubled her efforts on Rick's cock, reaching her hands up to pull on his ass and trying to signal for him to let go and fuck her. His hips surged, and he drove inside over and over. She felt him get harder and his cock pulsed, but just before she was sure he was going to climax, he pulled away and swung around on the side of her.

Rick laid down on his back. "We're going to do this a little differently, angel. I want you to lay on me but face up to Conor."

Calleigh settled over the top of his body. Her soft skin rubbed against him from head to toe. Her honey coloured hair draped over his shoulder. Conor helped spread her legs.

"Now stay here and relax while Conor gets you ready, love."

He looked over her shoulder and saw Conor pick up the tube of lube, click open the cap and squeeze out a liberal amount onto his fingers. Rick held Calleigh still while Conor put his fingers to the closed rosette and pushed his way through the ring to stretch her opening.

Rick was so damn hard he hurt. It had taken everything within his power to not come down her throat a few minutes ago. Conor held up the bottle of lube with a question in his eyes. Rick nodded, signalling that it was okay. When Conor's large hand surrounded his cock to slick it up for Calleigh, Rick's eyes rolled back inside his head. He and Conor had never touched each other sexually before, and he was able to admit the strong grip on his cock felt damn good.

When he opened his eyes, Conor nodded his head that they were ready. Rick lifted Calleigh's hips and guided his cock inside the clasping heat of her ass. He groaned as he slowly entered her welcoming body, mesmerised by the way her body flared open to accept him. Calleigh's moans guided him as he nudged deep inside.

Holding her in position, he signalled to Conor that he could begin his entry. Conor leaned over their bodies and slowly fit his cock to Calleigh's pussy. Her channel surrounding Rick got tighter as Conor filled her.

Being filled by both her men was a feeling she could never eloquently describe. Their bodies joined, their breaths mingling, their skin sealed together as they moved as one. Conor thrust up, the head of his cock nudging her cervix, as Rick pulled back. Their countering thrusts made sure her body was never empty. Conor grabbed the back of her head and slammed their lips together. His tongue drove into her mouth in the same tempo of his cock. Ricks hands separated her cheeks as he drove forcefully deep inside her body. Groans and cries echoes through the room.

Their strokes became less rhythmic as they neared orgasm, their hips jerking, her straining into every thrust, milking out each sensation. Calleigh screamed into Conor's mouth as a tremendous orgasm ripped through her body. She felt every tissue in her pussy and ass contract around the thick shafts buried deep inside her. She ripped away from Conor desperate to fill her lungs with air. Rick and Conor both slammed into her one last time and held deep. Their cocks pulsed as they released their seed deep inside her body.

Chapter Nine

Calleigh opened the door to the ladies room and ran smack into Carla. It took a moment for her eyes to focus on the swimming letters of her friend's scrub shirt.

"That's it. I'm taking you to see someone." Carla grabbed Calleigh's hand and pulled her down the hall.

"Carla, stop! What are you doing?" She pulled her hand from her friend's firm grip.

"I heard you throwing up again. You swear up and down that you're not pregnant, but this is not going away. So we're going to find out exactly what is going on." Carla picked up Calleigh's hand again and tugged.

Carla dragged her to the doctors' lounge door and knocked before walking in. Several doctors looked up, and a couple of questioned their presence, but once Carla gave them the evil eye, they shut up. Her friend was so good at that. Calleigh let out a little giggle.

"Davie, I need you to examine Calleigh," Carla said to her brother.

"Umm, why?"

"Because she's been throwing up and has a loss of appetite. She swears up and down she's not pregnant. Oh, and she's not been sleeping through the night for the past three weeks."

Calleigh turned to Carla in shock. "How do you know that?"

Carla faced her best friend and took hold of her hand. "I called Rick and Conor a week or so ago, and they told me."

Calleigh yanked her hand out of Carla's grasp. "Why are you calling them behind my back!"

"Because I'm worried about you! Now stop changing the subject." She faced her brother again. "Please, Davie?"

David walked over and looked closely at his sister's best friend. "What makes you think you're not pregnant? I see the ring on your finger, congratulations by the way. So I assume you're having sex."

"For multiple reasons. Number one, I take the Depo shot and have for years. My last shot was administered approximately two and half months ago. Two, I had a period approximately a month ago. Granted, it was light, but that's not unusual for me since starting the shot after my sons were born. Finally, three, I'm not throwing up every morning or after I eat. It's just random. I've been under a lot of stress. Miles has been stirring up trouble with the administration, although I think that's settled now, and my mother-in-law is threatening to sue for custody of my children because she doesn't approve of my fiancés."

"Okay, I agree there's some stress there. Any number of things can cause those symptoms. Come down to an exam room, and let's run some tests."

They left the lounge and walked down the hall. Calleigh heard her name called over the speaker asking her to come to the nurses' station. She told Carla she would be right back. Walking up to the desk, she saw a delivery man with a bunch of flowers. Her heart flipped over at the idea that maybe Conor and Rick had sent her some. In the two weeks since their proposal, they'd left little love notes all over the house for her to find. Her favourite was when she stepped into the shower the other morning. There had been a large piece of paper taped to the tile that said *Wish we were here.*

"You paged me Melissa?" She saw the young woman point to the delivery man as she wrote a chart note. "Can I help you?"

"Are you Calleigh Wells?"

She looked at the pretty flowers and inhaled trying to catch their scent. "Yes. Are those for me?"

"Yes." He handed her a clipboard. "I just need you to sign please."

She accepted the pen and signed on the line next to her printed name. When she looked up, the man had taken off his delivery hat and held out a piece of paper.

"You've been served. Have a nice day."

Calleigh stared at his back as he walked out the sliding doors of the department. The whole desk area was silent. She heard several comments about what an asshole the guy was. When she looked down, she saw the word subpoena in big bold letters. Her hands shook as she opened the document, and as she read the first few lines, a raw animalistic sound escaped her throat and her world went black.

Her senses were muddled as she slowly opened her eyes. After she blinked several times, the room came into focus. Her brain tried to remember what had happened, and suddenly awareness snapped. She sat up quickly and grabbed the railing on the side of the bed as her head swam for a few seconds. Looking around, she found herself lying on a gurney in one of the curtained-off prep areas for surgery patients. Carla and her brother stood next to her.

She fell back onto the bed and flung an arm up to cover her eyes from the bright, fluorescent lights overhead. "What happened?"

"You passed out," David responded. "Apparently after being served a subpoena. When you came to a moment later, you started crying hysterically and yelling for Rick and Conor, so I gave you a sedative."

"Oh my God," she moaned.

How embarrassing that she acted that way in her place of work, but she couldn't stop the tears from filling her eyes as she looked over at her best friend. "She's trying to take my babies away. Rick swears it won't happen, but what if he's wrong? What if his lawyer friend didn't get it right? If I lost Rick and Conor, my heart would shatter all over again, but if I lose my babies I just might die."

"Calleigh, calm down. It won't happen. She's trying to stir up trouble. Besides you shouldn't get overly upset. It's not good for the baby." Carla's lips twitched, making every effort to keep a straight face.

"How do you know it won't happen? You can't guarantee... What do you mean 'baby'?" *Did I hear that right? It's not possible.*

David picked up Calleigh's hand. "You are pregnant, Calleigh. I ran a blood test while you were unconscious. I did an ultrasound to confirm because of the bleeding you reported. I suspect the bleeding occurred at the time of implantation."

She couldn't wrap her mind around it. She'd taken the shot. Granted, she and her lovers had never used any form of protection, but what were the odds that the Depo shot would fail? One and half percent...maybe? "But what about the shot?"

"Well, I looked up your electronic records, and they showed you receiving a flu shot back in September but nothing about your Depo."

She shook her head. "That can't be right. I declined the flu shot. They asked me that same day, but I said no. Told them to just do the other."

"Regardless of how it happened, you are pregnant. Judging from the ultrasound, I would estimate around eight weeks."

"Oh my God," she whispered right when Rick and Conor came running into the curtained area.

Rick rushed the bed where Calleigh lay. She looked so pale. When he'd gotten the call at work that she had passed out then started screaming for them, his heart had nearly stopped. He'd run through the building to Conor's office and told him what happened. They'd raced to the hospital as fast as possible. He even gave the cab driver a huge tip to make it as fast as he could.

"Angel? What happened?" He cupped her cheek and placed a soft kiss on her cool lips.

"*Muirnín*? Are ye sick again?"

She held Conor's hand on one side of the bed and Rick's on the other. "I don't remember what happened after I woke up. They told me I went into some kind of hysterics. Loves, she served me papers. Susan actually filed a dispute of custody."

Rick couldn't believe it. He'd never thought the woman would actually go so far. He was furious. How dare she disrupt their home? How dare she hurt Calleigh this way?

He knew no better mother than his angel. Her love for those boys was stamped into every action of every day.

"*Go n-ithe an cat thú, is go n-ithe an diabhal an cat,*" Conor spat under his breath.

"Um, Con? Did you just put a hex on the woman? Can you teach me one?" Rick tried to lighten the tension.

"Sorry. I said 'may the cat eat ye and the devil eat the cat'. 'Tis an auld family curse."

Calleigh smiled. "I like that one. One thing about you Irish is that you're very creative with your cursing. Give me a kiss, and whisper sweet nothings in my ear."

Rick watched Conor lean over and thoroughly kiss their love. He did whisper something in her ear, and it made Calleigh giggle. It warmed Rick's heart to see a smile back on her face.

"Calleigh, I think we need to face this head on. Why don't we contact Susan? Tell her to come over to the house to discuss this idiocy. If we drag lawyers into this, it's going to turn into a nightmare. Why don't we try talking it out with her first?"

"I'll try, but you saw her that night. There was no talking to her rationally. For now, I have to get back to work. I'll meet you at home later."

"Oh no, you are not, missy," Carla scolded.

"Carla! Have you been listening this whole time?"

She poked her head through the curtain. "Sue me. You *are* going home. You *are* going to bed. And you will call me and tell me *everything*." She gave Calleigh a pointed look.

Rick looked over at Conor and sensed there was something else going on. What was Carla talking about? Was there something Calleigh wasn't telling them? "Angel?"

Calleigh twisted the sheets on the bed between her fingers. "Um...well...the thing is..."

"'Tis okay, *mo ghrá*. Ye can tell us. This is about ye still gettin' sick, isn't it?" He saw the shocked look on Calleigh's face. "Aye love, we knew. We didn't say anythin' cos we wanted ye te come te us. Please tell us. What's wrong?"

She took a deep breath. "Apparently, I'm pregnant. Somebody screwed up. I never got my shot, and David thinks I'm about eight weeks along." She rushed it all out in one breath.

Rick sat heavily on the bed next to Calleigh's legs. She was pregnant. She wasn't sick. She was pregnant! He scooped his arms around her back and pulled her up into his embrace. She latched onto him, and he felt tears wet his shirt. Conor was moulded to her back, and his arms were around her waist. Their heads lifted and gazes caught. Rick saw joy and love radiating from Conor's blue-green depths.

"Angel, those had better be happy tears. This is the best thing we've ever heard — next to you agreeing to marry us anyway."

She pulled her head up off Rick's shoulder. "Really? You're not upset? I didn't know if you were ready for something like this. I know it's shocked the hell out of me."

"We're havin' a babby. 'Tis a blessin' to celebrate." Conor held Calleigh's face between his hands and kissed her. Their lips welded together as he wiped the tears from her cheeks.

"Let's go home. We have to plan how to tell the boys to expect a little brother or sister. I think we should make it a game." Rick rubbed his hands together as plots started forming in his mind. Scooping Calleigh up off the bed, he carried her out of the hospital to her embarrassment and the cheers of her co-workers.

* * * *

Conor paced around the living room. He looked up at the clock on the mantel and grimaced. *It couldn't possibly be two minutes since he last looked.* He turned his back to the clock and walked to the bow windows to peek between the curtains.

"Con, stop pacing. She'll get here when she gets here. No matter how fast you turn in circles, time doesn't actually speed up."

"Ask me bollocks. I just wanna get this over with. I'm afraid the *bitseach* is goin' te make this as difficult as possible. Calleigh disna need any more stress."

It had taken them a week since Calleigh had been served the papers to get Susan to agree to see them. He and Rick had repeatedly called and left messages. At first, she had refused to talk to them at all, telling them to contact her lawyer. When Calleigh tried, she spent twenty minutes on the phone, half the time holding the receiver away from her ear as Susan harangued her. She'd finally gotten fed up and yelled for Susan to shut her mouth. She'd told Susan unless she wanted the tape recording of the conversation to make its way into her lawyer's hands she would agree to meet with them.

The doorbell rang, and Conor jumped forward to open the door. Rick's hand landed on his shoulder to stop him.

"Make her wait. Don't appear too anxious or aggressive."

Conor took a deep breath and attempted to calm his racing heart. He knew Rick was right. This was not an occasion to let his Irish temper get the best of him. Turning his head, he looked at the stairway. Calleigh had paused on the middle step. Her face was pale and her eyes filled with anxiety. He forgot the door and walked up the few steps separating them.

"It 'ill be gran', *muirnín*. We'll sit down an' talk this out like rational adults." He placed his hand on her flat belly where their child nested. "How is *ár caragan*? The little darling is not giving you any trouble today?"

She placed her hand over his. "We're good." She looked over Conor's shoulder at Rick standing by the front door. "Go ahead and let her in. Once you're in the living room, I'll bring the boys down to the playroom and get them settled."

Rick opened the door and saw Susan on the front stoop, but she wasn't alone. He held the door wider to allow them to enter. One by one, they filed through, and he accepted their coats.

"This is my lawyer, Mr Nielson, and Ms. Waterman from the Department of Children and Families. I brought them so they can see for themselves what is occurring in this house."

He couldn't believe Susan's audacity. "We invited you here to discuss your concerns as a family. We did not authorise you to bring anyone else into our home."

He saw the surprised looks on the faces of the lawyer and social worker. It appeared Susan had given them some misinformation.

She pointed her finger at the man before her. "That's precisely why I wanted them here. So they could see just what this place is like when you haven't coached Kevin's children on what to say." She looked around. "Where are my grandchildren? I demand to see them."

Calleigh stepped forward so she was face-to-face with her mother-in-law. "Our sons are just getting up from their nap. They will be given their snack then they will go to the playroom while we speak. If after getting to know Ms. Waterman, we are agreeable, she will be allowed to speak with them, but *you* will not until I am assured you can control the venomous words from spewing out of your mouth."

Rick guided the three interlopers into the living room. "Can I offer you something to drink?"

"I would love a coffee if you have it ready, and please call me John," Nielson responded, settling into the club chair near the windows.

"Make that two please, and you may call me Jamie," Ms. Waterman answered.

Rick nodded his head in acknowledgement. "Susan?"

All he got in return was a haughty stare as she sat primly on the sofa.

"In that case, Calleigh and Conor will be down in a moment after they've gotten the boys settled. I'll have your coffees shortly."

He walked through the archway into the kitchen. Grabbing two mugs from the cabinet, he attempted to release some of the rage boiling though him. The addition of the officials put an entirely different tone on this meeting than they were intending. He knew he shouldn't act defensive, but it was hard not to when his family was being threatened. He placed the mugs, sweetener and milk on a tray then carried it back into the living room.

He handed the two officials their coffee. "As I said earlier, we invited Susan here to discuss her concerns. We respect her as Mikey and Brandon's grandmother," he looked at her, "but we want to make sure you understand that we are their parents and as such will be making decisions regarding their upbringing."

"That is exactly why I've filed the suit. People like you have no business raising children. You perverts will poison their minds and give them no moral code."

Calleigh entered the room, catching that last statement. "And I suppose you believe being raised in a house where you preach hate and bigotry is a more nurturing environment?"

"It is not wrong to teach a child morality based on Christian values. I did so with Kevin, and he grew into an upstanding man who became a national hero."

Calleigh nodded her head. "Yes, he did. He also understood and accepted alternative lifestyles. Our relationship was a direct reflection of that."

Rick stood next to the mantel and addressed the room. "Our argument with you has nothing to do with Kevin's character. It's truly a tragedy that he never had the opportunity to raise his sons. I'm sure he would have made a great father, but that is neither here nor now."

Conor held up his hand to halt the conversation. "'Tis obvious we dinna agree on certain aspect of our lives. Ye may not approve of our lifestyle, but what I don't understan' is why that entitles ye te involve the legal system in a custody dispute."

"Let me take this," Jamie responded. "It was explained to us at DCF — and from speaking with John he was given the same information — that Mrs Wells feared for the safety of her grandchildren. She reported possible abuse of a sexual nature."

Rick was shocked. He knew Susan disapproved, but he'd had no idea she would tell blatant lies to get her way.

"That is the most preposterous accusation I've ever heard! I would never put my children in jeopardy!" Calleigh yelled.

Susan stood up and got in Calleigh's face. "How do we know you're not forcing my grandchildren to watch or even participate in the sexual orgies that no doubt occur in this den of depravity?"

"Susan, sit down. Now," John said from the corner of the room.

Rick was impressed by the steel hardness in the attorney's voice despite its quite nature. Obviously, he was fed up with the whole proceeding, and that eased one of the knots in Rick's gut.

Conor went to stand next to Rick at the fireplace. "Again, that supposition goes back to your opinion of our lifestyle. There is no evidence of physical, sexual or emotional abuse in our home."

Rick glanced over as Jamie set her coffee cup down on the tray and stood. "Mr Connor, Mr McGuire, Calleigh, I believe I've heard enough of this conversation. Would you be agreeable to me speaking with Michael and Brandon so I can make a complete report?"

Rick thought the idea had merit. If she spoke with the boys, he was certain any lingering questions would be put to rest. He looked at Conor and Calleigh to determine how they responded to the request and saw them give a slight nod. "I believe that would be acceptable, provided one of us supervises the visit." He again looked to Conor and Calleigh. "I believe I would like to volunteer."

Calleigh watched the social worker and Rick walk back to the playroom. She was ready for this evening to be over. The sleepless nights and stress were catching up to her. Most likely the pregnancy contributed to her lack of energy as well. Conor must have noticed her wilting because he came to sit next to her on the sofa, and she leaned against him. He slipped his arm around her shoulder and placed a soft kiss on her temple, pulling her in closer to his side.

Susan gave her a dirty look from the chair across the room.

"Calleigh, I notice the ring on your finger. Are you planning to remarry?" Susan asked.

Calleigh looked down at the beautiful ring that still took her breath away. Her first smile of the night appeared. "Yes, we are planning a spring wedding on the Cape."

Susan leant forward. "I notice you have quite an accent, Mr McGuire. May I ask if you have a current visa?"

Conor rolled his eyes. "Naw, I don' require one."

"Why ever not? Did you manage to complete the naturalisation process?"

"Actually, I'm a natural-born citizen. Me da is a retired colonel in the United States Air Force. Me ma is Irish, and I lived in Ireland most of my life with the exceptions of summers in England where Da was stationed. I moved here te attend university an' decided te stay."

"Oh I see."

Calleigh heard a slight chuckle from the corner. For the most part, the man sitting there had been silent throughout the exchange. There was a knock at the door, and Conor stood to answer the summons. Looking over her shoulder, Calleigh saw her mom enter the room with Conor.

She stood and walked around the edge of the sofa. "Mom. So glad to see you." She gave her a big hug. When she let go, she turned and introduced her mom to John. "And I'm sure you remember Susan, Kevin's mother."

Lilly nodded her head in acknowledgement. "Susan. Can't say it's nice to see you under these circumstances."

Calleigh sensed her mother's anger at the other woman. She backed away, and Conor pulled her into a backwards hug as he propped himself on the wall.

"Lilly, I don't understand how you can condone this situation. Michael and Brandon are your grandchildren, too. What happens in this house is—"

"Stop right there. I have no problem with Calleigh's relationship with Conor and Rick because I've seen them interact with each other on nearly a daily basis for the last three years. Did you know they were the ones who brought her home the day she found out about Kevin? It was their arms that held her as her heart tore in two. They were the ones who stood beside her, helped her with the boys when they were still infants, made her smile again. They healed her heart, and she stole theirs. I know how much they love Calleigh and Michael and Brandon. They would give their lives for them, and that is all I need to know. I don't care what occurs in their bedroom. Frankly, it's none of our business."

Calleigh heard footsteps and saw Rick and Jamie enter the living room at that moment. Rick held the boys' hands, and they stopped in front of Susan.

Susan sat down and tried to pull her grandchildren into her arms, but they stepped away. "Michael? Brandon? Why don't you give grandma a hug?"

"Why you take us away?" Mikey asked.

She saw tears in their eyes and scowled at Rick. "Sweeties. I just want to make sure that you grow up to be like your daddy. Big, strong, happy, good men."

"Wick is our daddy. Conna is our da. They are big," Brandon replied.

Susan shook her head. "They may be big, but I'm afraid of what they are teaching you. They may be bad men."

Mikey scratched his head. "Conna teach us to bike."

"They just got tricycles. They're learning how to pedal on their own," Rick explained.

Brandon nodded his head in agreement. "Wick make smiley takes. Bad man no make smiley takes."

"The boys' favourite Sunday breakfast is smiley pancakes," Calleigh clarified.

"They kiss our boo-boos." Mikey pointed out the band-aid on his knee.

"They read stories." Brandon held out a book to show his grandma then walked over and gave it to Conor. "This one."

Conor lifted Brandon in his arms and accepted the book. "Ye bet, *mo grian*." He kissed him on the forehead then put him down. "Go give *mamó* a hug."

Calleigh had tears in her eyes as Brandon ran over and hugged her mom. Hearing the boys defend their daddies in the simplest terms pulled at her heart strings. She put a hand to her stomach and rubbed their unborn child. She may have been afraid of how Rick and Conor were going to react, but it was clear from the very mouths of babes what good, loving fathers they were. She felt bad for second guessing their desire to raise more children.

She went over and stood beside Rick. He pulled her into an embrace as she looked down at Susan sitting in the chair with a stunned look on her face as Mike turned around and joined his brother at her mom's side.

"Susan. I will fight you to the death to keep my family intact, but I ask you to drop this ridiculous suit. It will only lead to heartache on both sides. I think we've shown you here tonight that, although we may be a unique family, we have all the love and nurturing abilities of a traditional home. If anything, there is more to go around."

Susan stood and walked to the closet to retrieve her coat. "I will never approve of what you've turned into, Calleigh

Wells. In fact, I'm ashamed to call you my daughter-in-law, but I will not hurt my grandchildren, and it appears that they have the misguided notion that these men are their dads. I dearly hope you don't come to regret your actions as they grow into adults and learn just what you are. When they start asking questions about their real father, please send me notice." She walked out the door.

Calleigh couldn't believe after all Susan's pontificating on family values that she'd turn her back on Michael and Brandon without even saying goodbye. Calleigh shook her head in regret.

Nielson stood from the chair where he'd taken residence and addressed the room. "Calleigh, Rick, Conor, I wish to apologise to you. Had I know this was a witch hunt, I never would have agreed to represent Mrs Wells. It's obvious to me this is the perfect home for your sons. In fact, I hope this is not too presumptuous, but I was hoping that I could call you sometime. You see my partner and I recently adopted a little boy a year younger than Michael and Brandon. We may need some advice from time to time." He smiled.

She laughed at the blush on his face. "I think that would be fine, but I hope you remember that we're learning as we go as well."

"I, too, will be filing my report and officially closing this file. You have my respect for the way you handled this situation," Jamie said.

Calleigh showed both of them to the door and leaned her head against it for a moment after it closed. Strong arms wrapped around her, and a kiss was placed on the back of her neck.

"Ye see, *mo ghrá*, everything has worked out. I'm sorry the boys willna have their other grandma in their lives, but I think there's enough of us te make up for the loss."

"That's just it, Conor. I feel that not having her in their lives is no loss, and that makes me sad because Kevin was a good man. He would have been a good father. With her reactions, she's denying them the relationship with that half of their family."

She stepped away from the door and turned to face everyone in the room. Rick came over and held her between him and Conor. She raised her head and received a kiss.

"That's her choice, angel. You aren't denying them, she is. Kevin would understand that. I don't think he would find fault with you."

She leaned her head on Rick's chest for another minute then stepped away. Kneeling down, she held out her arms and both boys ran to her. "My little loves, mommy is so proud of you. You said very nice things about your daddies." She wiped away the errant tear that slid down her cheek. "Now how about we get some dinner then we all have movie night?" She looked up at her mom. "Are you going to join us?"

"I would love to, but I promised your father I'd bring him home dinner from *Mirabelle's*."

Calleigh stood and gave her mom another hug. "Thank you for coming. For saying what you did."

"I only speak the truth. Now, have a good night with your family. I'll see you all this weekend. How about we all go to the aquarium? You want to go see the big fish and turtles, boys?"

Calleigh smiled as their eyes lit up and twin heads nodded in unison. They loved the aquarium. They all said goodbye, and the group headed into the living room.

"Mikey and Brandon, you pick the movie tonight. Daddy can help you with the names. Da and I will get dinner started."

Epilogue

Conor leaned his head back against the sofa. He absently ran his thumb over the wedding band on his finger as he and Calleigh watched the most recent blockbuster to come out on DVD. Calleigh's head was in his lap, as was customary, and his other hand stroked through the thick, honey tresses falling over her shoulder.

His lowered his hand to smooth it up and down her back, lifting the tail end of her shirt as he caressed the soft skin. Calleigh turned her head and nuzzled his crotch, rubbing her face against him like a cat. The touch caused all the synapses in his body to spark. He craved her touch like the most addicting drug—her nimble fingers on his skin, her soft lips and wet little tongue meeting his as her taste invaded his senses. And there were no words to express how it felt to sink deep inside her body.

Her fingers came out to play with his rapidly thickening shaft. She put enough pressure behind the movement to drive fire bolts racing through him. He groaned.

"*Muirnín*, yer playin' with fire."

The material of his jeans dampened as her pink tongue traced the ridges of his erection. He was about to unzip and beg her to swallow his cock when Rick came into the room.

"Sorry, Con. Someone else needs Calleigh's special skills right now."

Baby Alannah Nicole was transferred into Calleigh's arms. Conor pulled her between his legs to support her back. He loved sitting behind her and looking down when his child nursed from his wife's breast. The tiny, rose coloured lips latched onto Calleigh's nipple for nourishment and tugged deep on his soul.

Rick sat next to Calleigh and Conor. He felt bad about interrupting their play, especially since opportunity for such interludes had been limited lately, but his daughter wanted food. He stroked Calleigh's legs and watch as her fingers smoothed the static flies of black hair on Alannah's tiny head. Conor hummed as he wrapped his arms around their wife and daughter.

Calleigh looked up at Rick. "Were the boys still asleep?"

He nodded. "Out like lights. I think I actually managed to wear them out today."

They'd been out in the backyard of their new home, building the boys' first tree house. The family had chosen to relocate to Roslindale and had found a wonderful home in a neighbourhood surrounded by old growth trees in the Metropolitan Hill area. The place had beautiful hardwood floors, French doors, and custom built-ins. But Rick, Conor, and Calleigh's favourite spot was sitting out on the deck, late at night, listening to the crickets. For now, Calleigh was staying home with the kids, and he and Conor were able to catch the commuter train on a daily basis. This was a quiet neighbourhood with all the advantages of being near the city they loved so much.

Calleigh lifted Alannah to her shoulder and burped her. When she handed her back to him, he looked down into the sapphire-blue eyes that were wide open and staring at him. "I'll go put her back to bed. Why don't the two of you head upstairs, and I'll meet you in our room shortly."

Calleigh proceeded Conor up the steps. His hands were on her hips the whole way. She had a surprise for her men tonight. She'd finally gotten the all clear from her doctor to make love again and was ready to experience the mind melting pleasure Rick and Conor always provided.

"You go ahead, and get in bed, love. I'm going to slip into the bathroom and wash up first." She gave him a hungry kiss and groped his reawakening crotch. "I'll take care of this when I get back."

He speared his hand through Calleigh's hair and captured her lips in a bruising kiss. "Dear God, I want ye Calleigh. I'm beggin' fer ye touch."

"Don't worry, I'll make sure you get what you need. Both of you."

She turned her back and sauntered into the master bath they'd renovated when they'd bought the house. She stripped from her clothes and, after pinning her hair up on top of her head, jumped in a quick shower. When she got out, she lathered her skin in lotion and slipped a sheer, baby-doll nightie over her head. She left off the matching panties. When she peeked out the bathroom door, she saw Rick and Conor both in bed with their eyes glued to the doorway. She opened the door and struck what she hoped looked like a sexy pose.

She guessed she achieved her purpose with the negligee because Rick and Conor were staring at her as if she were a feast and they were starving men. She knew the sheer fabric didn't conceal any of her attributes, and she gave them a sultry little smile.

"Heaven preserve us," Conor whispered.

"Uh-huh," Rick agreed.

Calleigh stepped onto the padded bench they had at the end of the bed. She stood looking down on her men. Slowly, she started to sway her hips. Her arms rose above her, lifting the ribbon edged hem. She tilted her head and let her long hair drape down her back. Spreading her legs a little, she undulated to silent music. She heard the raspy breaths of Rick and Conor. Occasionally, a soft moan could be heard. She turned her back to them and bent at the knees, slowly straightening. Her right arm slid up her entire body as she arched her back to once again raise her hand over her head. She circled her hips like doing a rumba.

"Sweet God, have mercy on us," Rick agonisingly whispered.

Turning to face them again, she stepped over the footboard and stood with one foot between each man's spread legs. The darkness of the room was broken by the light of the moon, streaming through the skylight and large French doors leading to their small private deck overlooking the backyard. In the muted light, she saw the fires blazing in her husbands' eyes.

Each man sat up and latched onto the leg in front of him. Conor's hand caressed up the front and Rick's up the back. Their lips and tongues played with the skin of her thighs. She reached down to grasp the hem of her nightie and slowly pulled it up and over her head. When she looked down, both men stared up at her as if paying homage to their empress. She rested a hand on each of their cheeks, and they nuzzled into her palms.

"*Muirnín?*"

"I got the okay from my obstetrician this morning."

She stepped out from between their legs and knelt on the bed. Rick's hand clasped hers and jerked her forward only to catch her in his arms and slowly lower her onto her back. Her vision filled with his large, hard body leaning over her.

"Are there any restrictions, angel?"

"Well, yes. You can't...umm...you know...go down there just yet. The doctor said we'd have to wait a couple of months for that, but anything else is fair game. She also said we may need a little assistance in the moisture department." Calleigh knew she was blushing but hoped the dark room covered her embarrassment.

"I think we can work well within those limitations, don't you, Con?"

"Absolutely."

Conor's hand rested on her waist and slid up to cup her breast. Lifting the heavier mound, he manipulated the tips softly. Calleigh closed her eyes and let out a sigh. Her breasts were more sensitive since she was nursing. Rick's finger dipped between her folds to play with her clit, rubbing back and forth, stimulating the bundle of nerves. Conor's head lowered and his lips claimed hers. She opened readily, and his tongue flicked against hers.

One of Rick's fingers slowly circled in the opening of her pussy, dipping in partially only to pull back and circle hungry flesh some more.

"Please, Rick," she begged. She wanted to feel him inside her again.

The finger pushed through once again, but this time didn't stop until it was fully embedded inside her. She cried out in pleasure. Rick added a second finger. Slowly, he stretched her. Conor licked at her breasts, occasionally flicking over the tips. She had already warned them about leakage, but neither one of them expressed concern over it. Rick removed his fingers, and she whimpered. He rolled her on top of him. She straddled his legs down by his knees.

"I think we should do it like this. So you can go at your own pace for now, angel."

"Put your hand out, *ár ghrá*." Conor put a dollop of lubrication in Calleigh's hand. "Now slick up his cock so it slides in real nice and easy."

Her hand wrapped around Rick's length and smoothed the cool gel up and down. He hissed, and his fingers dug into her hips. She pulled up and gave a little twist over the plum shaped head. Fluid freely flowed from the slit at the top.

"Angel, you'd better stop, or this will be over before we begin."

She scooted up so she could straddle his hips. Rick's hands were at her waist, and Conor's supported her hips. She slowly sank down onto the long, thick cock waiting for her. It took her several minutes before he was fully embedded, but once their groins were flush, she let out a sigh.

"Okay, *muirnín*, when you're ready, rise up and take a few strokes. Let us know if you have any problems or if we need to change positions."

She rose on her knees, and when just the tip of Rick's cock remained inside her, she slowly lowered herself down. She was pleased there was no pain or discomfort. Doing so again, she let her weight carry her down harder. This time she cried out but only because it felt so exquisite. Her fingertips dug into Rick's chest as she moved up and down. Closing her eyes, she concentrated on sensations. With each downward movement, his cock rubbed against her g-spot. She started moving up and down in shallow little strokes so the head kept sliding over it again and again.

Conor stilled Calleigh's strokes and leaned her forward to lie against Rick. He picked up the bottle of lube and released some on his fingers. He smoothed it onto the skin surrounding her back entrance then dipped a finger inside. Adding a second a few moments later, he stretched her as best he could. When he thought she was sufficiently ready, he guided the head of his cock to her opening and slowly pushed forward. When the head popped through the ring of muscle, he cried out at the intense heat and tightness clenching around him. He slowly worked his entire length in. Calleigh panted against Rick's neck the entire time.

He and Rick began to move. He felt Rick's cock through the thin membrane separating them inside Calleigh's body. It had been so long since he'd been inside her that he knew he wouldn't last long. His climax boiled low in his spine, and he thrust through the tight, hot, velvet lined channel.

"Gu sealladh saelbh oirnn!"

Conor cried for heavens to preserve his sanity for his wife owned his soul. Calleigh's moans echoed in the high ceiling of their bedroom. Rick's groans rumbled beneath their bodies.

She was going to explode. The intense pleasure rippling through her body, combined with the teeming love for her husbands, overwhelmed her entire being. Her orgasm was only seconds away. She was riding that elusive crest and just needed something to send her tumbling over.

Rick slipped his fingers between his and Calleigh's bodies. His fingertip found her clit and rubbed it tiny circles. He and Conor thrust hard inside her. He felt Conor plunge deep and hold. Looking over Calleigh's shoulder, he saw his best friend's neck strain as he found release inside their wife. Calleigh's pussy clamped down as she exploded around their cocks, sending Rick over the edge into oblivion.

Long minutes later, when their breathing even out, they separated their bodies and tucked Calleigh between them. Hands and lips crisscrossed and soothed their sensitised skin. Reaching over he picked up the damp cloth by their bed and tidied Calleigh then himself before handing it to Conor.

Rick turned on his side and gathered Calleigh to his front. Her head rested on the pillow beside him, and their noses rubbed. "Angel, I love you."

Conor scooted forward so he spooned behind Calleigh. He slid the hair from the side of her neck and whispered softly in her ear, "*Is tú, mo ghrá.*"

Calleigh lay between her husbands filled with peace and joy, her love for them beyond anything she'd ever experienced. Their journey together might have started with a tragedy, but in her best friends, she became whole again. She was their love, and they were her salvation, their hearts and souls blending to form a more perfect union.

THE PERFECT BALANCE

Dedication

To anyone who has ever had to make a new beginning. I applaud your courage and strength. Hopefully your life is now filled with happiness.

Prologue

Miranda slowly made her way back to Evanston from where she worked in downtown Chicago. She looked to her right and could make out the blue of Lake Michigan beyond the grass of the park as she drove down North Lake Shore Drive. Twelve hours ago her phone had gone off, waking her from a sound sleep, to summon her back to the hospital for an emergency.

When she'd arrived, it was to find the place inundated with patients from a massive fire at a club located in the warehouse district. Miranda's hospital had been swarmed with casualties from patrons, employees and several fire-fighters who'd been trapped when a section of the building had collapsed with them inside.

She'd spent the next ten hours in surgery, working two different cases. The first had been a young man whose chest had been crushed when panic had ensued and he'd been trampled by those trying to escape. He hadn't made it, and Miranda had watched through a glass window as the doctor informed the family of their son's death. The mother had collapsed in her husband's arms, crying for her baby boy. Her wails could be heard outside the closed room and the sound of her anguish had torn Miranda's heart in two.

Later, the other case had managed to stitch part of the edges back together. Miranda had been part of team that had worked on a young woman, who'd started to haemorrhage after going into early labour when the restaurant, next door to the club, had been evacuated. They'd managed to not only save the mother's life, but her son as well. The baby was born at thirty weeks gestation and would have an extended stay in the neonatal intensive care unit, but mother and fathers couldn't have been happier. That last little bit had thrown Miranda for a loop. At first when she'd stood with the surgeon to impart the happy news, she'd assumed the man standing with the woman's husband was a friend, but it turned out he was actually the couple's partner.

As Miranda had later prepared to leave, she'd walked by the woman's room, unable to get the threesome off her mind. It may have not been the most professional behaviour on record, but she couldn't help but stare in fascination as the two men hugged and kissed each other while sitting next to their wife's bed. Her hand had been secured between theirs, and even through the sedating effect of lingering drugs in the woman's system, the love she shared for her two men had been obvious.

Miranda had never had much exposure to anyone who was gay, and had been a little shocked by the tingle that went through her while she watched the two men kiss. Knowing that those men also made love to the woman, maybe even at the same time, had caused Miranda to clinch her muscles below as she felt moisture seep from her folds.

Miranda jolted back to the present as she realised she had almost missed her turn into Sheridan, she'd been so caught up in the memory of watching the family celebrate their good fortunes earlier. She made sure to pay closer attention as she continued to wind through town. It was three in the afternoon and traffic was busy with early commuters and carpools making their way home from school.

Finally Miranda pulled into a parking space outside of her condo complex. The green grass and flowering trees were bright against the aged red brick and brownstone façade. She'd been lucky to find a spot right outside her building. Maybe that meant good fortunes for the rest of the day. After shutting off her engine, she gathered her purse and slowly made her way down the sidewalk towards the iron gate enclosing the courtyard in the centre of the buildings, from which all entrances were reached. It seemed now that she was home, exhaustion hit her as if it were a tsunami. All she wanted to do was climb in bed and sleep for at least a few hours. Maybe Drew would let her nap till it was time to make dinner. She carefully slid the key into the lock of the gate. It seemed to take all her strength to twist the little piece of metal.

Their condo was on the first floor of the north building. Miranda made her way inside the building then unlocked the front door. When she pushed it open, she knew immediately that Drew wasn't home. She felt a little guilty at how relieved that made her. She carefully hung her jacket and purse in the closet beside the door. A few more steps and she was in the living room. As she looked around, unbidden tears came to her eyes. There were magazines littering the floor, and a pile of clothes scattered all over the floor between the living room and kitchen. It looked as though a tornado had been through their place, with the cushions of the sofa strewn all over the place, and the rug scrounged up in front of the entertainment centre.

Miranda made her way into the kitchen to get a glass of water, and found the sink full of dirty dishes. Dishes that hadn't been there when she'd left in the middle of the night. Enough dishes that she wondered if Drew had had a dinner party while she was gone. It seemed a nap was out of the question. Miranda knew that if she didn't get the place cleaned up before Drew got home, she'd never hear the end of it. Never mind that it had been spotless when her phone had gone off.

She picked everything up on the floors, straightened up the cushions and rug then vacuumed and ran the duster across the hardwood floors. She smoothed out the sheers on the windows in the living and dining areas. Miranda picked up the pile of mail that had come from their box and set it on Drew's desk for him to sort through, flipping through the envelopes to see what had come. When she saw the logo of their bank at the top left corner, she was tempted to open their statement to find out exactly what the status of their finances were, as she was every month. However, couldn't bring herself to attempt steaming open the envelope then resealing it so Drew wouldn't know she'd been snooping. He handled all the bills. Miranda was given a weekly cash allowance for gas, groceries and incidentals.

She'd tried not to remember the only time she'd gone through her money and asked Drew for some more, a few months into their marriage. Her ears had rung from the virulent insults reverberating in her brain for days. Now days Miranda was much more careful with keeping track of money in her wallet.

Miranda picked up a glass sitting beside Drew's laptop, which was sitting on the kitchen table. She must have knocked the mouse because the screen came out of hibernation. It wasn't unusual for Drew's computer to be on, since the man did most of his work as a web designer from home. But when Miranda looked down, instead of finding the work project she'd expected, the screen was filled with a picture of giant penis being shoved inside some woman's vagina.

The phallus was huge, dripping with secretions from the woman's body. Thick ropey veins snaked up the length of the column. She collapsed into the chair and stared at the image, trying to deduce whether or not it was artificially enhanced. Could something that colossal really exist in nature? She rested her arms on the table to lean in for a closer inspection, and the next thing she knew the image came to life. The penis started thrusting into the woman's body, violently. So not fake apparently. Miranda had never seen what sex looked like up close. It was messy, raw, primal and arousing.

The faceless woman was really in to it, by the moans coming from off camera. She made sounds Miranda had never heard from another human before. What would it feel like to have something that large inside her? Drew was the only man she'd slept with, and he was nothing like that thing pummelling the poor woman on screen.

Sex with Drew consisted of twice monthly interludes in the dark, under the covers. The episodes over almost before they began, after which Miranda was more glad Drew was finished than wishing it could have lasted longer. While the idea of sex aroused her, the reality was so far from her fantasies as a young woman that the quicker it ended the better in her opinion. There was nothing pleasurable about Drew pushing his way inside — while Miranda was still dry — never mind the painful twists of her nipples or the fast paced thrusts that had Drew straining in a matter of minutes. Her husband would vacate the bed to go clean up almost immediately. He always reported that being inside Miranda made the skin of his penis burn, which was why he also refused to go down on her.

Miranda jumped at the sound of a key turning in the front door. She scrambled frantically to get the video to stop. Moving the mouse arrow around, she tried to find the pause button. She looked over her shoulder and clicked the bottom of the screen, blindly. The video stopped, but in the process another window popped up. It was an instant message, and there was one line.

NSA meet. 2:00pm...same place.

Miranda heard the door open. She quickly picked up the glass from the table and ran into the kitchen. Turning on the water, she began to do the dishes. Her hands shook as she tried to move the soap around a plate. She was more focused on the sound of Drew's footsteps behind her, not the task at hand.

"What the fucking hell were you doing on my computer?" Drew screamed.

Miranda dropped the plate as she spun around. Water and soap suds splashed all over the floor.

"I've told you over and over, not to touch my stuff. An idiot like you has no business messing with this kind of equipment. If you fucked anything up on here, I'll beat your ass. I have important stuff for work on here. It's only with the money I make we're able to live the way we do. You think the measly amount of money you earn is enough to support us? I lose this account, and it'll be your entire fault, you fat cow!"

"I didn't Drew…honest. All I did was —"

"All you did was put your nosy ass where it doesn't belong. Now clean up that mess you made. Don't think I didn't hear that dish break. What are you making for dinner? I'm hungry."

"I planned on making lemon herb baked chicken and new potatoes. Your favourite."

"Trying to buy into my good graces? What did you do wrong? As if you ever do anything right."

"I just thought you would like —"

"Well that's your first mistake. You and thinking are never good companions. Never mind, I'll find out eventually what you did. Now get to work. On second thought, go take a shower. I can smell the stink of that hospital from over here."

Miranda picked up the shards of ceramic on the wood floor. She knew tears would do no good, so she kept them inside. In fact, the sight of tears only made her husband angrier. When he got like this, it was as if her husband turned his ears off and put his mouth into overdrive. Not an unusual occurrence in their two and half year marriage.

Had she known the man with the face of an angel actually held within him the temperament of the devil, Miranda never would have agreed to marry him in the first place. When she'd met Drew in a club three years ago, the man's shining black hair and mesmerising violet eyes had put her under a spell almost from their first dance. Their courtship had been filled with romantic dinners and walks along Lake Michigan. Drew had been attentive and sweet, and Miranda had fallen harder than a two ton anvil. Six months later they were married in a small ceremony at the courthouse. They'd decided to forgo a honeymoon, since Drew had just started a new job. Then, almost from the moment they moved into their condo, the benevolent mask fell and the true Drew was revealed.

* * * *

Miranda couldn't get the instant message out of her mind. A few days after the computer incident, she was at the hospital during her normal shift and decided to use one of the computers to dig a little deeper. She opened a search engine and typed in the letters she'd seen in the message. The first hit was for the National Security Agency. Miranda was pretty sure her husband wasn't a government agent. Given the nature of the video behind the message, she typed the letters and added the word 'sex' behind them. The first several websites that popped up on the search engine were for partner swapping and no strings attached hook-ups.

She didn't dare open any of the sites for fear of the hospital's nanny programmes catching on to her private investigation. She sat at the nurses' station numb, oblivious to the sounds of the intensive care unit around her. Her fingers shook as Miranda closed down the internet search. It seemed that Drew had been cheating. She couldn't quite find the appeal in having sex with Drew, but it was still a break of the vows they'd spoken. Vows that, no matter how loudly Drew screamed at her, or how much Miranda found herself hiding in their bedroom to avoid her husband when he was in one of those moods, she'd never gone back on.

So while she'd been at work, Drew had been getting his groove on. Her gut clenched as she remembered later that very night Drew had taken her, the whole time whispering that he was sorry for yelling earlier, he loved her, and he was really stressed out on the most recent job he'd been working on.

Miranda ran to the bathroom to release the bile churning in her stomach.

* * * *

Almost three months had passed since Miranda discovered Drew's extracurricular activities. She hadn't confronted her husband that first time, or the second she'd come home to find him missing, or even the third. Sure, Drew wasn't perfect, but she was hardly the first woman to have an unfaithful husband. Drew had even been more relaxed lately. He didn't yell as much or call her names. So maybe it could even be looked at as a good thing.

Drew had been gone again yesterday when she got home. He'd come home a couple of hours later, demanding dinner and smelling of perfume. Once again, Miranda had put her head down, fixed his meal and kept her mouth shut. They hadn't had sex in a month, and much to Miranda's relief, she'd started her period that morning so she knew she wasn't pregnant. She'd always been irregular and when she'd skipped last month, she'd been a bit panicked.

Miranda sat in the hospital cafeteria, picking at her salad. The other day Drew had watched her as she got dressed for work, and made several comments about how round her hips were and the pooch at her belly. Miranda had never been reed thin. From the time she hit puberty, her chest had blossomed and her hips flared. She tried to keep everything else in proportion by good diet and semi-regular exercise but try as she might, Miranda never fit in anything smaller than a size ten.

She flipped through a magazine at the table and came upon an advertisement for Valtrex, a drug used in the treatment of herpes, and froze. Holy shit! She'd never even thought of STDs. She worked in a hospital for God's sake, she should know better! From the beginning of their marriage, he'd refused to use condoms. So what were the chances he used anything with his tricks? She really didn't know how long his little trysts had been going on. Had he ever been faithful? They'd crossed the three year mark a couple of weeks ago, and who knew how many times in those three years Drew had blithely exposed Miranda to all kinds of sexually transmitted diseases.

Miranda looked at her watch. She had another ten minutes of her break. She threw her uneaten salad in the trash and ran out of the cafeteria. The other employees probably thought she was running to get to an emergency, and that was fine with Miranda.

She slid to a stop at the station desk in the OR department. Jessica, one of the other nurses on her team, sat there getting the charts ready for the afternoon cases.

"Jess, oh thank God!" Miranda exclaimed, breathing heavily.

"Miranda, what's wrong!"

"I...I need your help," she said, looking around for anyone in the vicinity. She leant in close and whispered, "I need you to draw some blood for me."

Jessica leant in. "Who am I drawing on and why are we whispering?"

"Because you're the only one I trust with this. Nobody can find out, promise me." She nibbled on her lip. "I'll have to do it under an assumed name," she said distractedly.

"On you? You're running a panel on yourself? Why? What's wrong? Oh my God, are you sick or something?"

"Or something," Miranda mumbled. "Look, will you just do the draw?"

"Yeah, sure." Jessica looked at the clock. "Let's go now. The next case is in prep, we've got a few minutes. I've already got the room set up."

Jessica led Miranda to a bed in the recovery area. She pulled the curtain around them and got out the supplies they'd need. The mission was quickly accomplished. Miranda thanked the one person she considered a semi-friend, even though she and Jessica didn't hang out outside the hospital. Miranda didn't have friends outside the hospital. She did before her marriage, but after Drew performed his transition to Mr Hyde, it'd been impossible to maintain the relationships. Miranda had one of the doctors sign the work order, telling him it was for another case, and put a fake name on the order. Now all she had to do was wait.

* * * *

The last ten days had been the longest of her life. That morning, Miranda had got notice she had a clean bill of health. She'd spent a lot of time over the last week and half thinking about her situation. It was time to put an end to sticking her head in the sand. For the sake of her physical and mental health, she needed to confront Drew. Up till now, it had seemed easier to avoid the problem. Easier to stick with the status quo than to risk another tirade from her husband or, if worse came to worse, the loss of her marriage. Part of Miranda had always thought that, despite his faults, Drew was the best thing she could hope for. The love she'd felt during their courtship had slowly died, but Miranda was committed to her marriage.

She believed in the vows she'd spoken, and if Drew chose to divorce her, it would mean she was a failure.

Then what would she do with her life? It's not as if she could attract another man easily. Miranda knew she was no belle of the ball. She was short, plain, overweight and even though she felt competent at her job as an operating room nurse, she'd never had the smarts to go to medical school like she dreamed as a little girl. When her mom had met Drew, she'd pulled Miranda aside and told her to marry the man before he came to his senses. Her father had simply sat in his chair in the living room and buried his face in the newspaper, as he had for as long as Miranda could remember.

Several hours later she opened the front door and found Drew watching television. Miranda put her purse away in the closet and took a deep breath. She stood to the side of the sofa and stared at the man she married.

"Are you going to say anything, or just stand there and stare at me?"

She swallowed slowly. "We need to talk."

Drew didn't look away from the programme he was watching. "Oh yeah? It'd better be about what you're making for dinner."

"I planned on—" Miranda had started with her normal response, but stopped before she completed the thought. "No! You're cheating on me."

Drew looked away from the TV, but his face had a rather bored expression.

"Your point being?"

"Why?"

"Because I get more pleasure from fucking a blow up doll than I do between your fat legs."

Even prepared for the insult, it still hurt.

"Oh, Jesus, don't start the crying shit. Look, some women are made to fuck and some are made to do everything else around the house. I have needs."

Miranda wiped her damp cheeks. "Then why...why bother having sex with me at all?"

"Because you're rather convenient. It's not like I can go out all the time and you *are* my wife. A bad fuck is a fuck after all. I still get a load off."

Drew looked back at the TV and started clicking the remote. Something in Miranda snapped. She strode over to the sofa, ripped the remote out of Drew's hand and shut off the television. She faced her husband with her fist clenched. "I am not some mannequin who exists simply to make your life easier! I am a living, breathing human being. I have feelings and desires and needs just as you claim to have. I'm tired of being your servant and receptacle for your frustration and hate. Your whoring not only demeans the vows we spoke to each other, but you've risked my life, you stupid, selfish son of a bitch!"

Miranda gasped at her outburst. She'd never shouted at Drew before. And by the redness of his face, the outcome was not going to be good.

Chapter One

April 2006

Miranda dragged the roll of packing tape across the top of the box then secured the end. She twisted and turned, looking for the roll of pink duct tape. Pink meant living room, and she knew if she waited to label the box, it would get lost and end up in storage somewhere. She could have sworn it was lying on the floor beside her a moment ago.

"Axel!" she called out, warningly. "Did you steal my tape again?"

There was a loud noise in the kitchen and Miranda rolled her eyes, not even wanting to imagine what the cause behind that sound was. She heard the click of her two year old boxer's nails on the wood floor.

Axel's head peeked around the corner of the kitchen island at the other end of the room, purloined tape clutched firmly in his jaw.

"Bring it here," she commanded, holding out her hand.

Axel's head tilted as if to question what Miranda meant. "Come."

With a sigh, the all-white boxer crept towards her. But where Axel's white coat should have been there was instead a fine layer of blue fuzz. When he stopped in front of her, Miranda couldn't help but laugh at benign expression on his face. Those giant black eyes swam with innocence. She brushed at his coat. The short hair of his fur tickled her hand, and little blue puff balls filled the air.

"I don't even want to know where this came from."

Axel sat on his rear haunches and leant into Miranda's touch.

"Okay, drop it."

He did as ordered then lifted his head and gave Miranda a big kiss on her cheek.

"Ugh!" she cried out, wiping her cheek, then wrapped her arms around Axel's sturdy neck.

"I love you too, boy."

Suddenly tears leaked from the corners of Miranda's eyes. They'd spent a lot of time together like this over the last three months. One minute Miranda would be fine and the next she'd be weeping as if she were her mother watching the latest lifetime movie of the week. However, when everyone else in her life had abandoned her, Axel was never far away. Always up for a jaunt to the park to let off some steam, or simply lay on his bed while Miranda cuddled up on the couch to watch a movie or read a book.

Now a year after she'd confronted Drew about his abuse, and Miranda was finally able to admit that Drew's behaviour was abuse, his treatment of her had got so much worse. The malevolent whirlpool her life had become finally managed to suck her under. Months of fighting, silent treatments and every other form of verbal abuse that Drew could sling at her took its toll, and

Miranda's depression hit an all time low. Low enough that even a doctor she'd only worked with a couple of times asked if she was okay during one shift at the hospital.

She'd suggested to Drew that they go to marriage counselling to talk about their problems, but when he'd not shown up for their first two appointments, Miranda had apologised to the psychologist and left, more defeated than ever.

The final straw had been when Miranda had got a call at work from the police saying that Drew had been arrested for propositioning sex to a minor in a night club, and would she come bail him out. She'd hung up, finished her shift, gone home, packed all of Drew's clothes in his matching five piece luggage then dropped it off at the police station where he was being held. The next day she'd found an attorney and used the savings she'd been putting away for the past year to put down a deposit on the divorce proceedings. Failure or not, she couldn't take any more.

Three months later, Miranda had been driving, her mind a swirling fog of self recrimination, pain and anger after signing the final divorce papers, and had passed an animal shelter not far from her condo. There was a huge banner outside that advertised for adoptions, and in a rash but ultimately perfect decision, she decided to find a companion to take home with her.

Miranda had strolled up and down the concrete aisles, peering in the chain linked pens at all the homeless animals. A chorus of barks echoed off the concrete walls, acting as her soundtrack on the expedition. Her heart had gone out to each one, part of her wishing she could take them all home. Well, all except maybe the Brittany Spaniel doing his best to imitate the Tasmanian devil from the cartoons in the corner. She'd been about to give up, convinced that the errand was impulsive and that's why none of the animals really called to her, when her eyes landed on Axel's cage. He'd sat quietly, almost as if he'd been waiting just for her to show up. When Miranda had squatted down to his eye level, he'd tilted his head, and if dogs actually had the ability to smile, she would have suggested his jowls had spread wide from one floppy ear to the other.

He'd come home with her that day after a quick stop to the local pet store to pick up supplies and a couple of toys. The moment they'd entered the condo, the atmosphere instantly felt homier than it had in the three and half years she'd lived there.

Miranda sat back and wiped her eyes. "Enough weepiness. A few more boxes and we'll be finished. Then tomorrow it's off to the spa for me and you." She rubbed the back of Axel's ears and he let out a low moan. "We have to look our best when we arrive in our new home. I think you're going to like Boston. It's a city, like Chicago. There's a huge park we can play in, and it's on the ocean so there's still water nearby. It's not the same as the lake, but I hear there's lot of stuff to do down by the harbour. Not to mention we'll probably learn all kinds of new stuff, since the city played such a big part of the country's history."

She ripped off a piece of the pink tape and stuck it on the box in front of her. Miranda looked around at the piles of cardboard surrounding her. Sadly, there wasn't much. Drew had made her get rid of most her stuff when they got married. Miranda had managed to squirrel away a few boxes of mementos from her childhood, teens and years at college. She'd kept them at a storage place not far from the house, paying each month's rent out of her allowance. Drew had never been the wiser, thank God. After Drew had moved out, she retrieved the boxes and brought them home.

Rocking back on her heels, Miranda stood with a soft groan and only one crack as she stretched her arms overhead. She walked into the kitchen and found the box of utensils that she hadn't yet sealed shut tipped over on its side, the contents spilled onto the floor. The remains of one of her kitchen towels lay shredded in a pile. That must have been the source of the blue fuzz.

"So that's what you were up to." She peered over her shoulder, knowing Axel would be right behind her. "Did you find what you were looking for?"

Axel let out a little whine, and Miranda scoffed. Axel had the *I'm the adorable puppy please don't punish me* routine down pat. Unfortunately she also knew — thanks to the puppy training classes they'd been to — punishing Axel now would do no good, so she cleaned up the mess and put the box on the counter so he wouldn't be able to knock it over again.

Miranda shut off the light in the kitchen, made sure that the front door was locked and sent the living room into darkness with the flick of the last switch. She headed for the bathroom off her bedroom, in need of a long hot shower to loosen up the muscles stiff from packing over the last week.

Miranda tilted her head back for one last rinse from the hot water then shut off the valve. Stepping out of the shower she dried herself, using the last towel not packed away, brushed her teeth and combed out her hair. Miranda was tempted to go to bed without drying the long tresses, but knew come morning she'd regret that decision, not to mention, who wanted to snuggle up to a wet pillow? After her plain brown strands crackled with static electricity from her dryer, she slathered on a layer of lotion—the bitter Chicago winter had wreaked havoc on her skin. Finally Miranda slipped on her PJs. She'd already taken Axel out for his last potty break, so she climbed into bed. She heard Axel get settled on his big dog bed against the wall.

"Good night, Axel," she whispered.

Tomorrow morning Miranda would pack the boxes up in her ten year old Jeep Grand Cherokee, and after her and Axel's appointments, they'd hit the road for Boston. Drew had taken all the furniture in the divorce except the bed, and Miranda had a donation company coming to pick it up in the morning. She'd sold the condo, thankfully at a profit, and after splitting the equity with Drew still had enough leftover to get her new life started in Boston. She'd flown out to Massachusetts to interview for a position at Mass General a month ago, and while there, toured a couple of apartments within her price range. She didn't plan on buying right away, not until she got a better feel for the city and its neighbourhoods. Two weeks ago, she'd got the call that the position was hers. She'd turned in her notice and brought home boxes that very afternoon.

After three years of dreading the next day, Miranda knew that tomorrow when she woke up it would be the beginning of a new life. One she planned on celebrating each and every day.

* * * *

Miranda clocked in for her first shift at the hospital after orientation. She pushed open the door to the women's locker room and pulled a set of scrubs off the stocked shelves. She usually wore a medium, but when she slid the top over her head it was apparent that either this manufacture sized differently or the label was incorrect because the material was exceeding tight across her chest and came to a halt a good two inches above her waist line. Miranda wiggled her way out. She probably looked ridiculous to the other staff in the room, twisting her way around as she tried to get the material back over her head. The material magically disappeared and once free, Miranda spun around. Another woman stood next to her with a smile on her face and Miranda's removed garment in her hand.

"Looks like you got the lucky shirt today. There's always one that never fits the way it should."

Miranda picked up her shirt lying on the bench and covered her chest. "Thanks."

She picked up another top from the wire shelf and this one slid over her body the way it should. Great way to start a new job, looking as if she were a moron who couldn't dress herself. Miranda slid on a pair of bottoms, drawing the string tight so they wouldn't slip during the day. She wanted to get out of there as quickly as possible, so she hurriedly put her tennis shoes back on. She'd spent a little over a hundred dollars on the New Balance product, but Miranda swore by them. She'd worn New Balance in the OR for years, and despite having tried others, never found a more comfortable set for the long hours spent on her feet. She slid a pair of covers over her feet then slid the pony hat over her head, making sure her long hair was secure under the material before tying the cord at the base of her skull.

Walking through the halls she started to get a little nervous, but excited at the same time. What would the members of her new team be like? Would they welcome her, or would they behave as some elitist society Miranda didn't have the pedigree to join? Would everyone get along, or would there be a bunch of smiling masks in place until a person's back was turned? Miranda had been part of more than one team where snide gossip and comments flew through the sterile hallways faster than the germs they tried to protect their patients from contracting.

She made her way to the charge desk to find out what surgeries were scheduled for the morning. As she turned a corner there was a blur of white and blue then Miranda found herself smashed up against a hard chest.

"Oh!" she cried, putting her hands up to catch herself before she fell.

"Shit! I'm sorry," the deep voice above her head growled, and a pair of arms came around her. Miranda stiffened at the unfamiliar male touch.

"Hey it's okay. I'm not going to hurt you."

The hands around Miranda's waist let go and rested gently on her shoulders. She looked up and found herself staring the base of a man's neck. The tendons were smooth and long beneath the skin. Her gaze travelled upwards and came to a sculpted jaw line that held a rough growth of hair that spoke of either determined perpetual grooming, or a busy doctor's schedule. A pair of lips with just the right amount of softness rested below a set of high cheekbones and a straight nose. She took a step back and got a better overall picture. Standing before her was a living breathing god of masculinity with shaggy dark blond hair and a pair of sky blue eyes. Miranda was both amused at herself and little scared. After her experience with Drew, she knew good looks were often veils for darker attributes in a human.

"Are you okay? I really didn't mean to nearly run you over. I wasn't paying attention."

Miranda took another step back. "No, it's my fault, Doctor."

rina Lane

Miranda moved around the tall man and quickly made her way down the hall. She found the door labelled as the staff lounge and ducked inside. Inside were several other nurses, most drinking coffee and chatting.

Miranda went over the coffee pot and poured herself a cup. She didn't really need more caffeine, but at least it gave her something to do with her hands. She ripped open the packet of sugar substitute and added it and a dash of creamer to the dark brew.

"Hi! You must be Miranda. I'm Jenna."

Miranda found herself looking at a young woman with really short black hair and green eyes that could only be the result of contacts. The green was enhanced by heavy black eyeliner that made the girl's eyes appear even more cat-like. At least the woman was smiling, quite brightly in fact. Brighter than anyone should at five in the morning, in Miranda's opinion.

"Yes, I am. It's nice to meet you."

"You too. I checked the desk and it looks like we'll be working together most of today. You're the scrub nurse and I'll be on circulation.

"Did they show you how to read the schedule? I heard you worked at Northwestern before moving here, so it's not as if you don't know the ropes, but sometimes it varies from hospital to hospital." Jenna took Miranda's hand.

Miranda jerked away and took a step back. Jenna frowned for a second, but then pointed to the door to the lounge.

"Let's go to the charge desk, and I'll show you the screen."

"Jenna I'm—"

"No worries. I know I can be a little much for some people."

60

"No, no. Um…it's not that…well I guess maybe a little, but really I get a little jumpy when someone grabs me." Miranda looked at the ground and whispered, "Sorry."

Miranda felt Jenna's stare and that of everyone else in the room. She hated being the centre of attention, and it seemed as though everything she did that morning somehow brought her into focus to everyone in the hospital. How many times had she wished she could simply push a button and a magical force field would surround her and cloak her presence from the rest of humanity?

They left the lounge in silence, and Miranda followed Jenna to the desk. The coffee in her stomach churned from the anxiety boiling in her gut.

Jenna pointed at the screen. "So today we have a total knee replacement with Dr Martin, a tonsil and adenoidectomy with Dr Krieghauser, a tumour removal with Dr Fischer and last but not least a double breast reconstruction with Dr Pruitte."

"Sounds as if we have a full day ahead of ourselves," Miranda said.

Jenna nodded. "Lots of variety too. You picked a good day to start."

Jenna and Miranda headed for the operating room that had been assigned for the first case. Both women gloved up and entered the theatre to begin the first scrub for the day. Despite twelve years of experience, the almost arctic air in the room made her shiver as the measly scrubs didn't really provide much in the way of warmth. Miranda and Jenna quickly prepared the room for surgery. They damp dusted the overhead lights, mayo stand and back table then worked their way to the outer edges of the room. She grabbed the sheets to make the OR bed, folding them perfectly with no wrinkles or kinks just the way she liked them, while Jenna switched on and tested the various pieces of equipment. When Jenna flipped the switch on the overhead lamps, Miranda hadn't been prepared and was blinded for a moment. She rolled her eyes at herself. You'd think this was her first time or something.

A scrub technician came in with the instruments, and he and Miranda began to open the sterile field. Miranda watched as Jenna did a count of the sponges, sharps and instruments. It didn't take long and soon the room was ready for the doctor and patient who'd been in the preparation area for the last thirty minutes. Jenna left to go get the necessary paperwork and talk to the patient.

Another nurse came in, one Miranda hadn't met yet, and started get the equipment ready that was used for anesthesia. A pair of bright, golden brown eyes looked up and caught Miranda's stare.

"Hi, I'm Calleigh Wells. I'm the nurse anesthetist on this case."

The soft voice was slightly muffled by her mask, but Miranda had no difficulty understanding her since she'd earned her OR ears years ago.

Miranda held out her gloved hand. "I'm Miranda Green. Scrub nurse and newbie to the hospital."

"Is this your first case with Dr Martin?"

"Yes. I met him during my orientation period, but haven't worked with him yet. How is he?"

Calleigh tapped the touch screen of the anesthesia machine. "He's actually one of the good ones. Likes to keep the room relaxed and always chooses good music. He expects the best, but he won't ream you out if something doesn't flow perfectly. I need to go check the patient, then we'll get this show on the road."

Miranda waited quietly for Jenna and Calleigh to wheel the patient back. The ten minute rest gave her a chance to rapid charge her batteries and get mentally psyched up for the next several hours. She closed her eyes and took a deep breath. There was a loud clunk as the gurney was pushed through the swinging doors. Miranda stood and things quickly got down to business. Jenna got the patient positioned on the table, placing the foam for the arms and feet, attaching the sequentials to the legs and making sure the safety strap was on.

Miranda took her place beside the patient. The doctor came in and said a few words to the patient before he left to scrub. The scrub tech helped Miranda don her isolation gown and a fresh pair of gloves. Dr Martin returned and said a few words about which sizers he wanted to use. Calleigh induced the man to rest. Then a couple of minutes later when she was happy with her readouts, she nodded. Jenna called the time out to be entered in the log, and the doctor started the procedure.

Miranda slid into what she referred to as her surgical persona and throughout the procedure felt as though she did a respectable job. It was by no means her first knee replacement, but working with new players was always a little nerve wrecking at first. At one point in the surgery the patient started to bleed heavily and Miranda was able to identify the bleeder quickly much to the surgeon's appreciation. A medical student who was assisting the doctor cauterise the leak.

After placing the implants into the patient's leg, the doctor verified the full flexion, extension, and ligament balance. Miranda cleaned the bone with saline and applied cement to the joint replacement components. The medical student closed the incision while the doctor looked on. Jenna was off to the side doing the second count.

"Nice job, Ms. Green," said Dr Martin. "I appreciate your help this morning. I think you'll make a fine addition to the staff here, and look forward to working with you again."

"Thank you, Doctor. It was enjoyable working with you as well."

Miranda dressed the knee while Jenna finished her paperwork and called recovery to let them know the patient would be arriving soon. A few minutes later, Calleigh signalled that the patient was breathing on his own and ready to be transported. Miranda helped take the patient to recovery and Jenna called the turnover team. The entire procedure took about an hour and half. Now, time to send in the clean-up crew and get ready for the next case.

Chapter Two

Miranda sat at a corner table in the cafeteria, eating her apple. The flatbread turkey sandwich had tasted as if it were actually made from cardboard, and she'd not finished half of it. That'd teach her to buy the cheap stuff again. It was still a little bit of an adjustment to be the master of her own finances again. When Drew had taken care of everything, all Miranda had to worry about was her weekly allowance. Now she had to make sure to remember to pay all the bills and put money into savings. One of the first things she'd done after the divorce was final was go out to buy a laptop and a software programme that allowed you to set up a household budget. Her bank sent her email notices when a bill was due, and that really helped. Especially now that Miranda actually had the means to check her email on a regular basis.

When the truth about hers and Drew's financial status was brought to her attention by her attorney, Miranda had been in shock. It seemed that Drew made about thirty thousand less than Miranda's annual earnings at the hospital. When her attorney had told her she'd basically been supporting them, Miranda had cried remembering all the times Drew had told her it was only by his good graces that she got as much of an allowance as she did, since it all came from his earnings.

She'd also learned that Drew had racked up quite a bit in credit card debt, which Miranda had known nothing about, even though two of the cards had been opened in her name. She used part of her equity from the sale of their condo to pay one of the credit cards off, but still had another which would take her at least three years to pay down. Every month when she looked at that statement, she cursed Drew a little louder. Miranda had contacted the company and explained the situation, but they informed her that since the account was in her name, and during the division of assets during the divorce that portion of the debt had been placed on her, she was responsible for the balance. Miranda's lawyer had said they could fight, given that the card was opened without her knowledge, but there was no way to prove that without a doubt since Drew had put both their names on the account. The credit company had worked with Miranda to lower the interest rate so she could pay it down quicker, but frankly it still sucked.

The extra money she earned by taking this job was basically sucked up by the higher cost of living on the East Coast, but Miranda was still glad she come out here. Axel was adapting to his new environment well, and they'd had fun exploring the city together over the last month.

"Hey! Are these seats taken?"

Miranda was dragged from her mental ramblings by the voice coming from her left side. She looked over and found both Jenna and Calleigh standing there with trays of food. Miranda shook her head, and the two sat with dual sighs of pleasure.

"Man, my feet are killing me. Is twenty four weeks too early for them to swell?"

Jenna shrugged. "No idea. I've never been preggers, but you are carrying a matched set, so logic would suggest that your symptoms would be twice that of a normal pregnancy."

Miranda quickly looked down at Calleigh's stomach. There was most definitely a protrusion to her stomach that Miranda hadn't noticed earlier. How she'd missed it Miranda wasn't sure, because the roundness beneath Calleigh's scrubs mimicked a half inflated beach ball. In fact, she wore maternity scrubs that flowed over her baby bump compared to the straight shooters Miranda and Jenna had on.

"Congratulations. When are you due?"

"September fifteenth. I'm having boys. My husband is so thrilled, but unfortunately he's going to miss their birth."

"Why is that?"

"He's on deployment in Iraq. He'll be home early next year."

Miranda couldn't imagine being left home alone and pregnant while your husband risked his life on the other side of the world. Was it possible Calleigh ever got scared at the prospect of going through the process alone? Miranda didn't think she could do it, but then again the likelihood of her ever having children was slim. While being married to Drew hadn't been ideal, and the thought of having his children had scared her, the concept of being a mother was always something she'd envisioned as part of her life. Now Miranda was thirty-four, alone, and quite frankly scared of putting out her for sale sign in the dating market.

"Calleigh, are you on Dr Pruitte's case this afternoon?"

"Yep." She sighed. "That man is...he's so..."

"Fuckable?"

Miranda's eyes went wide and she looked around at the other tables to see if anyone nearby had overhead Jenna's comment.

"Jenna!"

"What? He is. You can't tell me that if you weren't married to the world's most perfect man, you wouldn't want a slice of that heaven."

"Kevin is not perfect, believe me. And as to having a slice, haven't you ever heard of the perils of eating a bite of forbidden fruit?"

Jenna smiled as she took a sip of her fruit juice. "I like to live dangerously. What about you, Miranda? Are you married?"

Once again the spotlight had swung her way, and Miranda squirmed in her seat. "No."

"Are you looking? We have some fantastic looking guys here."

Miranda actually shuddered with Jenna's description. She couldn't help it, whenever she thought of good looking men, her mind flooded with images of Drew's angelic face contorted in rage as he screamed obscenities at her.

"Miranda?" Calleigh asked, softly. "You okay?"

"Yeah, fine. Sorry. Um...no, I'm not looking."

Miranda peaked through her lashes and saw Jenna watching her with an expression of concentration. She didn't know what it was. It was almost as if Jenna were studying her, which made Miranda want to jump out of her chair and run, but that would only bring more attention to herself. So she studied the cracked lines of the laminate on the table and waited for either Jenna or Calleigh to start their conversation again.

"Jenna, you don't have plans to try and land Dr Pruitte, do you?"

Jenna leant back in her chair and looked at Calleigh. "No. He's hot and everything, but I heard through the rumour mill that he's actually involved with someone. One person said that he and Dr Burns are getting it on, but then a nurse up in intensive care said that she and Dr Pruitte dated for a couple of months." She shrugged. "Who knows what to believe around here?"

Calleigh was quiet for a moment and Miranda saw her brown eyes dance mischievously. "He could be bisexual. That would seriously hot!"

Miranda quickly looked over at Jenna who in turned stared at Miranda, then they both swung their heads in Calleigh's direction, mouths agape.

"What? It's the hormones. I swear."

Jenna smiled, widely. "Beneath that sweet and innocent exterior lies a kinky little minx. Damn girl, wish I'd known that before. I've been keeping my exploits rated PG-13 in deference to your delicate sensibilities."

Calleigh laughed and tossed her wadded up napkin at Jenna. "You never asked. I have stories from Kevin's and my years at Boston College that would probably send you into cardiac arrest."

Miranda knew she was blushing. Her experience with men was nowhere near what these two women were talking about. Having only had one sex partner in her lifetime, she felt that much more inadequate. She had no sexy stories to share, no tales of decedent excess filled with midnight orgies and sipping champagne from body parts. Her mind flashed back to that threesome in Chicago the night of the club fire. Seeing those two men kiss at their wife's bedside had stirred something inside Miranda.

What would it be like? How it would feel to be surrounded by two men who not only loved you, but loved each other? There had to be love in Miranda's imagination. She could never envision herself having sex simply for the sake of sex. Despite all the rumours, she didn't think the act itself would ever be good enough to take part in without caring for your partner. Wasn't that the whole point of having sex? Besides the whole procreation thing, you wanted to share intimacy with a loved one. Sex for sex's sake didn't make much sense to her.

She looked at the clock on the wall and noticed her lunch break was over, so with a quiet goodbye she gathered up her trash and headed back to the OR floor. Miranda pushed open the doors and walked over to the desk to check for any changes to the afternoon schedule. There was a doctor standing at the computer, looking at something on the screen. Miranda didn't want to bother him, so she went to the sink to wash her hands.

"Excuse me?"

Miranda turned and found the doctor looking at her. "Yes?"

"Do you know who's working Dr Fischer's gastrectomy this afternoon?"

"I'm the scrub nurse. Is there something you need?"

The doctor pointed at the screen and his white coat moved enough that Miranda caught a glimpse of his name. It was Burns. Was this the same person Jenna and Calleigh had been talking about? Although it was possible that there was another Dr Burns in the hospital, but they had said Dr Pruitte and Dr Burns were supposedly involved, and this was a man standing in front of her. A very attractive man, at that.

"I have the patient's most recent PET scan results, and there's something he needs to see before the surgery."

Miranda pointed at the computer. "May I?"

Dr Burns nodded and Miranda stepped up to the computer. She pulled up the programme that called up the status of all the patients on the docket for the afternoon. "The patient is already in prep. Let me see if I can track down Dr Fischer." Miranda looked at the list taped to the back of the desk beneath the counter. She punched in Dr Fischer's number into the pager system. When it started ringing, she handed the phone over to Dr Burns.

While Dr Burns talked to his colleague, Miranda took the opportunity to examine the specimen in greater detail. Probably somewhere around six feet tall, with dark brown hair with light blue eyes that reminded her of Hugh Laurie from that show House. Arresting combination actually. The man's physique ran towards long and lean, but Miranda sensed an underlying strength was hidden beneath the stylish button down shirt and tailored slacks. Her glance moved up and she found those blue eyes watching her. Miranda quickly turned her back and moved away.

"You're new, aren't you?"

Miranda nodded. "I started my orientation last month. Today's my first independent shift."

"Would you look at me, please?"

Miranda did so, reluctantly. She knew to ignore the request would be extremely unprofessional, but it didn't stop the embarrassment from being caught looking at the man a moment ago flooding through her.

"That's better, thank you. You're not new to nursing though. You seem too confident."

"No, I moved here from Chicago. I worked at Northwestern for twelve years."

"I'm Dr Victor Burns, radiology." He held out his hand.

She slipped her hand into his. It was warm and that warmth spread up Miranda's arm. "Miranda Green."

She found herself staring into Dr Burns' eyes once again. It was with a mental slap that she realised what she was doing and began to panic. She would not go down that road again, would not be sucked in by a man's presence only to learn too late it was all a lie. A painful, humiliating, soul crushing lie.

Miranda jerked her hand away from Dr Burns'. "I'm sorry. I have to get ready for the next case."

She took off down the hallway where the ladies' room was located. She locked herself in a stall and leant her forehead against the door, breathing erratically.

"Are you okay?"

She groaned at the sound of Calleigh's voice? God, why couldn't she have one moment today where she didn't make a fool of herself in front of her new co-workers?

"Hey, whoever's in there? Is everything all right? Do you need me to get help?"

"No, I'm fine. Please. I'm fine."

"Miranda? Is that you?"

She nodded but then realised that Calleigh wouldn't be able to see her behind the closed door. "Yes," she said softly.

"Will you open the door?"

Miranda wiped at her cheeks, satisfied at least to find that she hadn't started crying. She slowly pulled back the latch to the stall then pulled the metal shielding back, exposing herself to the world.

"What happened? You sounded terrified when you came barging in here."

172

"I'm sorry. I didn't realise there was anyone in here."

Calleigh laughed softly and rubbed her protruding stomach. "Ever since these two have taken up residence, the ladies' room has become my favourite hangout. At first it was because I was puking for the first three months, now I swear I have to pee every half hour."

"I bet that makes those long surgeries difficult," Miranda said smiling.

Calleigh rolled her eyes. "You have no idea. So you're good?"

"Yeah. I had a mini panic attack, but it's nothing to do with work. I'm fine."

"Hmm. Something to do with why you're single and not looking?"

Miranda didn't respond. She went over to the sink and washed her hands, looking for any excuse to escape those too-knowing golden eyes.

"I know we just met and all, but with Kevin gone I can get kinda lonely, so if you ever want to grab a bite or hang out or something that'd be fun."

Miranda knew what Calleigh was trying to do. The offer to talk was nice, but she didn't think letting someone at work know just how stupid she'd been with Drew was in her best interest for professional growth.

"Okay, well...I'll see you in there."

Miranda leant against the counter top and stared into the mirror for a moment. "Calleigh?"

"Yeah?"

"I appreciate the offer, and...maybe."

Calleigh smiled and Miranda really wished she had the guts to take a chance on making a new friend. A real friend, like she'd had before her life with Drew. She told herself she was going to live each day in thanks for her new beginning, but she didn't realise at the time how hard that would be. She had to choose whether to accept the hand being held out for her, or fall back into the abyss of isolation. She guessed what they said about the first step being the hardest was true after all. Then again, she'd taken that step the morning she'd called the lawyer. So, then why was this so hard?

* * * *

Vic dropped down onto the sofa in his apartment. Closing his eyes, he leant his head back and loosened his tie. It'd had been a long day. He'd had a young woman who came in for her eighth treatment of whole brain irradiation. She'd been diagnosed with neurofibromatosis II on her twenty-sixth birthday. The vicious genetic disease that riddled a person's body with multiple tumours in the brain and on the spine was one of the worst things he encountered as a nuclear radiologist. The latest PET scan had showed a reduction since the beginning of treatment, but the bright eyed, happy young woman who'd showed up in his office full of positive thoughts and courage had been replaced with a wan ghost of her former self. Her beautiful blonde hair was a thing of the past, and in addition to the terrible bouts of nausea and vomiting, she'd lost forty percent of her hearing. He'd been on the phone consulting with her oncologist for half an hour, discussing the use of stereotactic radiosurgery to address the new lesion which had showed up in her spine with the latest scan.

It was cases such as these that left him feeling strung out at the end of the day. Sometimes Vic was able to identify diseases early enough that the patients were able to have treatment and go on to live full and happy lives. And sometimes he felt as though he felt as though he was as effective as trying to slap a band-aid on a slice to someone's carotid artery. While he loved his job there were times when he wished he hadn't chosen to specialise. He could imagine worse things than reviewing films of broken bones or scans of nameless emergency room patrons.

He opened his eyes and heaved himself off the sofa. He needed to change and grab a bite to eat. Maybe a shower to help slough off the remnants of the hospital would help. Then he'd spend the night vegetating in front of the television. Was there anything good on? It'd been so long since he watched a show with regularity that Vic had no idea what shows were even on the air anymore.

He stepped into the bedroom of his Charlestown condo and heard the water running. Vic leant to his right to look through the opening into the bathroom. From this angle he could see straight to the shower. He smiled and leant back against the wall to enjoy the show. The fog free glass door allowed Vic an unobstructed view of a vision that would tantalise anyone's senses, and he got to not only look, but touch and taste the skin of the occupant whose dusky flesh was slick with moisture raining down from the ceiling mounted shower head.

Vic removed his tie and unbuttoned his shirt. He couldn't decide if he wanted to join the occupant, and share a hot round of shower sex or wait patiently, spread out on the bed in offering. The occupant's hands ran down their wet body, soap trails left in their wake. Vic licked his lips, thinking about tasting the throat exposed to his view. It was always a heady mixture of flavours.

Vic undid his belt and released the closures of his slacks. The garment dropped to the floor with a thud. Vic knew he should pick them up to hang back in the closet, but couldn't find the willpower to look away from view before him. He toed off his shoes and socks then took a couple of steps forward, moving slowly so not to bring attention to his presence. He stood there in his boxer briefs and shirt, which hung open. Vic's cock was hard, and he pressed his hand over the mound, stifling the groan that threatened to escape.

The water shut off and the glass door opened. The occupant stepped out, back towards Vic's bedroom. Vic got a perfect view of the high, tight ass he loved to grab. Vic traced his eyes up the spine. Straight, healthy and strong. He frowned as one of his navy blue towels covered part of the body he'd been ogling. Another towel floated through the air to land on top of his lover's head, covering their face which was now in profile.

Vic found himself walking closer. He'd reached the doorway when the towel over the head was dragged away and a pair of bright sky blue eyes met his.

"Hey love! When did you get home?"

Vic didn't answer. He closed the distance between him and his lover. His arms wrapped themselves around the strong neck and tugged the wet strands at the back of Chase's head till their lips came together. Vic put all his thanks for their shared past and hopes for their future into meshing of their mouths. If love and passion had actual flavours, Vic imagined it would be what he tasted in Chase's mouth.

Chase's arms came around him and their bodies pressed tightly together. Chase's chest was warm and wet from the shower, Vic's nipples hardened between the edges of his shirt. Their heights were almost an exact match, so their groins pressed together. The towel around his waist fell to the floor, and Vic's hand slid down that strong spine he'd been admiring to grasp the ass he loved in his palms.

Chase moaned into their kiss and pulled Vic's shirt away from his shoulders. Vic reluctantly let go of Chase's butt to get the sleeves off his arms. Chase pushed at the waist of Vic's underwear, and he shimmied enough to let the last barrier fall from his body. As soon as he was free, Vic pushed back against Chase's body. Firm muscle and hot skin touched him from head to toe, relaxing away the last of the day's stress.

They clung to each other, one hard cock pressed against the other. Vic wanted Chase inside him, that link to his lover. Needed to feel their bodies connected, their hearts beat against one another through the walls of their chests. He had to reaffirm they were both alive, together. Vic loved to stare into Chase's blue eyes, the blue darker than his own, but the emotions swimming in their depths a reflection of the ones buried deep inside him.

Chapter Three

Chase guided Vic backwards towards his bed, the path they'd crossed many times familiar enough that neither needed to look where they were going. The back of Vic's legs hit the mattress. He sat and scooted across the mattress, Chase's body coming over the top of him, refusing to release their connection. Vic's head hit the pillow, and he arched his head back, exposing his throat to Chase whose firm lips kissed a fiery path down the tendons. When they landed on Vic's throbbing carotid, Chase nibbled on the pulsating artery. Vic's fingers dug into Chase's broad shoulders. His legs opened and he moaned as Chase's hips rocked against his own.

"Need you. Please. Make me feel, make me forget."

Chase reached into the bedside drawer and pulled out the bottle of lube. "You have me, love. Always and forever."

Vic nodded. He and Chase were both bisexual and from time to time they did bring a woman into their bed.

However, none lasted. None became more than a passing fancy. Vic enjoyed the softness of a woman. He loved their delicate scents and plush bodies, but his heart belonged to Chase.

The man who currently was spreading cool gel around his opening. The man whose finger slid deep inside him. Vic wanted a harder touch. He needed to feel consumed.

"More," he demanded.

Chase added a second finger, the stretch and burn absolute bliss to Vic's senses. Chase wasn't a small guy and it had been a few weeks since Vic bottomed, so as much as he wanted to tell Chase to get the show on the road, he knew that too much too fast would push him over the blurring line between pleasurable ache and real pain.

Chase's lips attached themselves to one of Vic's nipples. His cried out at the sharp sting from Chase's teeth on the sensitive protrusion. Chase repeated the treatment to the other side, and it was Vic's breaking point. He flipped their bodies over and straddled Chase's legs. Vic grabbed the condom that Chase had placed on the mattress. He tore the foil packet open and smoothed the polyurethane barrier down Chase's cock. The latex-free material was crucial for Vic's allergy. He moved forward and rose up on his knees. Vic reached behind him and stabilised Chase's cock as he pushed downward. Chase's hands held Vic's hips and after the head popped through the ring to Vic's channel he paused. Vic looked down at Chase and saw the slight nod. He braced his hands on Chase's pectorals and in one swift downward movement took Chase's entire length within his body. Their moans mingled in the air as Vic's fingers dug into the resilient skin of his lover's chest.

Vic set a quick pace. Chase's possession filled the gaping spots in his worn-out psyche from the hellacious day. Chase braced his feet on the covers and thrust up in counter to every one of Vic's downward stokes. Vic adjusted the tilt of his hips and cried out when Chase's cock came in contact with his prostate. He became a man possessed with finding that spark over and over. His heart raced, his lungs and legs burned. Endorphins flooded his bloodstream as no workout could. Sweat dripped from his body onto Chase's chest.

He climbed higher, Chase's moans telling Vic that his lover was right there with him. Their pleasure built upon each other, their desire fed off the other's responses. It was symbiotic, it was perfect.

"Now!" he screamed.

Chase's hand wrapped around Vic's cock, and he bellowed out as cum spouted from his slit. He shot so hard it was almost painful and his orgasm kept coming. Wave after wave tumbled over him and Vic held on, clinging to Chase's body and seeking out his cry of pleasure to know that they'd reached the summit together. Chase lifted Vic's lean hips up and thrust up rapidly over and over. Seconds later Vic heard the cry that was music to his ears. He felt Chase's cock pulse inside him, and knew his lover had found the ecstasy of release.

Vic collapsed over Chase's chest. Large hands calmed the skin of Vic's back as he peppered kisses along Chase's jaw line.

"Love you," he whispered.

Chase rolled them over onto their sides. He removed the condom then Vic rolled back into Chase's arms. Chase's chest spooned against Vic's back. Their hands latched together as the echoes of the storm that had consumed their bodies faded away.

Chase kissed the back of Vic's neck. "Love you too. Not that I'm complaining, mind you, but what brought this on?"

"Saw my NF2 patient today. She's not doing well. I came home expecting to maybe get a bite to eat and stare mindlessly at the television, but when I saw you in the shower something hit me with the gale force of a Nor'easter. I wanted to feel alive."

Chase's arm tightened around Vic. "Then I'm very glad I decided to come by. I almost went home myself. My last surgery went longer than I expected."

"Everything go okay?"

"Yeah. It was a double reconstruction, and she had some fluid collection issues but it all resolved. I think she's going to be very happy with the outcome. There was a new scrub nurse. I think she recently joined the staff, but seemed competent. Hell, she was actually really great, kept a cool head unlike that twit I had to work with last week. I know everyone has to start somewhere, but does it always have to be in my operating room?"

Vic chuckled softly. He'd heard all about Chase's experience with the nurse fresh into her fellowship programme. "I may have run into your nurse myself. I was down in the OR with the latest scans for one of Fischer's patients. She seemed nice enough, but a little jumpy."

Chase rose up and braced his head on his palm. He tugged Vic over onto his back. "Really? I thought that was just me. I actually literally ran into her early this morning."

Vic arched an eyebrow and wiggled around so he was more comfortable.

"I came around a corner and smack, we collided. When I tried to steady her she froze, and I swear I saw her cringe as though I was about to hit her or something."

"I wonder if there's a story there. She said she moved here from Chicago. Bad relationship maybe?"

Vic saw Chase's frown and smoothed the lines from his lover's forehead. "I know that look."

"I've never understood why some spouses feel it's okay to abuse their partners. Men, women, gay, straight. I've seen the aftermath too many times to count. Thousands of sutures over the years putting their bodies back together, but their hearts and heads never heal as easily."

"That's one of the reasons why I love you. Your patients are more than body parts, you really consider the whole person and what your actions and how you treat them will affect their lives. We can't fix everything, babe. If we put that kind of pressure on ourselves, it'll lead to nowhere except a mental meltdown. That or an endless sea of empty bottles."

Chase leant down and kissed Vic. "Look who's talking."

"Sometimes, maybe. I enjoy nuclear medicine but it can be tough, especially when I'm dealing with cases like today. It helps to mix it up with my other duties as an attendee."

Chase squeezed Vic then rolled off the bed. He walked over to Vic's dresser and pulled out a pair of shorts and T-shirt. They'd started keeping changes of clothes at each other's condos years ago. Vic often wondered why they'd never officially moved into together. It wasn't as if they were unsure of their relationship, and when either of them felt like company of the female persuasion it was simply a matter of informing the other. Two men over the age of thirty-five living together wouldn't exactly draw an eye in a large city such as Boston. Vic knew that rumours about him and Chase floated around the hospital, but they were discreet about their relationship, and it had never been a problem.

"Move in with me," he blurted out.

Chase froze with the T-shirt half way over his head. "What?"

Vic chuckled at the sight of Chase's arms bent at awkward angles over his head. The dark blond head popped through the neck opening and Chase's wide eyes met his. "I'm serious. Why have we never moved in together?"

Chase sat on the bed beside Vic's legs. "You never asked, for one."

"Neither have you."

"Things are good. We love each other. We share our lives to the extent that we want."

"The extent that we want? We've been sleeping with each other more often than not for twelve years. Committed since we finished our respective residencies and took our positions at Mass General three years ago." Vic was a little hurt. Here, he'd thought his and Chase's relationship was good, solid. Did Chase's comment mean that he wasn't as happy with Vic as Vic was with him? Had Vic's presence become a convenience for Chase?

Chase leant over Vic and kissed his lips softly. "Hey. I know that look. I didn't mean that the way it sounded. Never doubt that I'm happy with you. I love you, Vic. No man has ever given me as much or made me feel as happy as I do when I'm with you."

Vic relaxed a little bit. "I hear a 'but' in there somewhere."

"Not a 'but' exactly."

"Is it the woman thing? You know I'd never begrudge you those desires. Hell, I have them myself. We bring women home when we want to. You've dated women outside of us, and I've done the same on occasion. As long as there's honesty about it, why would that pose a problem?"

"But can you see how that would continue to work, if we lived together? Say one of us went out on a date. Wouldn't it be a little awkward to come home and find me necking on our couch with a stranger? What about sex? Do we hang a sock on the door knob? What if she's not into threesomes? Or one of us isn't attracted to her as much as the other?"

Vic sat up and pulled the comforter over the lower half of his body. He felt too vulnerable lying there naked still replete from his and Chase's loving. "All good points. I don't know what I was thinking."

Chase cupped Vic's cheek. "You were thinking that what we have is special and right and you want to make it permanent. There's nothing wrong with that, and you're right to an extent but can you honestly tell me that you'd never crave the feel of a woman beneath you, or her soft hands on your body ever again? Because if we did this? Really committed to spending our lives together, all of our lives? That's what it would mean. The scenarios I described earlier would only lead to anger, pain and resentment. I won't do that to us. I can't. I need you, just as much as you need me."

"Damn it. Why do you have to be so smart?" Vic leant his head on Chase's broad shoulder.

While they were virtually the same height, Chase had a more muscular build while Vic ran more to the lean side. Vic kept in shape by running and swimming, while Chase preferred kick boxing and weight lifting. Vic preferred having a man who was different from him. During his residency—while he and Chase had lived in different cities, only occasionally meeting up for sporadic weekends of blistering hot sex then falling back on the friendship that never seemed to change despite months apart — Vic had dated men with similar builds and interests as him. In the end, he became bored. Who wanted to date themselves? The premise seemed a little narcissistic to him.

"Hey, maybe someday we'll find a woman who could actually manage to fall in love with two doctors who love not only their crazy jobs, but each other. Then we can all move in together and create a perfect little family. We'll travel the world, have kids, maybe even a dog or two."

"Buy a cute little Cape Cod house in the suburbs with a white picket fence?" Vic teased.

Chase grimaced. "I was thinking more along the lines of early twentieth century Victorian. Blue with white shutters and river rock foundation. A huge yard for the kids to play on. We could build a fort in the trees and a clubhouse with attached swing set. The kids would run around while we sat out on our patio next to the fire pit, watching them play."

Vic was stunned. He'd never heard Chase talk about any dreams he had for the future. It was only natural. They were thirty-eight, and most men they associated with at the hospital were settled with families. "Wow! You've really put a lot of thought into that."

Chase stood and moved to walk away, but Vic grabbed his hand. "I love it."

Chase looked back and smiled weakly. "Someday, right?"

Vic nodded. "Someday."

* * * *

Miranda tried to keep her breathing even as she ran with Axel in tow. She'd gone online and looked up suggestions for great places to run in Boston. The posts had led her to the Emerald Necklace conservatory. The conservatory was a series of parks linked in a natural chain around the western half of the city. Today, she decided to explore the Arnold Arboretum. She'd read that there was a fabulous view of the Boston skyline from the top of something called Peter's Hill. Miranda actually hated running, but she had to do something to keep her figure in check. Otherwise her generous curves would move past the stage of hour glass figure to full-on fat. Drew had cautioned her often about letting her weight get out of hand, and while Miranda hated to admit the man had been right about anything, she reluctantly admitted in this case he had been correct. She grudgingly acknowledged that after a run she did feel better, and she had more energy at the hospital when she exercised on a regular basis.

It was a good thing she had moved to this city in the spring. Had it been winter, Miranda would never have found the willpower to trudge out in the snow. It wasn't as if she could afford a gym membership. And it was a way to get out and explore the city. So far she'd done five of the suggested seven loops on the website. Her favourite so far had been the riverway loop.

Miranda came to a clearing. Her legs burned after the trek up the hill and she paused for a moment, walking it out. She looked off to her right and there it was in the distance. Beyond the tops of green leafy trees stood columns of glass and concrete, lined up along the horizon as if they were matchsticks.

"It's a nice view, isn't it?"

Miranda quickly turned, right as Axel ran around her legs to greet their visitor. Miranda lost her balance and fell into the arms of the man standing beside her.

"Whoa!" Vic exclaimed.

Miranda managed to get her feet underneath her, but Axel's leash was wrapped around her knees, and she was stuck.

"Stand still. Let me help."

The man bent down and Miranda had a view of the top of his dark head. A pair of firm hands touched the skin of her bare thighs, and a shiver danced down her spine.

"Come here, boy. Hand me the end of his leash."

Miranda did, and the man began talking to Axel as though they were the best of friends. His hands rubbed the top of Axel's head, and inexplicably Miranda found herself jealous of her dog. That was silly because she didn't want some stranger's hands on her body, did she? No! Of course not. The leash around her knees loosened and slid down to her ankles.

"There now. Step out, one foot at a time."

Miranda followed the instructions of the deep voice, mortified at her predicament. The man stood, Axel's leash still within his grip. Miranda looked up and gasped. This man wasn't a stranger after all.

"Miranda Green, right?"

Miranda nodded. "Dr Burns. I'm so sorry. You must think I'm a complete klutz."

"Not at all. Your dog got a little excited at meeting a new friend, that's all. He looks young, probably forgot his manners. Kids do that you know," Vic said smiling.

Miranda looked down at Axel who now sat as though he were the most well-behaved animal on the planet. *Little snot ball.* "Yes. Apparently. We haven't had much interaction with guests."

Vic rubbed the behind the dog's ears, and received a moan for his efforts. "What's his name? He seems friendly."

"Axel. Normally he's a very well-behaved, if slightly mischievous, two year old."

Vic handed the end of the leash back to Miranda. "So you two were out having a run?" He rolled his eyes. "Stupid question, sorry."

Miranda shrugged. Her social banter skills were hardly suave so she let the obvious question go without a comment. "We're still getting to know the city. We've been trying the Emerald necklace trails one by one, searching for a favourite to make our routine. We try to get out at least three times a week."

"That's good. I love to run. Gives me a chance to clear my head of all the constant buzz at the hospital. Would you like a partner for the second half?"

"Oh, I don't want to put you off your pace. I run out of necessity, not enthusiasm, so the road runner I'm not."

"Nonsense on both accounts."

"What's that supposed to mean?"

Vic held out his arm, and they started back towards the paved trail. "You said you run out of necessity. I can only assume that means you feel you're out of shape. You're beautiful as you are, so therefore nonsense. Now as to putting me off my pace, I would gladly slow my stride a touch if it meant enjoying this gorgeous summer day with a friendly companion."

"How do you know I didn't mean by 'necessity' that I completely pigged out on pizza and Chunky Monkey ice cream last night and now feel like a slug, and therefore thought a good run would get my system back in balance?"

"Then I would ask, was it worth it?"

Miranda smiled and found herself no longer dreading each stride of her trainers. "And if I said yes? That I love to eat and sometimes a girl needs a night of self-indulgence while watching the type of sappy romantic comedies men cringe at?"

Vic smiled. "Then I would say do you like pepperoni or sausage and have you seen *Serendipity*?"

Miranda stumbled and Dr Burns' hand landed on her lower back. Axel trotted alongside, oblivious to the burning in his mistress's skin from the touch of the other man.

"You've seen *Serendipity*?"

"I'll tell you a secret. It's one of my favourites. I think there's something sweet about finding a person you have an instant connection with, only to be separated and end up back together to live happily ever after."

Miranda stared at the man running beside her. Was he for real? Men didn't think like that. Or if they did, they were usually gay. Oh wait, hadn't Calleigh and Jenna said something a couple of months ago about Dr Burns and Dr Pruitte? Thoughts like that were stereotypical, but then again, they became stereotypes for a reason. She decided to test the waters. "And your partner? Will he sit and watch these sappy movies with you?"

Vic laughed. "Sometimes. He doesn't like to admit it, but every once in a while he enjoys them."

They ran in silence for a couple of minutes, and Miranda felt much better knowing that she didn't have to read anything more into Dr Burns' quips than friendship. She'd never really had a guy as a friend before, it might be nice.

"That was very smooth by the way," Vic said with a grin.

"Thank you. I thought so."

"Let me guess. Hospital grapevine?"

"That and the fact that any man I've dated in the past would rather be hung with barbed wire than watch some chick flick. I wasn't even allowed to have them in the house with my ex-husband. One day he came home and found the rental box for *Kate and Leopold*. He got so furious he—" Miranda cut herself off. She couldn't believe she'd been about to casually blurt out something so personal to a man she wasn't even on a first name basis with.

"Miranda? It's okay. I know you moved here to make a new start. That's a very brave thing to do, and I'm proud of you. I'd like to be your friend if you haven't filled up your dance card already."

"I'm not sure how appropriate that would be, Dr Burns," Miranda mumbled.

"Please call me Vic, and there's no professional reason why we can't be close. I'm not your supervisor or anything. Unless of course, you simply don't like me," he finished with a smile.

"Oh, no that's not it! I mean you seem nice." Miranda looked down at Axel, who gave her one of his goofy, ear-flopping smiles. "And Axel seems to like you, but as you said I recently got out of a really bad...making friends isn't easy for me. Trust isn't easy for me, not anymore."

Chapter Four

They'd reached the end of the loop. Miranda walked out to the parking area and got Axel's bowl and a couple of bottles of water out of a portable cooler she kept in her car. She poured some out for Axel, keeping the rest of that bottle for herself, and handed the second bottle to Vic.

Vic took a long drink. "Thank you. We'll keep it simple and uncomplicated. You know one of the perks of having a friend who's bisexual is that we're kinda like having a girlfriend and a boyfriend all in one. You get the best of both worlds," he said with a wink.

The sip of water went down the wrong tube and Miranda started to cough. Vic patted her on the back, and she held onto his shoulder as she bent over, trying to catch her breath again. "Did you"—she coughed—"say bisexual?"

"Mmhm. Grapevine missed that part, huh? Both Chase and I are."

"But I thought you said the two of you were…"

"Committed? We are, have been for several years. However, neither of us is willing to give up women completely. So, we occasionally share a woman and on occasion date outside our relationship. Less now than in years past. Our policy is honesty always. That goes for both each other and anyone else we become involved with."

"And you plan to go on like that indefinitely?"

"If we could find a woman whom we both love, and who loves us, and accepts our love for each other then we'd probably get down on our knees and beg her to marry us. Until then..." Vic shrugged.

Miranda's mind once again drifted back to Chicago and the love between the two men and woman in the hospital. She sometimes wondered whatever happened to them. She knew she shouldn't, but her mouth opened before she could stop herself. "The sharing thing. How does that work?"

Vic arched a brow.

"Not that part! I have an imagination. I can count body parts and add two and two together. Or I guess that would be one plus one plus one. Or would it be... Never mind the number."

"Then what do you mean?"

"I mean..." What did she mean? Why did she care? Was it morbid curiosity, or a desire to climb out on a branch beyond her safe little nest and see the world from a different perspective? How she'd had the guts to ask Vic the question in the first place, she didn't know. Anytime Calleigh or Jenna started talking sex, Miranda would clam up or scurry away as if she were a frightened little mouse. There was something about him though. Something calm, easy, comfortable.

It didn't make sense. Miranda had sworn off attractive men after Drew. Promised herself she'd never fall for their lies or phony good nature ever again. Yet here she stood, discussing a man's private life with ease. A very handsome man.

Okay, be honest with yourself, Miranda. He's hot. Seriously mouth watering, spine tingling, wish you had a bottle of chocolate sauce to lick off him, H-O-T!

Long and lean with firm runner's muscles. Dark crisp hair she wanted to feel tickling the palm of her hand. Broad shoulders Miranda could rest her head against. Vic's damp T-shirt clung to his chest and Miranda had the unfamiliar desire to feel the skin below the fabric rub against her. Good God, where were all these ideas coming from?

"Miranda?"

She blinked a few times. "Sorry?"

"You had a question about Chase and me sharing a woman."

"I did?" she squeaked out.

"Yes, you did."

"Oh, well I guess maybe it was something along the lines of, what's in it for the girl? If the two of you are in love, what does she get out of the experience? It's not as though sex with two guys is any better than sex with one. Seems more like double the hassle to me."

Vic stepped closer. Their bodies stood only inches apart. Miranda detected the scents of sweat and man and instead of turning her off, she actually felt a pull deep in the pit of her womb.

"Then you've been sleeping with the wrong men. Sex is all about sharing pleasure between you and your partner, or partners in the specific scenario we're discussing. It's about a feast to the senses to be experienced by everyone present. The sensation of fingertips caressing your skin, of lips and tongues dancing on and inside your body. The rapture of being filled, possessed and driven to heights unachievable outside the act of making love. Whether I'm with Chase alone, bring a woman to my bed, or share her with my partner, it's always about making love. Never do we treat the women in our life with callousness or as disposable sex toys."

Miranda panted. She couldn't even imagine sex such as Vic described it, but suddenly she wanted to. Whether she was capable of the responses she imagined Vic demanded of his partners, Miranda had no idea. Drew had always called her a cold fish. Said sex with her was less pleasurable than fucking a blow up doll. But deep down, Miranda knew passion resided somewhere inside her. She felt it sometimes late at night, alone in her bed. She felt it now, standing inches away from a man who described the intimate details of his life.

"Come with me, Miranda. Let me show you how making love is intended to be."

"But I don't love you, and you don't love me. To pretend otherwise would be a lie. To be frank, we hardly know each other. How can one experience pleasure if beneath the pretty words there's nothing but the sound of a stranger's voice?"

"Tell me what you feel, right now. As you stand here with me, our bodies a hair's breadth apart. Don't tell me what you *ought* to feel, based on logic. Tell me what's happening inside your body, right now."

"I'm jittery. My blood is hot, my pulse is racing and there's a slight buzzing sound in my head."

"Are you wet?"

Miranda gasped. She'd never had someone be so blatant before. What kind of man asked such a question?

"The kind of man who wants his woman to experience every ounce of pleasure her body is capable of."

"How did you—" she whispered.

"What you feel is desire, arousal. There's nothing false about it. Right now your body craves my touch. Pleasure is the result of bringing your arousal to its highest peak, then taking it one step further till you tumble over the edge into ecstasy. We'll start there. As to us being strangers, I sincerely hope we won't remain that way for long."

The words sounded pretty. Hell, they made Miranda want to clinch her thighs together to help alleviate the foreign ache building inside her. But they were just words, and she'd fallen for them before. "I'm sorry. I have to go. I can't do this."

Vic leant a fraction of an inch closer. Their bodies skimmed each other, and his head lowered till their lips all but touched. "Can't or won't?"

Miranda was horrified to find tears swimming in her eyes. She wanted to believe Vic. Wished that she could believe him, that she had enough strength to take the risk. "Both."

Vic stepped back and Miranda immediately felt bereft with his withdrawal. She opened the back door to her Jeep and Axel jumped in. Miranda opened the driver door and paused. She looked over at Vic, who stood calmly with an unidentifiable expression on his face. Was he sorry she'd turned him down, did he really care? Or had his attentions been an easy afternoon flirtation, easily forgotten the moment Miranda drove away? He had Dr Pruitte to go home to, so it's not as if he was without someone in his life. Miranda didn't really understand what her acquiescence would have brought to his life. He had love, he had a partner. The addition of her couldn't possibly enhance anything. More than likely if she'd capitulated and gone home with him, he'd have discovered she really was horrible in bed and regret the decision. And what if Dr Pruitte was there? Could Miranda really make herself vulnerable to two men, only to be tossed aside later when they discovered their love for each other was more than anything either of them could ever feel for her?

Miranda climbed in then shut the door. Her fingers fumbled as she tried to pull down her seatbelt. Vic stepped up the window and Miranda rolled the partition down. The summer heat had made the interior stifling, and fresh air cooled the sweaty tendrils on the side of her face.

"Think about it, Miranda. You are a beautiful and brave woman. Don't let fear win, don't let him win."

"How did —"

"I may not be as much of a stranger as you think. Both Chase and I have been keeping our eyes on you since you joined the hospital staff. We've seen you slowly come out of your shell, watched in silence as you crawled out of the darkness that had consumed your life. We've been waiting for you. When you're ready, we'll be here. Till then…"

Vic leant into the window and pressed his lips to hers. They were soft, inviting. They moved over Miranda's, encouraging her to respond. Her nipples tightened almost immediately, and Miranda felt a funny tingle move down the length of her body. Miranda opened her mouth, and Vic's hand slid behind her neck. He slipped his tongue past Miranda's lips and laved at her mouth. The slow slide of his hot tongue caused Miranda's hands to tighten on the steering wheel. The tingle settled between her legs, and Miranda felt her body softening in response to Vic's attention. Holy cow! Her head buzzed until she remembered to take a breath through her nose. If this is how a simple kiss made her feel, what would happen if she allowed Vic or Chase to actually meld their bodies together with hers? Vic's mouth moved slowly over hers. His tongue softly commanded her attention, Chase was a lucky man if Vic put this much focus into kissing his partner. A flash image of Vic and Chase kissing each other ricocheted through Miranda's brain and a soft moan escaped from her throat. When she expected Vic to take the kiss deeper, he actually slowed and pulled back.

Vic's thumb smoothed over Miranda's cheek. "Beautiful and responsive. Your sweet taste is alluring. I'll count the days till I can hold you in my arms for real." He turned and jogged away.

Miranda turned on the Jeep and set the air conditioning to high. "Holy cow, Axel."

She heard Axel whine out a yawn and laughed. "Did we wear you out? You big baby. All right, we'll go home, and you can fall asleep in front of the television."

She pulled out of the Arboretum and headed back towards her studio in Cambridge. She'd been lucky to get the last furnished unit in the complex. Her place was only ten minutes from the hospital across the Charles River Basin. They'd met a few of their neighbours and everyone seemed nice. Miranda was more convinced than ever that the move to Boston had been her best decision. She loved the city, her hospital, and now that she and Axel had settled down, it seemed as though their lives were really moving forward.

Now all she had to do was decide if she wanted to risk her heart again.

* * * *

Chase paced his living room, waiting for Vic to get back from the Arboretum, and his attempted interception of Miranda. Chase had overheard her talking to one of the other nurses about her plans to run the Peter's Hill loop this afternoon. He and Vic had become increasingly interested in the woman over the past month. Whenever she was assigned to Chase's OR, he found himself wondering how her small hands would feel caressing his body. If her soft voice rose in volume when she came, or if she made a little hitch as her body unravelled around him. He cherished those moments when her deep brown eyes would meet his across the table. Chase had taken to stalking the halls of the OR floor on the days he did surgery simply for the pleasure of hearing her voice.

They decided to take the chance and literally run Miranda down to test the waters. Vic was the runner of the two of them, so he was the logical choice in their mission, but the wait was nerve-racking. Chase pushed open the door to his terrace and stepped out into the summer air. He leant against the banister and looked out at the curve of the Charles River as it snaked its way towards downtown.

Was Miranda ready? Would she even be interested in the type of arrangement Chase and Vic wanted to propose? Not many women would be, Chase knew that, but he'd sensed something special about the woman. Beneath the damaged psyche left from the asshole of a man who'd abused her, he sensed a heart capable of great love and openness. Would it be enough?

The door behind him opened and Chase immediately detected Vic's presence. "Did you find her?"

They hadn't even known exactly what time Miranda planned on going for her run, so Vic had left Chase's place early that morning to lie in wait.

Vic slid his arms around Chase's waist. "Yep. Guess what?"

Chase relaxed against Vic's chest. Vic may have been leaner than him, but he had the best arms to hold him with. Chase had loved how when Vic held him, it was with more than his body, Vic held him with all his heart. He had from the very beginning of their time together back in medical school.

Vic placed his lips at Chase's ear and whispered, "She has a puppy. Two year old white boxer named Axel."

Chase smiled. He'd always loved boxers and Vic knew it. "And?"

"She's scared, but intrigued at the same time. There's physical desire there, but I think she's afraid of trusting a man again, or men in this case."

"That's natural given what we suspect. How intrigued?"

"Enough that when I kissed her, she kissed me back."

Chase turned to see the truth of the statement in Vic's eyes. He looked at his lover's lips. Miranda's mouth had been there. Vic sealed their lips together. The slow kiss filled his senses, and Chase imagined that a hint of Miranda's taste lingered on Vic's lips. He wasn't kissing Miranda though, he was kissing Vic. His Vic. The only man he'd ever loved. Until now, the only person he'd ever truly wanted. Anyone else he'd ever slept with had been a place holder until he and Vic could be reunited, and part of Chase always felt the need to go back and apologise to them for that. It wasn't manly to pine for the person who was your first love, so Chase kept that little bit to himself. However, there were some nights when he and Vic would be lying together in bed that Chase would look into Vic's pale blue eyes, and suspect his partner knew the truth. The only consolation was that Chase saw the same truth mirrored back at him.

Chase wrapped his arms around Vic's waist and pulled their bodies together. He felt Vic's cock thickening behind the thin nylon running shorts. Vic's bare arms were wrapped around Chase's neck, one hand buried in the loose strands of his hair at the base of his skull.

Vic broke their kiss and nuzzled his nose alongside Chase's. "Come inside. It's hotter than Hades out here."

"You need a cool shower. Can't have you getting heat-stroke."

"That's okay. I have a doctor at my beck and call to save me."

* * * *

Chase saw Miranda at the end of the hall and stealthily tried to catch up with her. They'd just finished their most recent case. A young child with a bilateral complete cleft lip and palate. The little boy was only three months old, and it always tore a little piece of Chase's heart to see someone that young on his table, but now the boy would have a better chance of developing normal speech and he wouldn't have the complications of feeding that his parents had struggled with for the early months of his life. Time would tell if he'd have any complications from the congenital malformation.

Chase pushed open the door to the staff lounge, where he'd seen Miranda disappear. He was glad to see she was the only one inside. It wasn't exactly normal for doctors to hang out in here, since they had their own lounge. She was pouring a cup of coffee, and Chase watched those slim capable hands. He frowned when he noticed they were trembling, and when Miranda cursed as a splash of hot coffee landed on her delicate skin, Chase found himself racing over to her before he even realised what he was doing.

"Quick, get your hand under some cool water."

He turned on the faucet in the sink beside the coffee machine and pulled Miranda's hand beneath the flow. He stood behind her, surrounding her small body with his. Chase's thumb rubbed the soft skin on the back of her hand. "Better?" he asked, softly.

Miranda nodded and beneath her pony cap Chase saw the edges of her brown hair. He wanted to nuzzle the skin behind her ear and wallow in the delicate scent that was all Miranda beneath the antiseptic smells of the hospital.

He reached out and turned off the water with his other hand, refusing to let go of Miranda's recently singed skin. It was still slightly red, and Chase examined it to make sure the burn wasn't more serious than he'd first suspected.

"I think you'll be fine. What had your hands shaking?"

"You."

Chase's heart lurched at the single word. Did that mean Miranda was afraid of him? "Why do I make you tremble?"

"Because I'm scared. I...want you, and yet my mind screams at me that the last time I gave in to my body's and heart's desire, my life became a living hell."

The desolate tone of her voice made Chase's chest hurt. He turned Miranda around and pulled her close against him. "Honey, I need you to be honest with me. Does anything Vic or I do remind you of Drew? Really truly mimic the things he did or the way he treated you?"

She shook her head against his chest. "No, but he didn't change until after we were married. Once I was signed, sealed and delivered, it was as if the curtain rose and the real show began."

He and Vic had spent the last month gradually winning Miranda over. They'd convinced her to hang out and watch movies at their places, they'd all taken Axel to the park and played. In moments such as those, Chase had almost felt as if they were a family.

"I guess that's where the trust comes in. You keep talking about the risk of opening yourself up to Vic and I, but I think what you keep forgetting is that you have the same amount of power in this relationship as we do. I have to trust Vic not to break my heart just as he has to trust me, and honey, we have to trust you that you won't break either of ours as well."

The sexual side of their relationship hadn't gone any further than kisses, but they were kisses more pleasurable than Chase had ever encountered with another woman. In fact, when he kissed Miranda, he had the same emotional stirrings as he did when he kissed Vic. That and the camaraderie they experienced as a group convinced Chase more than anything that they were all meant to be together. That the elusive someday was closer than he imagined a few months ago.

She felt so right in his arms. Petite and curvy, soft with a spine of steel. He knew she thought herself to be plain, but to Chase and Vic, Miranda was beautiful. They'd tried to show her and said the words repeatedly, but he knew she didn't believe them. Chase had noticed that Miranda never actually looked at herself in a mirror. She would look at parts, such as when she put on eyeliner or lip gloss. She would check to make sure her shirt laid right, but he'd never seen her step back and admire the woman staring back at her.

Chase saw the door to the lounge open and there stood Vic. How his partner knew they needed him and where to find them he'd never know, but Chase was eternally grateful for Vic's presence.

"To be honest. You have more power than we do. What would happen if you fell in love with Vic but not me, or vice versa? Vic and I are good together, we always have been, but we've been incomplete as well. That is until we met you. You have the power to make us into a real family. It's a scary thing to know that I have to relinquish control, but I'll gladly do so if it means living out the dreams I hold deep in my heart."

Vic walked over to them. He placed his hands on Miranda's waist, and snuggled up behind her. His and Chase's lips met for a brief second then Vic leant down and kissed Miranda's temple. "We're falling in love with you, princess. Someday, I hope you can say the same."

"I already do. I think that's part of why I'm scared. My love wasn't enough to hold one man, how can I ever expect to hold on to two?"

Vic closed his eyes and took a breath. "Because that asshole you married never loved you in the first place. I'm sure he talked a big game, but it was all pomp and circumstance. One-sided relationships like that never work. He used you, whereas we'll treasure you. You were his servant, while we want to treat you as if you are our queen."

Miranda looked up between their bodies. The top of her head only came to their chests. Chase leant down and kissed her. It was brief and soft, with only the barest hint of tongue. When Chase pulled back, Vic leant over Miranda's shoulder and kissed her. This was something Chase found that he enjoyed, watching the two people who held his heart in an embrace. Before when he and Vic had shared women, Chase had found the sight mildly arousing but nothing more. However, when he watched

Vic kiss Miranda it was as if his heart actually beat faster in his chest and swelled to twice its normal size.

Miranda slid out from between Vic and Chase. "I understand better now. Please give me a little more time."

"As I said to you before, when you're ready we'll be here."

Chapter Five

Miranda picked up Axel's leash and her best friend trotted over at the familiar sight. She snapped the clip onto his collar and gave the back of his ears a good rub. "You ready to go play?"

Axel turned in circles excitedly till he faced their front door then stood at attention.

"Okay boy, let me get your rope." She scooped up the braided rope, her keys, phone and shoved her ID wallet with a couple of dollars stashed inside in the back pocket of her jean shorts. Miranda hated carrying her purse when she was out running or taking Axel to the park.

"Where should we go today? Do you want to walk over to Riverside or should we jump in the Jeep and go across the Charles into Back Bay?"

Axel wasn't much help. He stood waiting patiently at the door. When he looked over his shoulder at Miranda as if to say *what's taking so long*, she shook her head and chuckled.

"Okay, I get the message."

Axel spent the elevator ride being petted by one of the kids in the building, and by the time they walked out of the building he had a definite spring in step.

"You are such a pet-slut, you know that?"

Miranda turned her head up into the sunshine and took a deep breath. It wasn't too hot for mid-July. She'd spent Independence Day working, and while she would've liked to have seen the fireworks over the river, she understood that as the low woman on the totem pole she was destined to work all the holidays for at least her first year. It wasn't that big of a deal. It wasn't as though she had family to see. After Miranda had turned in the papers for her divorce, her mother had basically cut her off. Being a staunch traditionalist, her mother felt a woman should support her husband at all costs. When you married, you married for life, regardless of a good or bad situation. Miranda had called her mom shortly before she moved, and left a message on her answering machine with her new contact information, trying once again to mend the gap that had formed in their relationship, but never got a call back.

It was difficult knowing that her mother had moved from indifference to disappointment. Miranda had tried her entire life to live up to her mom's expectations. She'd studied hard and chosen the right group of friends. She'd got her first part-time job at the age of sixteen and never asked her parents for a dime of spending money thereafter. But despite everything, Eleanor Green never once gave any indication that she was proud of her daughter. Hell, Miranda couldn't even remember the last time her mom had said "I love you."

She shook off the depressing thoughts and looked down at Axel. "Let's go have some fun. I think we should go over to The Fens. That means we need to go over to the garage."

As they walked to the parking complex, Miranda thought about what Chase and Vic had said the other day about trust and building their relationship. Up till now, the men had been the ones to initiate any time they spent together. Miranda had enjoyed their outings, and in fact looked forward to their invitations, but she'd yet to reach out her hand. Maybe today was a good day to take another small step forward.

"Axel, we're making a detour."

She turned the Jeep towards Western Avenue so she could take the Three-A South towards Chase's condo. He lived only about ten minutes away from Miranda over on Mount Auburn Street. She knew Chase wasn't working today, but she didn't know about Vic. He was scheduled to be on call, so he may be with Chase or he may have been called to the hospital. Then again, this was a gamble because there was nothing to guarantee that they'd even be at Chase's home. They could be at Vic's, or not home at all, but Miranda felt as though she needed to take a chance.

She looked in her rear view mirror. "We're going to see if Chase and Vic want to play with us."

Axel gave a little bark then stuck his head out the window Miranda had lowered for him.

The dark blue of the Charles whizzed past her and she smiled when she passed a cruise boat.

"I want to go on one of those, Axel. I think it'd be a nice way to see some of our new home. I know we're locals now, but sometimes I still feel as if we're tourists."

She cranked the lever to lower her window as well and sighed as the air rushing past the car lifted the damp tendrils from her temple. She'd tied her hair up in a loose knot, but the midday summer sun was still warm. The air from the soft brushes of her hair against her skin reminded her of Vic's and Chase's soft kisses.

They both seemed to enjoy peppering her skin with little touches. Soft, alluring, almost innocent kisses. Were they afraid of scaring her should they actually express more ardent emotions? Miranda had to admit that she had been very nervous when she first met them, and it was apparent that they'd picked up on those nerves. However, now her hands trembled more often not from fear but arousal.

She wanted both of the men. She knew they were physically attracted to her. One nice thing about men was that they couldn't exactly disguise the physical reactions of their body when they were aroused. She'd felt the evidence of both Vic's and Chase's desire press against her on more than one occasion. With Drew, any time they'd had sex he'd ordered her to suck him to get him hard. It was a nice feeling to know that Vic and Chase wanted to make love with her. That they didn't see sex as a chore.

Miranda pulled into the parking lot for Chase's building. The white balconies for each unit's private terrace glinted in the sunshine. Miranda loved sitting out on the wide terrace at sunset. Chase had placed a couple of comfortable chaise lounges out there, and sometimes she and the boys sat outside drinking a glass of wine and looking down at the river rolling around the bend directly outside Chase's building.

She shut off the engine and climbed out. Axel waited patiently at the door, but was well-trained enough not to jump out until Miranda had hold of his leash. Thankfully dogs were allowed in Chase's building because there was no way Miranda would have left Axel in the car.

She pulled open the lobby doors and followed Axel inside. Chase's building didn't really have a lobby, just a foyer. The elevators were directly in front of them, and she pushed the button to go up. The doors opened right away, so Miranda didn't have a chance to rethink her impulsive decision.

It was a short ride up to the sixth floor, and when they exited the elevator, Chase's door stood in front of them. She took a deep breath and knocked.

"Just a second!"

Chase's voice echoed from inside. It seemed that part one of the gamble had paid off. Now she had to determine if she and Axel were welcome in Chase's home without notice. The door swung open, and Chase stood in the opening. His eyes lit up, and Miranda felt her chest relax with the breath she'd held until that moment.

"This is a surprise!"

"We were in the neighbourhood?"

Chase pulled the door back and gestured for them to come inside. Axel entered as though he were the pasha of the palace. Miranda timidly followed, pulled in his wake. Chase's arm came around her waist to steady her, and Miranda dropped Axel's leash when Chase's lips touched hers in greeting.

"Want to try that again, honey?"

"Yes." She tilted her head up for another kiss. Chase's smile lit the room, and Miranda could have sworn that the light could still be seen behind her eyelids as they closed when Chase's head lowered for another kiss.

"I believe I found something that belongs to you, princess."

Miranda pulled back from Chase's mouth and turned to find Vic holding Axel's leash. Axel sat dutifully beside

Vic, leaning his head against Vic's leg, searching for a scratch. Vic granted her best friend's request with a smile.

She backed out of Chase's arms and faced Vic. Closing the distance between them, she wrapped her arms around his neck and pulled him down for a sensual greeting of his own. She heard Axel's leash hit Chase's parquet floor, and Vic's arms gathered her tightly against his firm body. Where Chase's greeting had been sweet and tender, Vic's sent an inferno racing beneath her skin. She arched up against him and tightened her arms around his neck. Vic's tongue thrust inside her mouth. The slick muscle licked and teased her hard palate then massaged Miranda's tongue and encouraged it to respond. She could have happily continued as they were, but was brought back to her senses when Axel barked beside them.

Miranda sensed Chase come up behind them. He rested his chin on top of her head. "I was taking Axel to the park, and thought I'd come by and see if you were home."

"Are you asking us out on a date, princess?"

"Maybe."

Vic gave her a little squeeze around the waist and Chase's hands massaged her shoulders. The combination of their touches was heaven.

"Well what gentlemen would we be do deny our lady her wish? Let us get some shoes on, and we'll head out," Chase said.

Miranda looked up at Vic. "What about you being on call?"

Vic shrugged. "I have my phone if the hospital needs to get a hold of me. I'll take my car, and if we go to The Common or The Fens then I'll be only minutes away if they need me. Chase can ride with you and Axel."

"I don't want to make things complicated. I just thought..."

Vic rubbed his nose against Miranda's. "I'm glad you came over. Now let's go have some fun in the sun."

* * * *

Miranda lay in the grass laughing at Chase and Axel as they played a game of tug of war with Axel's rope. Every time Chase threw the rope, Axel would fetch it as he was supposed to and bring it back, but he hadn't yet mastered the art of releasing it so Chase could throw it again. Personally she thought Axel enjoyed the little game. His antics certainly seemed to indicate he knew Chase would run after him in their little game of keep away. Vic collapsed next to her, panting.

"That dog is wickedly fast. Are you sure he's not part greyhound?"

"Yep." She smiled and relaxed onto her back to watch the clouds float lazily across the late afternoon sky. "He has fun with the two of you, and you play right into his little games."

Vic rolled and came up over Miranda. His hand smoothed back the strands of hair that had escaped Miranda's knot with their exertions. She stared into his eyes, somewhere between the colour of the clouds and the sky above them. His head blocked the sun and the dark strands of his hair had a halo surrounding them from the backlight.

"You are so beautiful, princess. Your cheeks are flushed and your neck and chest glisten with exuberance. I love how brightly your brown eyes shine with happiness. I love knowing that spending time with us put that happiness in them."

She smiled. "I am happy. Thank you for coming out with us today. It's nice to spend a day off having fun...with you. I could get used to this."

"So could I." Vic looked over at Chase and Axel. "I think we all could."

Vic's hand settled on Miranda's stomach. His fingers inched their way beneath the thin spaghetti strap tank top she wore. She tried to shrink away from the touch. Not because she didn't want it, but because she was self conscious about the extra padding around her middle. Normally she'd never wear clothes that were so skimpy in public. Unfortunately, her normal looser fitting T-shirts and baggie cargo shorts were in the laundry.

"Shh. It's okay princess. Nothing more than this. I simply want to feel your soft skin."

"Too soft."

Vic shook his head. "Perfect. I love your curves. Someday I hope you'll let us feel them press against us from head to toe. I want to feel your nipples tighten within my lips, and dig into my chest. I want to find out how your round, luscious ass cushions my hips as I thrust deep inside you."

"Inside me where?"

Vic smiled. "Hmm. There are lots of possibilities. I could shove my cock inside your tight little pussy." He groaned and slid up alongside Miranda, so their bodies touched. "Or I could take that sweet virgin ass, while Chase drives himself into your dripping wet cunt. Maybe one of us would fuck your mouth, while the other licks your pussy?"

"Or maybe you could make love to Chase, while he makes love to me?"

Vic's hand settled in the curve of Miranda's waist, and his hips ground against her side. "That is a distinct possibility. There are all kinds of positions we can try. And our hope is that we have a lifetime to spend exhausting the options."

Chase dropped to the blanket, breathing heavily. "Tag, you're it."

Vic growled, and Miranda snickered.

"What?" Chase asked then turned his head to look at them. His eyes roamed from Vic's hand beneath Miranda's shirt to the way their bodies touched. "What are the two of you up to?"

Vic leant over and kissed Chase softly on the lips. "We were discussing all the various ways the three of us can make love."

Chase's eyes widened and Miranda saw the bright azure orbs deepen to an almost navy colour. He rolled onto his side, so that Miranda lay on her back between the two men. Right as Chase moved, Axel came bounding up and started jumping over and between their legs. They all received doggie kisses from a very happy puppy and three sets of groans and exclamations filled the air around them.

Miranda sat and held Axel's collar, trying to get him to sit still for more than a nanosecond. They heard a ring and Vic cursed, digging through his pockets till he pulled out his cell phone.

"It's the hospital."

Vic took the call while Miranda set out a bowl of water for Axel. Chase's hand rubbed Miranda's back and she leant in to his side.

Vic shut the phone. "I have to go. I'm sorry."

"It's okay, love. Miranda and I will head back to my place. When you're done come on back. Maybe we'll all watch a movie tonight or something?"

Vic braced his weight on his hands and leant over Miranda to kiss Chase. "Love you." He moved his head and captured Miranda's lips. "Love you too."

She sat stunned and watched as Vic jogged back towards where they'd parked. He'd said he loved her. It was the first time the words had been said. A few weeks ago they'd said they were falling, and so had she for that matter, but now the actual words had been unleashed. Vic had run away before Miranda had a chance to respond, and now she sat there with Chase who gazed at her intently. The obvious question lingered in his eyes. If only she had the guts to answer it.

* * * *

Miranda paced her apartment with Axel at her heels. She spun around when she reached the end of the entry hall and nearly stumbled over him.

Miranda squatted down and rubbed the back of Axel's ears. "I'm sorry, boy. You probably think I've gone off the deep end." Axel pressed his cold nose against her cheek, and Miranda gave him a big hug. "Love you too." She sat back on her heels. "Now what are we supposed to do about those two men? Do you like Vic and Chase?"

Axel walked away and Miranda followed him with his eyes. She started to laugh when he picked up his braided rope from the basket of toys in the corner of her living area, and brought it back to her. It was the same rope Vic and Chase had tossed all over The Fens Park last weekend.

"Is that supposed to be a yes? I don't speak boxer. Maybe we should call Calleigh or Jenna. No Calleigh would be better. She's more level headed, Jenna would just tell me to get my groove on then worry about the consequences later."

She hadn't made a call such as this in a long time. She scurried over to her sofa and picked up her cell phone. You'd think she could remember the phone number, since she only had four in her contact list. Calleigh's, the hospital, Vic and Chase. Her mom had stopped speaking to her when Miranda filed for divorce from Drew, her Dad did whatever her mom told him to, and Miranda didn't have any siblings. She'd lost touch with her friends from before Drew's time, and it would be really awkward to call them up out of the blue for the first time in over four years and ask for boy advice. Miranda flipped open her phone and scrolled through her contact list. When Calleigh's name was highlighted Miranda selected the call button on the keypad. She nibbled on the skin of her thumb while waiting for the call to connect.

"Hello?"

"Hi, it's Miranda."

"Hey! What's up?"

Miranda heard a clanging sound in the background. Maybe Calleigh was making some lunch. Her new friend was always nibbling on something as it got closer to the twins' arrival date.

"I was wondering if I could get some advice."

"Sure, although you should know that I'm not a great all-knowing wizard."

Miranda smiled. Calleigh had a weird but fun sense of humour. She always knew how to make Miranda's day a bit lighter.

"Dang. Do you know his number because this is a bit complicated?"

"I'm sorry, he's in a meeting right now. Can I take a message and have him call you back? Perhaps I can help you? I've been trained as his apprentice."

"Oh good. I have a problem with a man. Well, two men actually."

"Ah, it's a good thing I asked. The great wizard doesn't do relationship questions. He mainly deals with end of the world and *'what's my purpose in life?'* queries."

Miranda tucked her legs up on the sofa. Axel tried to join her but she snapped her fingers and pointed towards his giant pillow bed. If the sofa had belonged to her, Miranda wouldn't have cared but since the studio came furnished, she couldn't take the risk of losing her security deposit.

"So you know those stories you mentioned that would make Jenna go into cardiac arrest?"

Calleigh giggled. "Yes."

She took and deep breath and let it out slowly. "Did any of them possibly involve a three-way?"

"Yeah. Kevin and I were a bit adventurous in college. We invited a third to our bed on occasion."

Miranda's fingers went numb and she dropped the phone. It clattered on the wood floor and she scrambled to pick it up, only to send it sailing across the room with her foot.

"Hold on, Calleigh!"

She dashed across the small space and scooped up the little rectangular device. Axel looked at her as if he was trying to figure out if this was a new game.

"Sorry, I dropped the phone." Calleigh's laughter rang through the ear piece as Miranda walked back towards the sofa. "So glad *my* near heart attack causes you such humour," she said, smiling.

"I'm sorry, but I got this image of your mouth dropping open and your eyes bugging out of your head in a very cartoonish fashion. So back to the topic at hand. Yes, I've participated in a ménage. Our third was always another man, so if you're about to ask for tips on how to pleasure another woman, I'm afraid I can't give you any firsthand knowledge. Other than what we both knows feels good on ourselves."

"Umm. It's probably best to table that for another discussion. I think my brain would short circuit if we broached that topic right now."

"Suit yourself. So why are you asking about ménage? Morbid curiosity or do you have an ulterior motive?"

"I've been approached by two men, who shall remain nameless, to join them."

"In bed as a one-off or have they asked you to be a part of a permanent relationship?"

"I think the latter," she said while going back to nibbling on pad of her thumb.

"Well, with Kevin and I it was always about the sex. Our thirds never expected to become a part of what we had, so I can only give you advice about the physical side of things."

"That's fine. Physical is good. Is it worth it? Does it actually feel good?"

"Oh my God yes. Don't get me wrong—sex with Kevin is nice, great even, but when we brought another man into our bed, it was like taking sex to a whole another level. Two pairs of lips, four hands rubbing and kissing and damn, now you've got me horny."

"What about two of the other things?"

"What, their cocks?"

Miranda squeaked into the phone.

"You'll be filled like never before, and if they know how to use them, then you'll fly higher than you can even imagine. Then again if we're talking about Dr Pruitte and Dr Burns, you realise that one of them might make love to the other, while you get to enjoy the attentions of one man."

"How did you—"

"Please. I'm surprised the electricity arcing between you and Dr Pruitte in the OR hasn't made all the equipment go haywire."

"If I go through with this, do you think Chase, Vic and I having a personal relationship will cause a problem with administration?"

Calleigh snorted. "Doctors and nurses getting it on in the on-call room is a time-honoured tradition."

Miranda knew if she went through with this, it would be more than an affair. She didn't have it in her to sleep with a man, and not want the whole enchilada. Adding another man into the picture only made the situation bigger. If she found the strength within her to do this, to trust them as they said they trusted her, there would have to be some sort of agreement that the three of them would really make a go of things all together. How that would work exactly, Miranda had no idea.

"What about the whole two plus one aspect?"

There was the sound of crunching on the other end of the line. Was Calleigh eating some chips? A snack wasn't a bad idea. Miranda couldn't do chips, they go straight to her hips, but a few baby carrots or maybe an apple sounded good. She climbed off the sofa and went to the kitchen.

"It's really none of their business. Neither Dr Pruitte nor Dr Burns are your direct supervisors. You happen to live in one of the most liberal cities, so it's not as if the three of you will get stoned walking down the street."

She opened the refrigerator door and peeked inside. No carrots, but there were a couple of celery stalks. She took them out and placed them on the counter to cut up. As Calleigh continued to talk about why a relationship with Chase and Vic was feasible, Miranda's mind wandered as she picked up the large kitchen knife and set to chopping up her afternoon snack. She knew her perception of sex was probably skewed, so she'd have to take Calleigh's advice, and take a leap of faith that the physical side of things would be pleasurable. Everything else that went into making a relationship would have to be taken one day at a time.

Miranda carried her treat back into the living area. She didn't have a table, so all her meals were eaten on the couch. She looked up when Axel didn't approach for a sniff and found him sound asleep, laying on his back with his legs splayed wide open. "Thanks. I feel a bit better. So have you heard from Kevin recently?"

"I got an email last week. We were talking about names for the boys. He said things are pretty hairy where he is right now, so they might be in and out of communication blackouts. Did you know that this weekend is our three year wedding anniversary?"

"No, congratulations."

"Thanks. Did you also know that in the past thirty-six months, my husband has been gone for twenty six of them? I don't think I realised how hard this would be when Kevin said he wanted to sign up for the reserves. I supported him, I still do, but this isn't the easiest thing to handle. At least I have my parents and his mom. They've all been great about checking up on me."

"Do you get scared, knowing the kind of dangers he deals with over there?"

"Yes, but I try not to think about that. I tell myself Kevin's at work and he'll be home soon. This is his second tour so maybe we'll get a bit of break after this."

"Do you remember the invitation you extended when we first met? I'm in a much better place now than I was then, so I'd like to return the favour."

"I appreciate that, Miranda."

"I have some thinking to do, so I guess I'll let you go."

"Okay. I think I'm going to take a nap. That is if the tumbling duo takes a break from their Cirque du Soleil practice. See you bright and early tomorrow."

Miranda shut the phone and placed it on the end table. A nap didn't sound as though it were a bad idea. She went over to the closet and pulled down her pillow. It was too much effort to open her bed from its hiding place inside the sofa, so she snuggled down lengthwise in the surprisingly soft sofa cushions. She dragged the throw blanket down from its normal resting spot on the back and covered herself. Even during the height of summer, Miranda could never sleep unless she had some type of blanket.

Miranda scooted back till her back was up against the thick cushions of the sofa. What if instead of cushions it was a man's chest? She'd never slept in a man's arms. Drew had always slept on the far side of the bed, saying that he couldn't sleep if he felt crowded. It sounded legitimate to her, so she'd never made a fuss. The fact that Miranda had difficulty sleeping unless she had some type of covering, and enjoyed the warmth of another person wasn't her husband's — *ex-husband's* — fault. How it would feel to have Vic or Chase's arms around her while she slept?

When they all piled on the sofa at one of the boy's apartments to watch a movie, their presence was calming. She loved the heat that came off their bodies, and most of the time Miranda would end up relaxing against Chase's shoulder, his arm around her, while Vic stretched out across the sofa with his head in both their laps. Sometimes after a long day she'd end up drifting off during the movie, and it was on those occasions that she woke more rested than after an entire night in her own bed.

Their schedules didn't always match up, so often Miranda would end up spending time with either Chase or Vic. Chase was the more light-hearted of the two. They'd spent hours talking about his trips around the world. He loved to travel, and Miranda had been spellbound as she listened to some of his adventures over the years. Apparently his love of travel had been nurtured from birth, since Chase had told her that his mom and dad often travelled on business and as a young boy they'd carted him around to the far corners of the planet on a regular basis. She'd never been out of the United States. In fact, until her move to Boston, Miranda had never even been out of the Midwest. If they got together, would Chase take her exploring?

Miranda sighed. She was going to do it. She knew it. When she was with them, she felt special. They made her feel special, and that was a very heady and new experience. Her initial fears about being a third wheel ended up being completely unfounded. In fact, now that she'd got to know Chase and Vic better, Miranda felt a little ashamed of her first impressions. They *were* handsome, but they were also the most genuine men she'd ever met. They put so much into the care of their patients, who were complete strangers, it had been a revelation to Miranda to discover how they treated those who were important to them. So yes, Miranda would take a leap of faith and completely open her mind, body and heart to Chase and Vic. Now all she had to do was find the gumption to tell them. Her eyes got heavy and a little smile crept across her lips.

Maybe I should show them instead.

* * * *

A week had passed and it was once again Miranda's day off. She'd made plans to meet Vic and Chase later that night, but first a little pampering was in order. She tugged open the door to the salon and stepped inside. The traditional scents of a salon mingled with a light incense wafting through the air, resonating with soft pop music.

"Welcome to La Dolce Vita. How may I help you?"

There was a young perfectly made up woman standing behind the half circled counter. She was dressed in black from head to toe, except for the splash of lapis lazuli around her neck. The blue reminded her of Chase's eyes.

"I have an appointment at nine o'clock. My name is Miranda Green."

The attendant looked down and Miranda assumed a computer sat discreetly out of sight from the clients' view.

"Yes, ma'am. I see you're having the soothing package as well as a hair treatment today. Why don't you follow me and we'll get you started."

Miranda did as told and followed the receptionist through a frosted door that had a rose design etched into the glass. The corridor was painted a deep mauve colour, the hue calming to the eyes. That made sense given that the entire purpose of the spa was to relax and rejuvenate the body. The pop music became new age, and drifted to

Miranda's ears via invisible speakers when they entered what appeared to be a lounge.

"Since this is your first visit with us, I need you to complete these forms. We'll begin with your facial then your massage. After your manicure and pedicure we'll serve you a light lunch and finish out your day with the cut and style. Can I get you anything to drink while you wait? A bottle of water, cup of coffee?"

"No thank you. I'm good." Miranda sat in one of the overstuffed chairs and placed the clipboard on her lap.

"Your aesthetician should be with you soon."

The receptionist left and Miranda looked around the room. The dark mauve continued and there were muted abstract paintings on two of the walls. Wall sconces emitted a glow in the room and Miranda spotted a dimmer switch on the wall next to the door. She glanced down at the forms, it seemed as though they wanted the basic information. There were blank spaces for length of time since last massage, what did she hope to accomplish with today's appointment, significant medical conditions and so forth.

Miranda finished with the last question and as if they'd simply been waiting for the moment she set her pen down the glass door opened and another young woman entered.

"Hi, my name is Amanda and I'm your aesthetician." She held out her hand. "I'll take your forms."

Amanda looked them over and smiled then they left the lounge and started back down the dim hallway. They came to a series of doors and Amanda pushed the first one open. When they entered Miranda saw a draped table that was vaguely reminiscent of those in surgery, but the blankets looked soft and there was a bulge from a round pillow hidden beneath the blankets. A magnifying glass attached to a swinging arm was off to the side, and

Miranda shuddered internally to think about how her skin was going to look when every pore was exposed to Amanda's critical eye.

"Because of the chemicals we use it's really best if you remove your shirt. I'd hate for anything to drip or spill. There's a robe on the back of the door for you to wear. After you're covered you can relax on the table and I'll be back with you in a moment."

Amanda left and when the door closed Miranda saw the robe waiting for her. She'd never had a facial before, and was a little excited. When Jenna had recommended this place she'd said that the experience would be unlike anything Miranda had ever had before. So far it was definitely living up to its reputation. Miranda had completely blown her entertainment budget for the next several months on the extravagant pampering session, but she'd put in over twenty hours of overtime on her last paycheque, so she figured everything would be fine. Today was meant to bolster her confidence for her night with Vic and Chase. She would leave this salon and spa looking and feeling the best she possibly could then set out to capture her men.

* * * *

Five hours later, Miranda felt as though she glowed from the inside out. She'd let the stylist convince her to try a new cut and the long layers helped alleviate the weight of her hair. She didn't have the guts to cut it all off, as had been first suggested, but did let the man add some copper highlights that caught the light in the salon and made Miranda smile. Now it was off to find a dress designed to make her men drool.

She'd called Calleigh from the salon and got the recommendation of a small boutique on Newbury Street. When she opened the door, Miranda stopped short. This place was nice. Way nice. Expensive nice. Miranda, who spent most of her living hours in scrubs, never invested much in her wardrobe. Why spend a lot on money on clothes that didn't get much use? Not to mention she hated shopping. There was nothing worse than being forced to stand in front of mirror and have all your faults stare back at you.

"Welcome. Can I help you find something?"

Miranda looked at the saleswoman. She was a tall, graceful, elegantly dressed, and a perfect size nothing.

"Um I think I'd like to look around for a minute?"

"Sure. Let me know if you'd like to open a dressing room."

Right, like there's any chance I'm going to willingly get undressed anywhere near you.

It would look odd if she cut tail and ran, so Miranda turned right and started a slow circuit of the displays and racks that lined the wall. She flipped through a couple of hangers as though she were looking for her size then moved on. She'd almost made it back to the door when the saleswoman approached her again.

"Did you see anything you liked?"

In truth she had. There'd been some nice dresses, but Miranda had cringed when she saw the price tag.

"Are you looking for something in particular?"

"A dress," *Oh crap why'd I open my mouth, now she's going to want to get me into something?*

"Is this for a special occasion or casual wear?"

"A date?"

That was the most simplistic answer. It's not as if she was going to blurt out to a total stranger that she planned on sleeping with two men tonight.

"Formal?"

"No, but it is a first date." *Sort of, mostly.*

"Were you thinking sundress or little black dress?"

A little black dress? Miranda had heard women and fashion experts use the phrase, but had never owned one. Those were for models and society types, not short, overweight operating room nurses.

"Why don't I pull a couple of both so we can look at all the options?"

Miranda's eyes went wide. "Oh, I'm not sure. I mean…"

"Trust me, we'll have you looking resplendent in no time. I would estimate that you're a size eight, maybe ten depending on the cut."

Miranda nodded. Oh well, she'd try a few dresses on. What could it hurt?

Chapter Six

Vic sat on his sofa. His right leg was restless as the ankle rested on his left knee. He picked up the medical journal lying next to him and flipped open to an article he'd intended to read for the last week. There was nothing like research methodology to numb out a jittery mind.

"Would you relax, love," Chase said.

Vic leant his head back on the edge of the sofa and spied his upside down lover. "I'm relaxed."

Chase snorted. "You're as nervous as a virgin bride. Everything will be fine."

Vic twisted so he could face Chase. "How do you know? What if she's coming here to tell us that she's decided not to go any further?"

"Then we take more time to win her over."

"And if she's coming to tell us that she's moving away?"

"Then we convince her to stay, or chase after her. But she's not moving away. We would've have heard something at work."

Vic nodded. "I want her so much. I want to hold her while she sleeps. I want to sit at the breakfast table with the two of you and smile over bowls of cereal. I want to watch you make love to her. I want to feel her body between ours. I want to hear her cry out in pleasure. I want that *someday*, Chase."

Chase came around the sofa and sat next to Vic. He pulled Vic into his arms and kissed him. Chase's tongue slid inside, and Vic's arms came around Chase's strong neck. There was nothing in the world that could compare to the pleasure he received from Chase's kisses. Except maybe Miranda's, but even those were different. Miranda's kisses were sweet and alluring and sexy. They made Vic hard and desperate to sink inside her soft body. Chase's kisses were fiery and made Vic's body throb. He'd lost count of the number of times he and Chase had started out with a few kisses, and one or the other ended up tackling his partner till they writhed on whatever surface was available till they eventually bellowed out in mutual orgasm. God save him when he finally got both Miranda and Chase in bed with him. Vic wasn't sure he was going to survive.

Chase pulled back from Vic. "I must be losing my touch. Normally you'd be crawling in my lap at this point."

Vic brushed the strands of hair back from Chase's forehead. "I'm sorry. I just hate all this uncertainty."

Chase leant his forehead against Vic's. "Have a little faith. She's a strong woman, a survivor. We've both sensed the depth of her passion. We know she wants us. She's said that she's falling in love with both of us. That's seventy-five percent of the battle. All Miranda needs is a little time to wrap her head around the idea of opening herself up to a relationship again."

The doorbell rang and they both looked over at the door to Vic's condo. Vic stood and held his hand out to Chase. His partner took Vic's hand and pushed off the sofa. They walked, hands clasped, to the front door. He took a deep breath, Chase gave his hand a squeeze and Vic pulled the portal open.

Before him stood a smouldering angel. His jaw dropped and Vic heard Chase's soft exclamation of wonder beside him. Miranda stood in the muted glow from the lights outside his door. Her dark hair shone, almost chestnut in colour under the lights. The soft ends floated around her shoulders and down her back. Wrapped around her petite, curvy body was the most stunning dress Vic had ever seen. The dark indigo stood out from her lightly tanned skin. The neckline plunged to a point between Miranda's breasts, and what stunning breasts they were. Round, full and firm. He wanted to suck on the nipples that stood out beneath the silk material. The dress conformed to every curve of Miranda's hourglass form, ending a couple of inches above her knees. Her cute little feet stood atop a pair of stiletto heels that would be dangerously narrow on the sidewalks of the North End, where Chase and he had planned to take her to dinner. Vic smiled — of course that meant they would have to hold her close to stabilise her as they walked down the street.

Chase jerked Vic's arm. "Say something!" he hissed.

Vic looked over at Chase. "Your vocal cords work as well as mine do." He held out his free hand to Miranda. "You look — "

"Breathtaking," Chase finished.

Pleasure spirals sailed up his arm when her small hand landed inside his. Satin smooth flesh slid against his palm. Her nails were painted a delicate seashell pink, and Vic noticed they matched the toenails peeking out from the straps of her sandals.

Vic pulled Miranda into his home and into his and Chase's arms. She stood between them, those magnificent breasts pressed against Vic's chest, those delicate hands sliding around his waist to rest against his back. Vic's hands rested on the soft swell of Miranda's hips as he dipped his head and sealed their lips together. As with every time they touched, his heart softened and his cock turned to stone. Vic opened his eyes and watched as Chase's head dipped and kissed the tender skin behind Miranda's ear. Miranda's soft whimper goaded Vic on. His tongue surged into her sweet mouth, commanding her response. And when Miranda's little tongue lapped at his lips, seeking permission to play, he nearly cried out in victory.

Vic pulled back from their kiss and rested his lips against her temple. Chase's hands smoothed up and down the side of Miranda's torso, moulding the curves of her breasts and the dip of her little waist. Their hands linked together on Miranda's hips, and they shared a kiss over her head.

"I love it when you do that," Miranda whispered.

"Do what, honey?" Chase asked.

"All the little touches the two of you share." She looked up at Vic. "The way your fingers play in the back of Chase's hair when the two of you are bent over the computer and the way when we watch a movie your head ends up resting on Chase's lap. But I especially love when I'm standing between you and you kiss over the top of my head. It makes me feel surrounded, protected, a real part of whatever this thing is between us."

"It's love, princess. I was drawn to you from the moment we first met, and every day since, your charming smile and open heart have bewitched me."

Chase nuzzled up against Miranda's back. "You're intelligent and witty. Competent and compassionate. You are a perfect match for us, and now that we've found you, our lives are complete."

Miranda giggled. "Nothing like a little pressure guys. I'm not some paragon of virtue you're making me sound like. While it's true that I generally have a pretty submissive personality, I not above losing my temper or being in a bad mood. What if I mess up?"

"We're human. Perfection is an illusion. At some point in time, each one of us or even more than one of us are guaranteed to mess up. It's easiest to hurt the ones you love, but as long as we remember there is love, then we can work it out," Vic reassured both of them.

"Where is Axel, honey? Do you need to go home and take care of him tonight?"

Miranda shook her head against Vic's chest. "Calleigh is puppy-sitting. I dropped him off before I came here. I wanted to make sure that my *entire* evening was free."

"Thank you God," Chase whispered.

Vic chuckled lowly. "Before we lose our minds and our clothes, I suggest we leave for dinner. I want to show you off in this amazing dress."

Chase stepped back, and Vic saw the erection straining his dress slacks. He smiled, knowing the longer Chase had to wait, the more intense making love to him would be. Vic knew the three of them would sleep in the same bed that night, and the image of their bodies replete in pleasure further tightened the fit of his own trousers.

* * * *

Chase held open the door and Miranda followed Vic into the restaurant. She was immediately assailed by the scents associated with a good Italian restaurant. Fresh baked bread, oregano, basil, pasta and succulent lean meats. The rumble of muted voices and the tinkling of crystal chimed in the air. Miranda's steps were cushioned by the thick, dark brown carpet. The bright white linens contrasted against warm wood accents. Crème stucco walls wrapped around them, displaying colourful works of art. Miranda imagined herself transported to some far away villa on the Italian coast. If only she could looked out the window and watch the waves of the Tyrrhenian Sea roll towards the beach... Miranda's dream was shattered at the sound of a feminine squeal.

"Vittorio!"

Miranda looked behind her and tried to catch Chase's gaze to question what was going on, but when she saw his expression of restrained hilarity, she turned back around. Vic was being smothered in a bear hug by a heavyset woman quickly encroaching upon her golden years. Vic's arms were pinned to his sides, and he stood stick straight. Miranda couldn't help it, she started to giggle. When Chase's hand landed on the small of her back, she leant into the touch.

"That's Mamma Sophia. She and her husband have owned this restaurant for thirty years. Vic worked here as a server throughout college and the first couple of years of medical school."

Miranda's eyes went wide. "And she remembers him? That was what, sixteen years ago?"

"You know Vic. He's leaves an impression from the first moment, but aside from that, Sophia treats all her servers as though they are family. I can't tell you how many times she gave Vic leftovers to bring home with him. For financially challenged medical students, it was as though manna had dropped from heaven. I used to tease him that the only reason I started dating him was for the food he brought home."

"I heard that, signorino! That is a very naughty thing to say. You and Vittorio are, as they say, two peas and a pod."

Chase laughed and stepped aside to hug Sophia. "*In* a pod, Mamma. But you are right, Vic and I are a matched set. Now I'd like to introduce you to Miranda Green. Miranda, this is Signora Sophia Biachni."

Sophia stepped closer and took Miranda's hands. "Such beauty. You are as da Vinci's Madonna." She looked over at Vic and Chase. "She is yours, no?"

Vic smiled wide. "Si, Mamma. She is ours. We've come to celebrate."

"Eccellente! I will have Massimo bring out il buon vino. We have the special table all set for you."

"Thank you, Mamma."

Chase held Miranda's hand as they wove their way through the tables. They passed under a bricked archway and paused at the base of a wrought iron spiral staircase. Miranda placed her hand on Vic's back. The warmth of his body through the fine linen shirt seared her palm. Vic reached back and clutched her hand. He brought it around his body and kissed the back side of Miranda's fingers, then he turned back and gave her a wink. They climbed the stairs slowly, and when they reached the top, Vic pushed open a metal door.

Miranda stepped out into an enchanted land. Little white lights danced in the summer night's breeze. Pots of leafy trees and wine casket barrels overflowed with flowers in bloom. Tiny tea lights lit a pathway through the rooftop garden. A small fountain with four little cherubs playing amidst the double tiers bubbled happily. The water was illuminated to a bright blue. In the middle of everything sat a table set for three.

"Wow," she whispered.

Vic took her other hand and led her over to the table. Chase pulled out the chair that was meant for her, and with courtly manners that would do the blueblood families of Boston proud, seated Miranda in elegant style. Vic shook out her napkin and placed it gently in her lap then sneaked a quick kiss from Miranda's still stunned lips.

Vic and Chase sat on either side of her. Brilliant smiles lit up their handsome faces. Miranda couldn't stop looking around at the little slice of heaven found in the middle of what she'd thought was a heavily congested, if historic, area of the city. The traffic noise fell away and Miranda gasped as a solo violin started to play softly in the back corner.

"That's Gino. He's Sophia and Massimo's grandson, and studies at the New England Conservatory. I remember when he was a little guy running around the kitchen while his dad cooked."

Miranda closed her eyes and let the music drift over to on the summer air. The soft melody was so rich and hauntingly beautiful, it stole Miranda's breath. "It's so beautiful. I wonder what he's playing?"

"It's the love theme from Tchaikovsky's Romeo and Juliet," Chase said, sitting back to in his chair.

Miranda stared at him. Her jaw dropped. She had no idea Chase was a classical music enthusiast. When she glanced over at Vic, the man had a rather besotted smile on his face. It appeared both her men were full of surprises tonight. Miranda's thought screeched to a halt. *Her men.* That sounded rather nice.

"You seemed a little shocked, honey. Didn't know there was more to me than a pretty face?" Chase teased.

Miranda stood and stepped over to Chase's chair. She looked down at his lap. Chase smiled and opened his arms. Miranda sat, at first a little self conscious because she'd never actually sat on a man's lap before and was a little worried about being too heavy, but Chase pulled her close and she rested her head on his shoulder. The music floated over to them and when the last note rang true, Chase lifted Miranda's chin and kissed her gently. In that moment, she could have believed she was Juliet in the arms of her Romeo. Of course, Miranda hoped to have a better ending than the star-crossed lovers.

"Thank you for sharing that with me," Chase whispered.

Miranda smiled then went back to her chair. A moment later a big burly man who could have passed for Tony from *Lady and the Tramp* brought over a bottle of wine and presented it with a flourish.

"I have brought you something from our special collection."

"Massimo, that's a 1943 Burgundy!"

"Si."

"No, si. You can forget it, signor. That's a three thousand dollar bottle of wine. You've probably had that in your family since it was made. Absolutely not, I refuse!" Vic exclaimed.

Massimo's bushy eyebrows furrowed and he frowned. "You said this was a celebration, no?"

"Yes, but not on the level of justifying the consummation of one of France's greatest treasures."

Miranda heard soft laughter coming from behind a screen of potted trees. Chase's blue eyes twinkled and he tried to cover his chuckle behind his hand.

Massimo broke out into a loud laugh that rumbled from his massive barrel chest. "Oh Vittorio, I have missed you. It is always so easy to jack your chain."

Chase snorted and Miranda was tempted to throw her napkin at him.

"Massimo," Vic warned.

"Okay, okay. Here you go. I brought this for you." He pulled another bottle out from beneath his apron.

Vic squinted at the label. "That's better. In fact that's very good. One of the best years on record, if I remember my education from your cellars."

"Si. The 1997 Chianti Classico." Massimo pulled the cork and presented it to Vic.

Vic sniffed it and smiled. Massimo poured a taste into Vic's wine glass. Miranda watched as he swirled the ruby liquid then stuck his nose into the glass and took a big sniff. She'd seen people do that on television, but never understood exactly what they accomplished by the task. Vic took a sip. It appeared as though he let the wine reside in his mouth for a moment before swallowing, then he turned to Massimo with a huge grin.

"Excellent."

"Buon! I will have Michael bring up your appetizers shortly, but now I suggest you request the hand of your lovely lady for a dance."

Massimo stepped away, and as soon as the door to the building closed the sound of the violin echoed across the rooftop.

"Ah, a tango." Vic stood and held out his hand. "May I have this dance?"

Miranda twisted the napkin in her lap. "I don't know how," she whispered.

"That's fine, neither do I...not really. Come dance with me, princess." Vic took another step towards Miranda, keeping his hand out.

She slowly lifted her hand and placed it in his. They walked together a few feet away. Miranda heard a scrape behind her and looked over her shoulder to see Chase turn his chair so he could watch them. Vic stopped and stood still. Miranda stepped into his space. Her breath slowed and she raised her eyes till they met Vic's pale blue. His arm came around her waist, and his palm slid across the material of her dress. Their hands linked at the side of their bodies and Vic raised their arms into the position Miranda commonly saw with formal dancing.

She gently placed her left hand on the back side of Vic shoulder. Vic adjusted the grip of their unified hands, so he essentially cupped Miranda's palm and her fingers naturally slipped over the top between the groove of his thumb.

"The thing about the tango is that it's all about seduction. Close your eyes, don't worry about the steps. Listen to the music, feel my body movement and simply follow."

She closed her eyes and opened her ears. The light breeze of the summer night caressed her body as the heat from Vic's core crossed through the barriers of their clothes, relaxing the nervous tension from Miranda's body. Vic took a step back, and she stumbled slightly unprepared.

"Feel me, princess. Feel my chest expand, and breathe with me. Feel my hands guide you, and give yourself into my care. Trust me to lead you. Are you ready?"

Miranda nodded, but didn't open her eyes.

"Good. And on the count of three. One...two...three."

Vic moved forwards another step then took another to the left. Miranda found herself walking backwards for two counts then Vic turned their bodies and a few more steps followed.

"Very good. Let's try that again."

They did and this time Miranda found herself moving easier, not only blindly being herded, but anticipating the next step and, as gracefully as she was capable of, floating across the rooftop. This wasn't dancing as Miranda was familiar with, but almost as though she and Vic were taking a stroll. Miranda gave herself over to Vic's arms, and the music Gino played for them. After several repetitions, she became more comfortable and heard Gino pick up the tempo of the music. He must be watching them to know when they were ready.

This time when they paused, Vic opened his arm and stepped away from Miranda. She opened her eyes at the exact moment he yanked her back into his embrace. His tall, strong frame held her securely in his arms, and Miranda laughed as happiness unlike anything she'd ever experienced filled her. They made another circuit, but this time instead of pulling away from her, Vic tightened the hand around her back and dipped her back over his arm. Their bodies moved up and Miranda landed hard against Vic's chest. It was exhilarating. They played with their feet, neither one of them really making any pattern, but deep chuckles rumbled against Miranda's breast with their bodies pressed tightly against one another. Vic took them back to the original steps and they repeated the process all over again.

"You ready for our big finish, princess?" he asked with a smile.

She nodded enthusiastically. Vic quickly turned them in tight circles over and over till the world tilted on its axis, and Miranda felt as though she floated away. The music slowed and their bodies simply swayed together until very slowly Vic dipped her one last time. Miranda let her head fall back, her loose hair no doubt pooling over the surface of the roof, but she didn't have a care in the world and when Vic's lips placed a kiss in the valley of her breasts, Miranda thought she might finally understand what it truly meant to be in love with someone.

Her eyes flew open as the sound of clapping broke the still night air. Chase stood beside his chair and in the candlelight of their table, Miranda saw his eyes glow from within. Vic lifted her up and held out their arms. Miranda curtsied and he bowed. Chase came over and swung her up into his arms.

"You were amazing. A natural. Maybe we should all enrol in dance classes. I'd love to see you do a rumba or one of those other sexy Latin dances. And this hair! My God, I never realised how much of it there was under those pony caps. You have it tied up so often. It's gorgeous. I want to bury my hands in it and kiss you unconscious."

"Okay," she whispered.

Chase sealed his promise with a kiss. It was a good thing he had his arms around her because the intensity would have sent her shooting up to the stars. When Miranda's feet were once again planted on the ground, she let go of Chase and tilted her head towards Vic. Chase smiled and dragged Vic into his arms.

"That was so sexy. Powerful and graceful at the same time. I couldn't stop watching your hips move to the music." Chase placed his lips against Vic's ear. "I want to fuck you," he said softly.

Chase had said the words loud enough that they carried the short distance to where Miranda stood. Her face heated, the thought of Chase buried inside Vic sent her rushing over to the table for her glass of water. She had to cool off before steam began to vent from her ears. She unabashedly stared while Vic and Chase shared a slow, open-mouthed kiss. Their heads tilted, each instantly knowing the best way they fit together. Their lips clung together, and when they broke for air Miranda saw Chase feed Vic his tongue. They sipped at each other, exchanging possession as Vic's tongue followed Chase's back into his mouth. Forget about steam, Miranda was sure her blood had reached a boiling point. Any moment now, her body would erupt. Her nipples pressed against the thin material of her silk dress and moisture trickled down onto the satin panties the store clerk had convinced her to buy.

Her personal show was disrupted when the door to the restaurant opened, and a young man brought out their first course. Vic and Chase looked her direction and both men smiled, their eyes trained decidedly lower than her face. As if they were predators, they stalked her. Miranda stood frozen, unable or unwilling to move, she wasn't sure. Both men snaked an arm out and yanked her against their bodies. Two sets of lips attached themselves to either side of her neck, and Miranda's head fell back further exposing the column of her throat. Her hands rose to the backs of their heads. The fingers of her left threaded through the strands at the nape of Chase's neck. The trim nails of her right gently scratched at Vic's. Triple moans filled the air and Gino's violin matched the pitch as he began a new piece.

They all managed to get control of themselves, and her men assisted Miranda back to her seat. She took the first taste of her soup and a moan of a different variety escaped.

Chapter Seven

Miranda settled on Vic's couch, and pulled her feet up on the cushions beside her. The wine they'd drunk at dinner swam happily in her veins. She wasn't drunk or even tipsy, merely very relaxed and mellow. Probably best considering what was about to happen.

Vic was in the kitchen and Chase had disappeared into the bathroom as soon as they arrived. Miranda was glad they'd given her a few minutes alone. She needed the space to settle the last of her nerves without having the two men's machismo overwhelm her. What would happen? Chase had said he wanted to make love to — fuck — Vic while they were up on the roof. So she assumed that meant Vic would be inside her.

Please, whatever higher power exists in the universe, don't let me be a disappointment to them.

Vic came into the living room with a glass of water in his hand. "Hey, princess." He handed the water to Miranda. "You doing okay?"

Miranda took a sip, thankful for both Vic's caring and the moisture to help her dry throat. "Yes, I'm a little nervous but glad to be here."

"We don't have to make love tonight, honey," Chase said as he sat next to her and pulled Miranda's bare feet into his lap.

She moaned as Chase began to dig his thumbs into her arches. Miranda rarely wore heels, and by the time they'd entered Vic's condo, she'd been more than ready to be rid of the stylish torture devices. Vic knelt in front of the sofa and Miranda took his hand. "I want to make love to the two of you. I want to feel your bodies on top of mine. I want to experience your touch on my body. But, in my experience, sex has been more painful than pleasurable. I was happier to have it over with rather than wishing it would go on longer, so I'm a little afraid of taking something you obviously cherish and turning it into something you hate."

"Oh, princess." Vic surged up and pulled Miranda into a hug. "I promise you no pain. You're not a virgin, so there's no reason for you to experience any discomfort when we make love. I can reassure you till I'm blue in the face, but I think it would be better to show you exactly how Chase and I plan on giving you a night to remember. Hopefully, one of many."

Miranda nodded. She knew the longer they sat there and talked, the more nervous she'd become. It was best to get the show on the road. Close her eyes and take a leap of faith. Jump in with both feet, and whatever other clichés she could think of. Chase slid her feet to the floor and stood. He held out his hands and Miranda took hold of one from each of her men to help her off the soft cushions. They walked together into Vic's bedroom. The king sized bed took up the centre of the room, and Miranda had to admit that compared to her pull-out, the thick mattress and comforter did look inviting. Vic stepped away to pull down the covers, while Chase wrapped his arms around Miranda from behind.

"We're going to make you fly, honey. I can't wait to taste every inch of your skin." He pulled the tab to the zipper on the back of Miranda's dress, and placed a kiss on the newly exposed skin. "Delicious. Exactly as I imagined."

Miranda stood still as her dress slowly loosened around her. Chase's fingertips skimmed her spine as the zipper lowered to the base of her back. She felt the closure of her bra come undone. Vic came towards them, unbuttoning his shirt as he walked. Miranda was struck by the sight of his exposed chest. Lean, defined muscle rippled in the low light of the bedside lamps he'd turned on. He removed the shirt and draped it over a bench at the foot of the bed. Miranda sucked in a breath when Chase's hands slid inside her dress and around her waist. Vic stepped up to them and raised his hands till they rested on Miranda's shoulders. They slid the straps of Miranda's dress and bra over her shoulders and down her arms. As the garment fell to her waist, Miranda closed her eyes. It was the first time any man other than her ex-husband had seen her partially nude. Chase's hands moved to cup her breasts, weighing the heavy mounds in his palms.

"So beautiful," Vic whispered.

Miranda's body went lax and she leant back into Chase's embrace. Her eyes flew open when heat covered her left nipple and an insistent tug pulled at the hardened protrusion. Miranda felt the residual echoes of the suction in the deepest core of her body.

"Oh, God. That…that feels…"

"Good, honey?" Chase whispered. "Tell me. What does Vic's mouth on your sweet pert nipples do to you?"

"I feel all warm."

"You know what I feel looking over your shoulder as I watch the man I love feast on your magnificent breasts?" Chase rubbed his finger back and forth on the underside of Miranda's breasts. His thumb traced Vic's lips now wrapped around the nipple on Miranda's right mound. "I feel as though my heart may explode, it's beating so quickly. I wish it were my lips wrapped around those pert nipples." He rolled the abandoned nub between his thumb and finger. "They're blushing and damp from Vic's mouth. I want to throw you on the bed, and watch you writhe in pleasure as we force you to be at the mercy of our lips and tongues and teeth and, yes, sweetheart, our cocks as well. I want to hear you scream in pleasure, claw our bodies with those delicate nails and cry out our names as you explode into a million pieces. I plan on burning every moment we spend together this night into my memory for all time to come."

Chase's hands left her breasts and traced the curves of her body till they rested on her hips. A few gentle pushes and Miranda's dress fell to the floor.

Vic straightened. "Step out, princess."

Miranda did and moved into Vic's arms. She heard a rustle behind her and assumed Chase was removing his clothes. She was tempted to look over her shoulder and watch the show, but Vic's hand threaded into the hair at the base of her neck and merged their mouths together, while their bodies collided. Her breasts, already sensitive from Vic's mouth, brushed over the crisp hairs on Vic's chest. The sensation made Miranda want to rub against him. Little sparks of pleasure rippled up and down her body.

Chase's hands slid between her and Vic's bodies. Miranda opened her eyes and saw Chase behind Vic.

Chase dropped a kiss on the back of Vic's neck. A piece of dark blond hair fell across his brow. A flush of arousal blossomed across his cheekbones. The bare skin of Chase's shoulders peeked over the top of Vic's. Miranda wanted to dig her fingers into the firm skin, close her mouth over the protrusion of his collar bone and suck up a mark so the world would recognise her mark on this magnificent man.

Chase's hands smoothly undid the buckle at Vic's waist then opened the trousers. Miranda felt one of Chase's hands slip inside Vic's pants. A low moan from Vic brought Miranda's gaze to his face, and the expression of pleasure that crossed his face gave Miranda an idea of exactly what Chase's busy hand was doing down there. She wanted to look down see the evidence of Vic's passion first-hand, but her eyes refused to move lower than his face.

Chase's head dropped out of sight, and Miranda peeked around Vic's body to see him kneel behind Vic. Vic's pants and underwear were slowly pulled down, and length of his erection fell towards Miranda's stomach.

Vic gasped and clutched their bodies together. "Oh God!" He keened and rubbed against Miranda. "Warn...oh fuck...warn a guy before you do that."

Vic buried his hand in Miranda's hair and took her mouth in an explosive kiss. His tongue thrust inside and his hips alternately pushed into Miranda's stomach then backwards. Vic's large hands cupped her rear and lifted her up against him. The heat of Vic's penis seared the skin of her belly. He felt large, certainly larger than her ex-husband. Which brought to mind the question — was Vic the norm or a deviation thereof? A low growl rumbled in Vic's chest and his fingertips dug into the globes of Miranda's butt. Her mind spun out of control and her arms wrapped around Vic's neck, needing some type of anchor in the storm raging through her body.

Vic pulled back from Miranda's kiss, breathing heavily. "Are you okay, princess?"

Miranda nodded and shuffled on the balls of her feet. "What..." She swallowed. "What did he do to you? What made you so excited?"

Chase stood and came around Vic and Miranda. He moved behind Miranda and put his hands on her shoulders. "I kissed him, honey."

"But how, when we..."

She gasped and looked to Vic for confirmation. His dark head nodded, and Miranda felt as if she were a complete idiot. Of course, she knew in theory how men made love to each other, but she hadn't thought everything through apparently.

"You liked that?"

"I love when Chase rims me. His tongue is so slick and hot as it glides across my rosebud. His lips and teeth suck and nibble on my hole, sending sparks arc through my body. When he bends me over and actually gets his tongue inside, it's like nothing you've ever felt before. And he loves it too. Chase is very oral. Aren't you, babe?"

Chase let his lips skim down the column of Miranda's neck. "I am. I can't wait to taste you, honey. Your sweet juices spilling from your body into my mouth and down my chin. I want to lap at your clit and feel it swell against my tongue. I want to hear you scream as your hungry little pussy vibrates against my face when you come."

"Holy shit," Miranda whispered. Her vagina pulsed as if it understood Chase's deep hypnotic words. Her panties were soaked by her arousal.

"You've never had a man take such pleasure from feasting on you as Chase will."

"I've never had a man feast on me," Miranda mumbled. She nibbled on her lower lip. Vic tilted her chin up and searched her eyes for a moment. Miranda wanted to squirm under his scrutiny, but forced herself to stand still and meet his gaze.

"You've never had a lover go down on you?"

Heat infused Miranda's face and she was eternally glad for the low light of Vic's bedroom. Her eyes darted over his shoulder then towards the door leading out to the living room.

Chase slipped his fingers beneath the top edge of Miranda's panties. "Honey?"

Miranda whimpered when Chase's fingertips played at the very top of her slit. "No! Okay? I've only ever slept with one man. My ex, and he…he…it was…"

Vic smoothed his hand over the top of Miranda's head. "Shh. It's okay, princess. That's all over now. Chase and I are going to take good care of you."

Chase knelt behind her and slid her panties down her legs. Miranda closed her eyes and tilted her head back when Vic palmed her breast and gently tugged on her nipple. She let out a low moan when Chase's lips brushed against her lower back. Chase's hand encircled her ankle and Miranda lifted her foot out of the scrap of elastic and satin. She lifted out the other leg while Chase's lips touched the back of her knee. It buckled, and she fell into Vic's arms.

Vic swung Miranda up into his arms. She stiffened in his arms, fearful that she'd be too heavy, and Vic would either drop her or stumble, but with easy steps he crossed over to the edge of the bed and laid her down gently. Vic climbed up on the mattress beside her. His body blocked the bedside light from hitting her eyes. He rested on his side, bracing his weight on his forearm. Miranda looked down and got the first sight of the erection that had pressed up against her. It stood tall against Vic's flat, toned stomach, the skin of his penis a shade darker than the rest of his body and flushed with the blood that rushed through the interior, making it come to life. The head was round and plump. Miranda watched in fascination when Vic wrapped a hand around the base and stroked up the column, releasing a drop of clear fluid from the slit. Chase, who'd settled between Miranda's legs, leant over and swiped the fluid away with his tongue. Vic hissed and held his penis out for Chase.

Chase wrapped his lips around the cap and Miranda saw his cheeks hollow. At that moment, Miranda wanted almost nothing more than to know exactly how Vic tasted. If Chase's expression was anything to go by, Vic was delicious.

"You like seeing Chase suck my cock, princess?"

She nodded. Her eyes were unable to move away from the sight. Miranda had never thought of a man's parts in such base terms, but Chase and Vic always referred to their cocks as though they were a almost a separate entity from the rest of them. She rolled the term around in her brain, and liked the way it sounded. She wanted cock. She wanted to feel a cock fill her…her pussy as they called it. She wanted to lick at the rounded head and taste both Vic's and Chase's essences. It was almost freeing to let go of her mental restrictions of how she's been taught women should think and behave. Miranda imagined that the proper constrained spirit floated away, and an earthy nymph inhabited her body.

Chase lifted off Vic's cock and came up over Miranda's body. His weight settled on top of her and she sighed in pleasure. Chase braced his weight on his forearm and settled his pelvis into the cradle of Miranda's hips. Chase's cock rubbed between her thighs. Its length and girth made Miranda's brain a tad nervous while her body simultaneously tingled in anticipation of the impressive organ filling all her cavities. Vic's body heat radiated against her side and Chase's transversed the barriers of their skin. Chase's lips were wet as he brushed them against hers. Driven by instinct, she licked his lower lip. The electricity of their touch made every minute hair on her body stand and reach for Chase, as if begging for further connection. Chase tilted his head and their mouths connected. Through Chase's kiss, Miranda tasted Vic. In that moment, the three of them were truly one. Her arms wrapped beneath Chase's arms and around his back. She arched up into the kiss, and her fingers traced the curve of his spine. Chase shivered and deepened their kiss. Miranda sank into the sea of sensations and let her mind float on the pleasure. Her hand encountered another and Vic linked their fingers as they stroked Chase together.

Miranda opened her eyes when Chase pulled away from their kiss. She looked over at the other man who shared the bed.

"You're beautiful together. Your dark hair fanned out across my pillows contrasts perfectly to Chase's lighter shade when your heads come together. His larger body covers yours as though he's enveloping you in sensuality and protection. The sight of your small soft hands skimming his firm resilient muscles will be burned into my mind for eternity."

Chase looked to his left and shared a kiss with Vic. Miranda watched as the two men revelled in their bond. It may have been a little narcissistic but part of Miranda felt as though by agreeing to become a part of their partnership, she'd managed to bring the two men closer together. If nothing more came of her time with them, she hoped this situation deepened Vic and Chase's love for each other. They were perfect for one another, and Miranda was more thankful than she could adequately express that they allowed her to share in their private lives. That the two men had given her the opportunity to get to know them on a more intimate level than would have been possible if strictly relegated to colleagues.

A finger smoothed back a tendril of hair that had slipped low over her forehead, and Miranda blinked out of the mind drift that had taken hold of her.

"Where did you go, princess?"

She smiled as she met their concerned gazes. "Nowhere unpleasant." She tightened her arms around Chase and tilted her head up to place a little kiss on the underside of his chin. Their eyes softened and she saw both men let out a collective breath. Chase slid down her body, leaving a trail of tender kisses along the way. When he settled back between her legs, Miranda stared at the top of his head. His hands pressed her thighs apart, and she suddenly became very self conscious. Chase had a front row seat to Miranda's most private parts, and her muscles tensed as she waited for the verdict.

Miranda's pulse pounded in her ears, but she managed to hear Vic ask, "Tell me, Chase, how beautiful is our princess' little pussy?" Vic's voice was deep and husky, the need obvious as the sound rasped over her skin.

The sound that escaped from Chase sounded almost purr-like. His head moved closer. So close that Miranda felt a puff of air against her soaking wet folds. She'd never been like that before. Even from her position up on the pillows she scented her own arousal. Would it disgust Chase? She'd heard and read that men didn't always enjoy the intimate smells of a woman. Drew had expressed his distaste on more than one occasion.

Her muscles tensed as the silence continued. She sensed Chase's eyes trained on her, and couldn't take it another second. She turned her head away from the scene on the bed and stared at the far wall. She tried to close her legs, but Chase's hands exerted enough pressure on the sensitive surface of her inner thighs to prevent the movement.

Vic cupped Miranda's cheek and pulled her face around. "What's wrong?"

She couldn't answer. She couldn't do anything other than stare and concentrate on trying not to let tears fill her eyes, or her breath hitch with disappointment. She knew things had been too good up till now. It was at this moment that she always seemed to lose whatever attraction she'd held for men who'd come into her life. Which was why she'd been so afraid to open herself back up to another man. Allowing that kind of vulnerability in her life had hurt her before, but this time with these men, she feared that their rejection may actually destroy her. With Drew she'd managed to hold onto a small part of her herself, but with Vic and Chase she allowed her barriers to fall and now not only was her heart exposed without protection to their spears, but her psyche was one small insult away from shattering into a million pieces.

One finger slid through her slippery swollen flesh, circled her opening slowly then flicked back up to twist around her engorged clit.

"Aw, God damn, Vic. She's so sweet smelling, wet and hot. I predict she's going to burn us alive, but we'll die experiencing pleasure unlike anything we've ever imagined."

Miranda's gaze flew down to Chase, and she was struck by the heat blasting her from within the electric blue orbs. Their stare held as his finger rimmed the edge of her vulva then pushed the thick digit into her channel. Miranda couldn't maintain the look and her head fell back with a cry. It was the first time she'd experienced any kind of intimate touch inside her pussy in over a year. And the kinds of touches she'd experienced before held nothing to this. This was pleasure. True pleasure. *Oh God!* Her insides clamped down on Chase's finger, trying to hold it within her for all time.

Chase moaned and pumped his finger Miranda's walls, rippling with need. "Fuck, Vic, you have to feel this. She's so silky and soaking wet. And tight. God damn is she tight."

A pair of lips captured her nipple and Miranda jolted when another finger massaged her clit then dipped down to trace her folds. It explored for a second, skimming around the base of Chase's finger then pushed its way inside beneath the digit already lodged deep inside her. They were both inside her and the full penetration and width of their touch stretched her tissues to point of the most perfect burn. A surge of cream flooded from her womb. They pressed deeper and Miranda actually felt their fingers twist together inside her. Their fingers moved together through her spasming tunnel.

Vic sucked deeply on her nipple and Miranda was helpless to the vibrations rippling throughout her body. Her hips rolled as she tried to get closer, but Chase's other hand held her stomach down. Miranda climbed higher and higher. She was on a journey without end, but with each progressive step she knew she somehow got closer to the ultimate destination. A warm wet tongue flicked at her clit then a pair of lips surrounded the pulsating nub and sucked. One man nursed on her breast and the other at her clit, their motions so in sync Miranda felt as though the two were tethered together from one source. Their fingers rubbed against a spot high inside her and she nearly fell over the edge of the pathway she imagined in her head. The fingers left and Miranda was left empty, instantly missing the possession she'd been so nervous to accept.

Chase's hand captured her hips and Miranda felt the evidence of her pleasure dampen her skin. His tongue set to exploring every ridge and valley of her pussy with determination and exquisite attention to detail. It was better than she'd ever imagined. Vic moved to the other breast. His fingers picked up where his mouth had left and rolled the abandoned swollen hill. One hand held on to the back of Vic's head and Miranda's other buried itself in Chase's strands.

Chase suddenly pressed his face deep into her flesh and his tongue speared into her vaginal opening. He ate at her as if he were starving. He stroked and suckled, deep hungry growls vibrating against her slick flesh. His lips and tongue worked together as implements of sensual torment. Vic's head lifted from her breast, and Miranda opened her eyes long enough to watch him stare at Chase's head buried between her thighs.

"That is so fucking sexy."

Miranda's body tightened. "Oh God, oh God, oh God." Her fingers dug into Vic's shoulders, her nails no doubt leaving tiny half moons in his skin. Pressure built inside her and she knew if something didn't break, she'd explode from within.

Vic cupped her cheek and Miranda turned into the touch. She panted and cried out when Chase thrust his finger inside her again, finding some spot that made all the nerves in her body dance. Her eyes flew open and caught Vic's, begging him silently for help.

"It's okay, princess. Let it happen. Don't fight the pleasure, let it consume you."

She had no idea what Vic was talking about, but his heat-filled gaze and soft reassuring touches let her relax enough that when Chase once again pulled her clit into his mouth and sucked, she felt something inside her burst. With a wrenching sob, she clenched her eyes shut and lights burst behind her eyelids. The pressure that had threatened to squeeze her guts rushed from her body in a violent explosion. A gush of fluid escaped her body and Miranda cried out. Tears streamed from the corners of her eyes with the pleasure crashing over her in waves. Her body trembled, eventually sinking into the mattress when her muscles no longer held her rigid in ecstasy.

Chapter Eight

"Jesus, that was amazing," Vic whispered.

Chase looked up at Vic whose hand was wrapped around his own cock. It was so beautiful. Harder and darker than Chase had ever seen it before, and that was saying a lot given their history. "Please?" He wanted to feel Vic's cock throb inside his mouth, taste his lover's cum pulse down his throat as Vic's deep groans echoed over his head.

Vic nodded and they adjusted their position. Chase got on all fours, straddling Miranda who was still coming down from her orgasm. He wet his lips, still covered with Miranda's taste and leant forwards. Vic stroked his cock, squeezing hard as his fist climbed from base to tip. One of Vic's hands threaded through his hair and pulled him close. The tug had just enough force that Vic straddled that line between aggression and passion. Chase opened willingly and Vic's cock nudged his bottom lip. The silky head of Vic's cock pushed forwards, and Chase accepted the blissful intrusion. He laved and stroked all around the rim with his tongue, but Vic was in no mood to play. His hand held Chase still and he surged deep, knowing after years together exactly how much Chase could take. Vic fucked his mouth in smooth, long thrusts. Chase moaned at the feel of Vic's powerful cock taking its pleasure from his body. Vic was definitely the more even-tempered one of the two of them, and Chase loved it when his partner loosened the reins on his tight control of his emotions. It seemed to only happen when they made love, and Chase had often wondered why that was, but was not above exploiting the effects for his own pleasure.

"Oh my God," Miranda whispered.

Out of the corner of his eye he saw Miranda scoot down so she was closer to him and Vic. Her hand reached out and her thumb brushed his lower lip as Vic tunnelled in and out of his mouth.

"I want a taste."

Vic stopped moving and held himself deep inside Chase. He looked over at Miranda. "You want to suck my cock, princess?"

While Chase waited to hear what Miranda's decision would be, he swiped and played with his tongue up and down the turgid flesh possessing him. He was reluctant to give up his treat, but would do so willingly to make Miranda happy.

"I have an idea. I'm sure by now Chase is desperate for some attention." Vic took Miranda's hand in his and together they grasped Chase's cock.

Chase moaned around Vic's dick filling his mouth. *Jesus, God, please don't make them stop.* He spread his knees wider, signalling to Vic and Miranda without words that he wanted more. He needed more.

"You see? He's so hard, and he's been a very good boy. First he made you come so beautifully, and now his talented tongue is whipping against my cock, all but begging for my cum to shoot down his throat."

Miranda slowly stroked Chase's erection. Her thumb slid across the wet tip, which made Chase groan again, and his eyes tried to roll back up inside his head. Her softly exploring touch was almost more than he could bear. When her short little nails gently scraped on the underside of his balls, he almost came right then and there.

Vic met Chase's eyes. "It's okay, babe. I'm going to make sure that you're taken care of."

Vic pulled his cock from Chase's mouth then slid his hands beneath Chase's arms and lifted him up. Vic's arms gathered both Miranda and Chase close as they all knelt on the bed. Miranda nuzzled against Vic's chest and Chase found a nice spot on Vic's neck to kiss and nibble.

"My two loves. You're both so good to me." Vic tightened his arms around Chase and Miranda. "Now princess, I want you to lie on your back with your head hanging just over the edge of the mattress. Chase you're going to stand behind her and let Miranda suck you."

"What about you?" Miranda asked.

"I'm trying to decide if I want to find heaven inside your tight little pussy, or if I want to blast a hot rope of cum down Chase's throat."

Chase captured Vic's mouth and reminded him exactly how proficient he was at oral pleasure. He sucked Vic's tongue into his mouth and massaged it with his own. There was something deep inside him that needed to accept Vic's essence after having Miranda come apart at his mercy. He knew both he and Vic would eventually stuff Miranda full of their cocks, but right now he was convinced this is what the three of them needed.

Vic's hands soothed Chase's shoulders as he pulled away from the kiss. "All right, love, I hear you."

Chase backed off the bed and got into position. He helped Miranda get comfortable. His hands massaged her breasts, which rested heavily against her chest, exposing the valley between. They were full and natural, and part of Chase wanted to forgo the blowjob and create a perfect tunnel between the mounds to fuck through. Vic's thick mattress was the perfect height for this type of activity. Chase spread his legs a little wider and awarded Miranda with an up close view of his smooth balls.

Her tongue came out and lapped at the skin. It traced the contours of his sac, and when she sucked one of his balls into her mouth, Chase's knees started to buckle. Vic grabbed Chase's arms and steadied him. He helped guide Chase down over Miranda's prone body. Vic straddled Miranda's hips and Chase's position put him once again in perfect placement to suck Vic's cock.

Miranda grasped Chase's dick and angled so that the head slipped into her mouth. He couldn't prevent himself from looking down the cavity between their bodies to watch the scene. Miranda's graceful neck arched back. Her hands held onto Chase's hips and pulled. He took that as a sign and slowly lowered himself into her mouth. It was so hot and wet that Chase nearly forgot that he needed to go slow until they determined how much of him Miranda could take. He was basically the same length as Vic, but thicker. The sight of Miranda's lips stretched tight around his cock had his temperature skyrocketing and his balls tightening in anticipation.

"Oh fuck, honey, that a beautiful sight." His voice was rough even to his own ears. "Your swollen lips wrapped around my dick, and the heat of your mouth is so perfect."

His hips jerked and he slid another inch deeper. Miranda's moan vibrated along his length and had him tightening his fingers in the blankets of the bed. Chase felt the resistance of Miranda's throat against the head of his cock and paused.

"Relax your throat, honey. Just a little more. You can take me, I know you can."

Chase refused to move until he sensed the tension leave Miranda's body. The tiny puffs of air that landed on the underside of his cock as Miranda tried to breathe through her nose slowed. Chase fed Miranda more of his cock in incremental steps. He knew he'd reached her limit when her fingers dug into his hips.

"So good, honey. Now swallow around me. Use that sweet tongue to drive me wild." Miranda followed his instructions to the letter and Chase cried out in pleasure. "God, fuck yes!"

Vic yanked on Chase's hair and lifted his head up. Chase opened in anticipation and moaned deep in his chest when Vic plunged his thick throbbing flesh inside. Chase tried to tell Vic how perfect Miranda's mouth was by mimicking every movement she made. His avid tongue stroked around the flared head and his cheeks hollowed with fierce suction. Vic tasted of earthy musk and salt. Between the lingering flavour of Miranda's sweetness still reeling in his senses, Chase had everything he craved. He felt drugged on the pleasure. Vic's hands speared through his hair and his hips jerked, forcing more of his flesh into Chase's throat.

"That's it, babe. You're such a good little cocksucker. Show me how much you like being stuffed full of dick."

Vic's words overhead sent Chase into frenzy. They seemed to stimulate Miranda as well because she went absolutely wild on him. Chase could barely take it. The mind melting suction on his cock, the feel of Vic thrusting in and out of him... His shell of civility dissolved and Chase became a slave to the base demands of his body. From his position he detected the scent of Miranda's arousal. The sweet honey floated up from her body and assailed his nostrils, beckoning him to fall deeper under her spell.

Vic's fingers tightened in Chase's hair. "Fuck, Chase, I'm gonna come."

Chase felt his balls draw up—he was only moments away from filling Miranda's throat as well. His eyes met Vic's. The primal hunger in his partner's gaze snapped another one of the threads Chase was using to keep himself under control.

"Miranda? Princess. Chase is about to lose it. If you don't want his cum pumping inside you, pull back, sweetheart."

Miranda not only didn't pull back, but she actually sucked harder at his thrusting cock. Oh God, he was going to come. Any second now, his balls would explode with a force that would surely make him black out. He needed Vic to be there with him. He desperately wanted to feel Vic explode in his mouth while his cum jetted down Miranda's throat. If only...oh fuck, now!

Chase's orgasm ripped him apart, shredding all his preconceived notions of what it meant to make love. He shook violently and the muscles in his back seized. His cum shot from the head of his dick in powerful spurts, and the last neurons of consciousness worried that he might actually choke Miranda with the intensity of his climax.

He sucked Vic harder and a deep, hoarse groan signalled he was about to receive his reward. He stroked Vic's cock with his tongue, greedily demanding Vic unleash the power building in his tight, lean frame.

Suddenly Miranda screamed around his cock and Chase jerked his cock out of Miranda's mouth, fearful that he'd hurt her. He tried to pull off Vic's cock but his partner wouldn't let him go. Vic fucked Chase's face with an intensity that only came from years of knowing one's partner.

"Oh my God! Vic!"

Chase's eyes flew down and between Miranda's spread legs, Vic had three fingers buried inside her glistening wet pussy. Her cream spilled over Vic's hand and Chase moaned. Vic came with a roar and Chase swallowed every drop, sucking and stroking Vic with his tongue till every last drop was drained from his lover's body.

Vic managed to surface from his dazed fog of satisfaction. He moved up and lifted Miranda into his arms, carefully supporting her head as the three of them moved to lay lengthwise on the bed. He tucked Miranda in between him and Chase. His hands slowly traced the contours of her body, soothing her in the aftermath of the most powerful sexual experience of his life. The three of them lay in silence. Vic heart rate eventually calmed, and a pleasant lassitude took over his body. His fingers flexed as he remembered the astounding tightness and heat surrounding them as Miranda came a few moments ago. Vic imagined how that snug channel would feel rippling along the length of his cock and said organ jerked as it rested along the length of his thigh. Miranda's head rested on Vic's pillow. Her dark lashes created shadows against her soft cheeks, and Vic inhaled her delicate scent.

His fingers slid down towards Miranda's slit and he combed through the small triangular patch of hair at the top of her pubis. She moaned and her hips rocked up into his touch. When he dipped his finger between the folds, he found her still slick from her earlier orgasms. He took his time and slowly explored every ridge and valley of Miranda's labia. His thumb tucked inside and massaged her clit, which had begun to harden as Miranda's arousal increased.

Chase must have picked up on Vic desire for a second round of play because his head dipped to Miranda's breast, and Vic watched as Chase's tongue circled and flicked over the stiffening peak. Miranda's honey toned skin blossomed with a delicate blush and Vic kept an eye on the pulse at her neck. The artery throbbed as Miranda's heart rate increased, and that, combined with her little mewling sounds, convinced Vic she was as ready for this as both he and Chase were. Vic was surprised at his recovery time, but his cock stiffened with each second of watching Chase feast on Miranda's flesh. He hadn't been this horny since he and Chase started dating back in medical school. But at that moment, making love with the two halves of his heart became a biological imperative. Miranda and Chase's bodies cried out to him, and Vic was a slave to their siren call.

Miranda's eyes flew open and stared up at Vic. "You can't possibly…Again? Now?"

He tucked a long strand of brown hair behind Miranda's ear and smiled. "What can I say, princess? You're inspiring."

Miranda looked over at Chase, and Vic saw the same question in her eyes. Chase's response was to grind his pelvis against the outside of her leg. Vic looked down and smiled when he saw that Chase had obviously fallen under Miranda's spell as well.

Vic's finger dipped inside Miranda's vulva and met a fiery plush cavern he desperately wanted to feel surrounding his cock. Miranda let out a moan when Chase cupped both her breasts and brushed his thumbs across her nipples.

"Do you want us, princess?"

"Yes," She moaned when Vic added another finger to her pussy. "God yes, I want this. I want you."

It was as if her words were the sonic boom of a starting gun. Chase's lips attached themselves to Miranda's neck. Then her head tilted back on the pillow to give Chase more room as his lips moved down the graceful column all the way to her collarbone. Vic watched Chase place little licks across Miranda's skin, moving to the stiff tips of her swollen breasts. He caught a glimpse of a hickey from their earlier round on the side of the full curve.

Vic worked both his fingers in and out of her tight pussy, rubbing her clit and revelling in Miranda's increased cries of pleasure. Vic pulled his fingers out of Miranda's heat for amount of time it took to remove one of their condoms from the drawer and sheath his aching cock. As quickly as possible, he rolled back over and settled his body into the space between Miranda's spread legs. He nudged the crown of his cock against her pussy. He eased the head inside, and the polyurethane barrier did nothing to diminish the heat of Miranda's body. Vic gritted his teeth as he held his position. Chase helped Miranda lift her legs and place them on Vic's shoulders. He stared into the chocolate brown eyes of the woman he'd fallen in love with, and with one smooth thrust buried himself fully into her welcoming body.

Miranda gasped and dug her fingers into Chase's wrist. "Too much. It's been so long and we've already...I'm swollen."

Chase leant down and rested his forehead against Miranda's. "It's okay, sweetheart. Relax your muscles and your body will stretch to let Vic slide back and forth, in and out of your sweet little cunt."

Vic started to thrust, and at the rasp of Miranda's tissues against his already sensitised cock, he moaned. "You feel so good, princess."

He felt her getting slicker with every plunge, and what started out feeling good became incredible. It'd been a number of months since he'd fucked a woman, content for the most part to spend whatever time he could with Chase, but now all those dormant memories of how it felt to drive his cock into the soft, wet body of a woman came surging forward, and Vic's hips snapped as his momentum increased. Vic increased his pounding rhythm, driving his cock deeper with every stroke.

Chase's head descended to one of Miranda's cherry red nipples, and Vic saw his cheeks hollow as he sucked the treat into his mouth. Miranda screamed and her body bucked while her pussy clamped Vic's cock in a stranglehold of pleasure.

"Yes, princess! Squeeze me. Come all over my cock!"

Vic fucked Miranda through her climax, his body slamming in and out of her rippling channel with a vigour born from the deepest parts of his soul to claim this woman for his own. His balls pulled up tight to his body and his spine tingled, signalling his orgasm was only moments away. He wished he could have lasted longer, forever if possible, but physiology being what it was, there was only so much stimulation Vic could stand before he succumbed to the ecstasy clawing its way up from the depth of his body. The sight of Chase's head buried against Miranda's chest, and the way Miranda's pussy milked Vic's cock with each thrust, he knew he only had another few strokes left in him.

He closed his eyes and tried to recite the different types of radiopharmaceuticals in attempt to stall the moment when his cock would explode. He made it as far as fluorodeoxyglucose before his head arched back and Vic roared out his orgasm. He fell against Miranda, breathing hard before he gathered her smaller body close and kissed her with the same intensity at which his cock had recently claimed her body. The kiss rocked him to his soul and he held Miranda tight. Miranda moaned and moved into his arms. Chase's hand landed on Vic's shoulder and he opened his eyes to see his partner stretched out on the other side of Miranda.

Chase held up the bottle of lube, and Miranda stiffened in Vic's arms. He rubbed her back and tucked her head into the crook of his neck. "It's all right, princess. Chase is going to go nice and slow. We know your pussy can't take anymore tonight, but Chase is dying to be inside you. And we want you to get used to this because someday soon there will come a time when Chase and I will make love to you at the same time. We're going to fill you till there's no way your body will be able to separate our parts from one to the other. Then when we all come, Chase and I will fill your body with our seed till you overflow with our love."

"She's stretching beautifully, Vic. Her body wants this."

"See, princess? It's going to feel so good, I promise. I love it when Chase is inside me. He uses that magnificent cock to send you to absolute bliss. Is that what you want? Do you want to experience Chase's cock inside you, inside every part of you?"

"Yes," Miranda whispered.

"Good girl, I've got three fingers inside you, honey. I bet it burns a little, doesn't it?"

Miranda nodded and Vic smoothed her long brown hair away from her face. He kissed her softly. "It's a good burn though. I know it's a little scary, but as soon as Chase slides inside you, the burn will disappear and leave only pleasure."

Vic heard the crinkle of a condom wrapper and the squelch of the bottle as Chase slicked up his cock. Chase braced his hand on Miranda's hip, and Vic watched his partner move into position behind Miranda. Vic lifted one of Miranda's legs over his hip to open her further.

"Hold on to Vic, honey. I'm going to work my way inside nice and slow."

Miranda's hands flew to Vic's shoulders and her eyes went wide. He saw the dark orbs flare the moment Chase's head popped through the guardian ring of her rosebud. Tears pooled in the depths at the foreign invasion of the new experience. He kissed them away and murmured soothing words. Miranda's breathing grew very rapid and shallow, and her nails dug into his skin.

"Breathe with me, princess." Vic slid closer and let Miranda's chest rest against his. "Relax your muscles. It hurts more if you fight."

Vic looked over Miranda's shoulder, and saw the expression of utter concentration on Chase's face. Their partner's hips slowly sank deeper till they met the soft cushions of Miranda's ass. "He's in, princess."

"It's so good, honey. You're clamped tight around me. I can feel every little ripple of your body."

Chase's hips pulled back, and Vic smiled when Miranda tried to push back to follow the retreating cock. When Chase pushed forward once again, Miranda moaned, only this time Vic could tell it was from pleasure, not pain.

Miranda angled her head back and Chase met her mouth. He gave Miranda a slow, thorough kiss in the same rhythm that his cock sank into her body. Vic knew exactly how that slow possession felt, and his own hole fluttered in empathy.

His fingers slid down and gently stroked Miranda's clit, giving her another source of stimulation and pleasure. They took turns kissing her, and when Chase's hips began to move faster, Vic acted as an anchor for the storm of sensations whipping their way through Miranda's body. Groans of pleasure filled the room, and the intensity of emotion that swarmed Vic with the experience had him gasping right along with Chase and Miranda as they both moved closer to their orgasms.

Chase cried out and his motions behind Miranda increased. Miranda's nails dug into Vic's skin. Her body was slick with sweat as it rubbed against him. Vic worked her clit faster, keeping up with Chase's thrusts. The scent of sex was heavy in the air. Miranda's body went taught as a bowstring she screamed.

"Oh…God…Oh…yes!"

The sound that echoed from Chase's chest filled the room and Vic was very glad that his bedroom didn't share any walls with his neighbours.

* * * *

After they managed to get cleaned up, Vic had both Miranda and Chase tucked under the blankets as they all basked in the afterglow of an amazing night. He heard a soft sniff and opened his eyes. In the low light of the room, he saw a sheen on Miranda's cheeks. His heart slammed against his chest and his hand froze on Miranda's stomach. "What's wrong, princess?"

Vic saw Chase's eyes fly open, and his partner rolled on his side towards them. Their gazes met, and Vic saw a mirror of the panic that startled his system into full wakefulness. He looked back down at Miranda, watching a single tear track down her cheek. Another followed, and Vic's pulse kicked into overdrive. The woman he loved lay in his arms silently crying, and he had no idea why or how to stop it.

"Please, honey, tell us what's wrong," Chase pleaded.

"Did we hurt you?" *Dear God, please don't say that.*

"Was...was it something we did? Something we didn't do? Something—" Chase swallowed hard. "Something Vic and I did to each other?"

Miranda shook her head and wiped her cheeks. "I'm sorry. I didn't mean for you to..."

"Mean for us to what? To see you cry?"

"Ah love, never be afraid to tell us how you feel. Never be afraid to—"

Vic growled low in his throat. "He did that to you, didn't he? He forced you to shed your tears in silence. You were always subservient to his needs, his desires, never free to express your own."

Miranda blinked and her warm brown eyes so mimicked that of a lost little puppy that Vic howled internally at her pain.

"I had no idea it could be like that, is all. I was...I've never actually had a...let alone more than..."

Okay this was good. Vic could deal with this type of emotional overflow. He gathered Miranda close to his chest. Her head tucked into the hollow of his throat. Chase put his arm over the top of Miranda and rested his hand on Vic's hip. Chase nuzzled his lips against Miranda's temple then met Vic's for a soft kiss.

"We've only begun to show you the pleasure that can be found when you're intimate with a person you love. I promise you, princess, things will only get better from here."

"And as to the silent tears, sweetheart, no more. If you need to cry, you cry. If you need to scream, you scream. If you need to hit someone...aim for Vic, because I'm a big pussy."

Miranda laughed, and it was a balm to Vic's heart. Things were going to be okay. He rolled away for a moment to turn off the bedside lamp then the three of them wiggled around till each of them found a comfortable spot. Eventually Miranda ended up with her head on Chase's chest, and Vic spooned up behind her. "Goodnight my loves," he said.

Chapter Nine

Miranda's consciousness slowly swam to the surface. Every part of her body felt heavy, but amazingly enough her back didn't hurt as it did most mornings when she woke. She'd love to lie in bed and languish the morning away, maybe by reading a good book, but if the brightness of the room was any indication, most of the morning had been and gone. Axel must be crossing his legs and doing a little dance at this point.

Her eyes shot open and instead of finding herself nose to nose with a desperate boxer in need of relief, she found her vision filled with that of a well-muscled chest as she lay sandwiched between two octopuses. It was then that her short term memory recalled the activities of the previous evening, and Miranda found herself smiling and a little giggle escaped before she slapped a hand over her mouth.

"And what has you giggling this morning, honey?"

Chase's sleep-filled voice was especially deep and husky in the morning. The gravely sound rasped across the top of Miranda's head, and she snuggled deeper against his chest.

"I was thinking about all the scandalous things the two of you convinced me to take part in last night. I've never been so thoroughly debauched in my life."

Vic tightened his arm around Miranda's waist. "Hmm, and you loved every second of it, didn't you, princess?"

She looked over her shoulder and smiled. Vic's eyes were still closed but he had a smile on his face. "Well duh!"

This had both men chuckling and Miranda felt two pairs of lips on her skin—Chase's at her forehead, and Vic's on the back of her shoulder. Last night Miranda had sensed an awaking of her sensuality, and this morning the last lock on her heart opened. She prayed that the love of the two men she shared the bed with would keep it beating with the life force necessary to let her heart grow stronger, along with herself.

"So what's the plan for today?" she asked.

Chase reached over Miranda and rubbed Vic's biceps. "I suggest a communal shower, some brunch then we go rescue Calleigh from Axel. We can figure out what to do from there."

"And how do you plan for all three of us to fit in Vic's shower?"

Vic rocked his hips against Miranda's butt beneath the blankets. His morning erection made itself known and despite the lingering tenderness from the previous night, an image of three twisting wet bodies flashed through Miranda's mind, and her pussy softened with need. A low animalistic purr vibrated against her back.

"Have you ever really looked at my shower, princess?"

"No. It appeared to look like any other so I saw no need to explore further. Why?"

Vic rolled away from Miranda's back, and she jumped when his hand smacked her butt cheek. "Come on then."

Miranda turned onto her back and watched as Chase walked around the end of the bed to meet Vic. Their arms went around each other and their mouths met. She watched the slow morning kiss in fascination. Vic's head tilted to the side and his mouth opened. Chase's tongue slid between Vic's lips. Chase's hands grasped Vic's ass and pulled their bodies tightly together. Miranda's breath turned shallow as Vic began to rock against Chase. They continued to feast upon one another. First Chase taking control, then Vic. Earthy moans floated on the air towards Miranda and she shivered in arousal. *God almighty, that's some sight!*

Chase pulled back from the kiss and nipped at Vic's earlobe. "Shower, love. Let's all get to the shower and then I'll fuck you."

The need and love made Vic's blue eyes glow as if they were some type of otherworldly crystal. Miranda saw their cocks, both so hard and long, duelling with each other between their bodies.

"Promise?"

Chase looked over at her and Miranda nodded. She wanted to see them make love to each other, to be included in that part of their relationship. She never wanted Vic or Chase to feel as though they had to hide their love for one another, or that she expected them to only have sex with her. That wouldn't work. The two of them had a rich history, so full of sexual experiences, closeness and camaraderie Miranda never wanted to diminish its importance. If the three of them were going to make this work, a balance had to be struck.

Both Vic and Chase were bisexual, which meant that not only did they need and want her, but each other. So she knew there would be times that they'd want to spend with each other, just as she would want to spend time alone with each of them. To her, it wasn't the hours that mattered but the days, the months and the years. She wasn't naïve enough to believe it would be easy — the blending of three lives would present significant challenges — but right now she was the happiest she'd ever been. And deep inside, she knew her love for both Chase and Vic was more than a fleeting attraction to a new experience or a residual high from her unimaginable night of passion. It was deep, it was true, and with the most elemental part of her soul, Miranda believed it was meant to be.

She bounced across the bed and leapt off the high mattress. She ran past Vic and Chase, who by now were staring at her, and into the bathroom. Opening the glass shower door she stepped inside to find the controls.

"Holy crap, look at this place!"

She stretched her arms and turned in a circle. None of her fingers found the edge of a wall. Miranda looked up and found two wide shower heads suspended from the ceiling. She was so intent on her inspection that when the glass door was pulled open with a whoosh, her eyes flew to the opening too quickly, and she got a touch of vertigo for a second. Chase entered the enclosure and gathered her into his arms.

"I love this shower. It's so much nicer than the one at my place." He bent down and placed his lips against Miranda's ear. "Don't tell Vic, but one of the reasons I've kept him around was so I could shamelessly abuse my shower privileges over here," he said loudly enough for the words to echo in the tiled space.

She saw Vic smirk and roll his eyes. He reached for the control, and Miranda stepped back, expecting to be hit with cold water Chase held her still.

"Wait for it."

The water that came down as if it were a gentle rain from the ceiling was warm and soothing and so perfect. Miranda closed her eyes and tilted her head back to enjoy the spray on her face. She lifted her head and looked over at Vic. "How?"

"Tankless water heater. It provides instant hot water. The people that owned this place before me redid the bathroom. I admit, it was a major selling point."

Chase was still hard, and Miranda reached down, wrapping her hand around his cock. He moaned and she took that as an indication she was doing something right. Slowly her hand stroked up and down Chase's thick cock. Its presence was as large in her hand as it had been inside her body last night, and Miranda shivered at the memory of the pleasure she'd experienced. Her thumb glided over the crown and picked up the drops of precum that had leaked from Chase's slit. Miranda smeared the liquid around the plush head.

"God, honey, that feels so...makes me want to throw you up against the wall and fuck you till you scream."

"No, no. You promised this cock to Victor." She looked over at Vic, whose eyes were glued to the sight of Miranda's hand massaging Chase. "He's hungry for you. He wants to have you inside him, just as I had you inside me last night." Chase moaned and Miranda's hand dipped down to cup his balls. She rolled them in the palm of her hand, and gave them a little squeeze. "You want that too, don't you? You love to fuck Vic." She went back to stoking Chase's cock. "To slide deep inside him." Her hand formed a tunnel and Chase's hips surged, sending his cock gliding through her grip. "To feel his hard body pressed tight against yours. You love to see the tight muscles of his back bunch as you thrust harder and faster, Vic taking every inch of you and begging for more."

"Jesus, Miranda! Stop or you're going to make me come right now."

She giggled, joy radiating through her at the knowledge that she held a special power, one she'd never experienced in any previous relationship.

She looked over at Vic to get his reaction, and was struck by the iridescent glow to his eyes. He stalked the couple of feet that separated them. Vic pulled Miranda from Chase's arms and slammed his lips against hers. Miranda parted her mouth and Vic surged inside, kissing, sucking, his tongue completely dominating Miranda's consciousness.

Vic broke the kiss and leant his forehead against Miranda's. "You are the most amazing woman we have ever met."

Miranda stepped back till she leant against the wall. The tiles were cold on her back, but they help soothe her heated skin. Vic came towards her and used his larger body to pin her in place. She looked over his shoulder and saw Chase bathe his fingers with saliva. Miranda knew what was coming, and looked into Vic's eyes.

Chase's fingers touched Vic's entrance. The pads of one digit rubbed in circles around his hole before pushing its way inside. Vic leant in and captured Miranda in another blistering kiss. His tongue thrust in the same gentle in and out as Chase's finger invaded his body. A second finger found its way inside and the burn had Vic moaning into Miranda until his muscles relaxed and the pain turned to pleasure. God he loved this. Loved the softness of Miranda's body pressed against him, while Chase's muscled frame rubbed against Vic's back. Chase's fingers scissored deep inside Vic, stretching him enough so he could accept a third. By now Vic was pushing back into Chase's hand. Chase's mouth latched onto the side of Vic's neck. His teeth scraped against the skin and Vic broke away from his kiss with Miranda to angle his head, giving Chase more room.

He pushed up and down on Chase's probing fingers, desperate for something more. "Please," he begged.

"So impatient, my love." Chase said into Vic ears.

He growled. "Yes. Fuck me."

Vic looked down into Miranda's clouded eyes. Her lips were swollen and wet. A small hand encircled his cock, stroking and pulling on his shaft. Vic didn't know what he wanted more, to thrust into Miranda's grip or to shove back and bury Chase's fingers deeper into his body. His mind fuzzed out. He reached beneath Miranda's ass and lifted her up.

"Put your legs around my waist," he ordered.

With Miranda's pussy open, Vic probed the opening with his crown. The wet, silky juices coated his head, signalling that Miranda wanted this as much as he did.

"Vic, wait!"

He growled and glared over his shoulder.

"Condom."

Vic cursed. He couldn't believe he'd almost forgotten to protect the woman he loved. He wasn't worried about disease. He knew he was clean, but they'd never discussed birth control. Plus he and Chase had sworn that, until the time came when they either found a woman to make their life complete, or decided to renounce that part of their sexuality and commit one hundred percent to each other, neither would *ever* have sex without protection. In Vic's mind, they'd met the terms of the agreement, but he knew the three of them should still have the discussion.

Chase quickly reached around Vic and sheathed him, squeezing the base of Vic's cock the way he loved. Vic looked deep into the warm depths of Miranda's gaze, and surged inside her to the hilt with one thrust. The tight clasp of her body and her pleasure-filled cry echoing in the enclosure had Vic dangerously close to orgasm.

"Hurry the fuck up, Chase," he rasped.

The knob of Chase's cock nudged his opening, and Vic imagined he actually felt the head throb against his fluttering hole. Vic arched his back, and Chase began to fill him one slow inch at a time till his rod filled Vic's ass completely.

"Oh God," Vic moaned.

Vic was so full, stretched, fucking and being fucked, and when Chase hit his prostate, Vic's control broke and he roared out. Chase's arm came around Vic's middle, above where Miranda's legs had latched around him. Chase's hips pumped in a steady rhythm, and Vic picked up his lover's tempo as he thrust high inside the velvet wet heat of Miranda's body.

"Vic! Oh God, Vic."

Miranda's soft chant rang over their heads and Vic tightened his grip on the soft cheeks of her ass. His fingers slide between the globes and he rubbed against her back entrance. She groaned and Vic pushed the tip of one digit inside. Vic shuddered, his body in the throes of ecstasy. Chase pulled back in a long, slow slide only to surge back with such force that his name was ripped from Vic's soul.

"You're so beautiful. Both of you, so gorgeous, and so mine," Chase said.

Chase pounded in and out of Vic, Miranda's pussy milked Vic's cock as her climax closed in. Vic's knees started to shake as his pleasure increased, and he wasn't sure if he was going to be able to stand upright much longer. Sensing his dilemma, Chase crowded Vic closer to Miranda and pressed him tighter against the wall. With his hips practically pinned, Vic couldn't thrust so he shifted his grip to Miranda's hips and pulled her up and down on his cock. Her legs loosened enough to allow the new movement.

Miranda's channel locked down, and Vic's cock was bathed in her release. The heat of her body scalded him, and her inner muscles contracted with a strength had him moaning. Once Miranda's pussy released its death grip on him, Vic bounced her up and down till the tingling in spine worked its way down to his groin and erupted in a gut-wrenching explosion. His head arched back against Chase's shoulder and he roared out his orgasm, coming so hard he actually worried for the integrity of the condom. Chase's fingers clawed at Vic's hips and Vic tried to protect Miranda as he jerked with the force of Chase's thrusts. Miranda's hands unlocked around his neck as she pulled Chase into her embrace as well. Chase impaled Vic with his rigid length one last time before Vic felt Chase's cock pulse deep inside him.

They all stayed still, one leaning against the other till their breathing slowed, and their heart rates returned to some semblance of normalcy. Chase slowly withdrew. The sting in his well-fucked ass made Vic hiss. Miranda's legs seemed to lose all strength, and if Vic hadn't been holding her up, she would have fallen into a heap on the floor of the shower. Vic removed his condom then handed it to Chase, who took care of disposing them outside the enclosure.

Vic held Miranda close, their bodies swaying in the warm water. Another benefit to the tankless heater meant no shortage of hot water. If Vic wanted to stay under the water till he became a prune, then he'd shrivel up under a waterfall of warmth.

"I love you," Vic whispered to Miranda.

"I love you, too," she mumbled into Vic's chest.

Chase came back in, stood to the side of them and wrapped both Vic and Miranda in his embrace. "My loves, my treasures. You've made my life complete."

* * * *

Chase leant back against the padded bench at the quaint little bistro in Beacon Hill where he and Vic had decided to take Miranda for brunch. His lovers sat across from him, and the sight of their clasped hands on top of the white linen made him smile. Vic was pointing out items on the menu that he recommended, while Miranda was playing footsie with Chase under the table. The waiter approached with the glasses of orange juice all three of them had ordered.

He set the glasses down on the table then pulled out his notepad. "Have you decided what to order?"

Vic looked over at Miranda and she nodded. "My girlfriend would like the roasted mushroom omelette with cheddar cheese, egg whites only please. And I'll have the roasted pepper frittata with onions, potatoes and cheddar cheese."

The waiter looked over at Chase. "And you, sir?"

"I'm going to have the open-faced grilled chicken with mint and almond pesto, and mozzarella. And a side of fresh fruit please."

Chase watched the kid scribble away before he flashed a tip-winning smile and said the food would be out shortly.

Once alone, he placed his hands on top of Vic's and Miranda's. "So loves, I was thinking that since it looks like today is going to be top out around eighty-seven that we spend the day in the pool at my building. You can bring Axel over, and we'll all spend the day drinking and frolicking in the water."

"Sounds perfect to me," Vic said.

Miranda chewed on her lower lip for a second. Chase could see the wheels in her brain spinning. He wondered what she was thinking about. Did she not want to spend the day with them? Were they moving too fast for her? He'd heard Miranda tell Vic that she loved him that morning and, while he thought she felt the same for him, he was still waiting to hear those all-important words.

"Honey?" Chase asked, softly.

Miranda smiled and met Chase's gaze. "I think that would be fun."

Chase released an internal sigh of relief. He gave Miranda's hand a squeeze then sat back against the cushions once again. Their plates were delivered in short order and the smells from the food made Chase's mouth water. He set the bread away on a side plate and proceeded to cut into his chicken breast. He moaned as the first bite hit his tongue, and the flavours of the pesto mingled on his taste buds.

Miranda and Vic appeared to be enjoying their meal as well since they both dug in with gusto. *Then again, we all did use up quite a few calories over the past fourteen hours.* He smirked and Vic lifted his gaze to Chase's with a questioning look in his eyes. Chase shook his head and stabbed a piece of cantaloupe then shoved it in before his mouth could get him in trouble.

Miranda's cell phone buzzed on the table. She'd set it down after calling Calleigh to let her know that the three of them would be over in about an hour to pick up Axel. When she picked up the phone and looked at the read out, she frowned. Chase set his fork down and took a sip of his water, keeping a watchful eye on Miranda's expression as she flipped open the phone and put it to her ear.

"Hello?"

Miranda was silent for a minute and Chase saw her fingers tighten on the napkin she'd placed on the table. When her eyes went wide and started to fill with tears, he kicked Vic under the table to get his attention. Vic looked up and Chase nodded at Miranda. Vic immediately put his fork down and placed his hand on Miranda's back.

"I understand. I'm not really sure what to say. We've been divorced since January. Are you sure there's nobody else?"

Chase didn't like the sound of this conversation. If it at all involved Miranda's ex, he knew nothing good could be a result. Since he and Vic had met and started to woo Miranda back in May, they'd slowly seen her shed the emotional baggage the bastard had left her with. The frightened and traumatised woman who'd run from them upon their first meeting had slowly blossomed into a vibrant person, whose self-esteem and confidence had grown incrementally day by day.

"Yes, I'll take care of it. I'll see about making arrangements and getting to Chicago as soon as I can."

Chicago? What the hell?

Chase met Vic's gaze and saw a mirror of shock and concern looking back at him. If Miranda had to return to Chicago, there was no way Chase would to allow her to do so alone. Either he or Vic would be going with her. Miranda shut her phone and stared down at the table. She pushed her half finished plate of food away.

"Princess? What's going on?"

Miranda swallowed once, then again, and when she couldn't seem to find her voice Chase pushed her glass of water towards her. "Take a sip, honey," he said softly.

Miranda lifted the glass of water and placed it against her lips, but didn't drink. She set it back down then looked at Vic and over to Chase. "Drew's dead. Apparently he slept with the wrong woman, and a jealous husband took offence. They've arrested the husband and he's made a confession. That was the police, they're asking me to come back and make arrangements since I was still listed as Drew's next of kin. They say there's nobody else."

Chase was caught off guard. This was probably the last thing he expected to hear. One part of him was glad the son-of-a-bitch was gone and out of Miranda's life for good, and another could see that despite everything, Miranda was upset by the news and that saddened him, making him want to reach out and comfort her.

"Okay so we're going to the windy city. I always have wanted to visit Navy Pier," Vic said.

Miranda's head jerked up and Chase smiled at her. "You didn't think we were going to let you do this alone did you?"

This time Chase could tell that the tears filling Miranda's eyes were of happiness and relief. He wished that the infernal table between them would disappear so he could pull her into his arms. Vic had no such restrictions and Chase watched as his partner gathered their woman into a hug. Miranda's head was turned towards him, and Chase gave her a wink to let her know that everything was going to be all right.

Chapter Ten

Miranda stood beside the hole in the ground where Drew would be laid to rest in a matter of moments. She looked up into the clear blue sky filled with the bright sun, and had trouble reconciling the beautiful day with what should be sombre moment in time. A warm hand rested on the small of her back and she leant into Chase's touch. She heard the minister's voice as if he spoke from a great distance, not really able to focus on his words.

Over the last few days, her emotions had run the gamut from anger at Drew's continued reckless behaviour to sorrow that such a young life had ended violently. However, deep in her heart—in the part she was actually afraid to examine—Miranda knew a black hole existed where a demon resided, laughing in glee that karma had caught up to her ex-husband.

"Ms. Green, are there any words you'd like to say?"

"No, Father. I've made my peace with Andrew Harper."

Chase pulled Miranda close, and she was thankful for his support. She was glad that Chase had been able to rearrange his schedule so he could be there. Unfortunately Vic hadn't been so lucky. Instead of focusing on Vic's absence, Miranda wanted to use this time to strengthen her bond with Chase. Her eyes widened as she realised she was contemplating using this little get away to spend time with her new boyfriend, while standing over the grave of her ex-husband.

Dear God, what kind of woman am I?

She tried to listen to the priest's words. To soak up their reverence and remember the good times she and Drew had before things turned bad, but unfortunately they'd had more bad times than good and despite wanting to find a kernel of warmth within her to mourn, all Miranda felt was numbness.

Finally the service — what there was of one with only her, Chase and the priest present — ended. Miranda stared down at the gunmetal grey casket.

Goodbye, Drew.

And that was all she could think of to say. Miranda turned and started walking back towards their rental car. The cemetery was one Miranda was unfamiliar with, but had been recommended by the police detective she'd met with upon arrival. Apparently it got used often for individuals who didn't own or have the means to pre-purchase family plots. Price was a concern because Miranda had to pay out of her pocket, and while she didn't intentionally want to cheat Drew of a comfortable final resting place or casket, neither did Miranda feel the need to spend more of her hard-earned money than necessary.

Chase opened the passenger car door and as Miranda moved to step in, a car came around the corner of the drive at a rather quick speed. Chase moved behind Miranda as though to shield her when the other car's brakes screeched when it pulled up behind them. A middle-aged gentleman with salt and pepper hair and designer suit quickly approached them.

"Mrs Harper! Please wait! I'm so glad I caught you!"

Miranda straightened her shoulders and turned to face the frazzled arrival. "It's Ms. Green. Drew and I were divorced as of January."

The older man stopped suddenly and had a confused look on his face. "Really? My client never mentioned getting a divorce."

"And you are?" Chase asked.

"Sorry, how rude of me. Albert Thomas. I'm an attorney Mr Harper retained about three years ago. I need to discuss with you his last will and testament."

Mr Thomas looked back and forth between Miranda and Chase. He frowned, but the expression disappeared as quickly as it had arrived.

"And you sir?"

"I'm Doctor Chase Pruitte, Miranda's significant other."

Miranda crossed her arms. "Chase will be present for anything you have to say to me. You're not the attorney who mediated our divorce. I didn't even know that Drew had a will."

"Be that as it may. It doesn't change the conditions of the will. Mr Harper, rest his soul, made some stipulations I think you will find very interesting."

"Mr Thomas I can't imagine anything about my ex-husband's life that I would find interesting. I divorced him for very good reasons, and if you truly knew your client then I think you'd probably not think so highly of him."

Mr Thomas stared at Miranda with a blank look, and she knew she'd made the man uncomfortable but at that moment she couldn't have cared less.

"I can't answer that for you, Ms. Green. However, the fact remains that Mr Harper did leave a will, and you are named as the beneficiary. When I read of his death in the papers I tried to contact you, but was unsuccessful with the information we had on file."

"I moved to Boston four months ago."

"Well, that explains a few things. It was when I called the police that they told me I might find you here, today. If you'd be so kind to accompany back to my office I'd like to go over everything with you."

Miranda looked up at Chase. She wasn't quite sure how to react. Was this guy for real? It wasn't too much of a surprise that Drew had made a decision such as this and never said anything to her. Miranda had accepted that she never really knew anything about her ex-husband's life.

"Let's follow him back to his office, and see what he has to say, honey. Then we can put all this behind us."

She looked back at Mr Thomas who stood there nodding and smiling. "Okay." She slid into the car and leant back against the head rest with her eyes closed. She'd developed a killer headache in the last ten minutes and wanted nothing more than to find a quiet place to rest for a couple of hours, but it seemed Drew had one last trick up his sleeve.

Miranda heard the driver's side door open and the car rocked as Chase sat in the driver's seat. After closing the door, he started the ignition and cool air blew over Miranda's heated skin. She sighed and opened her eyes when Chase lifted her hand to place a kiss on her knuckles.

"Hopefully this won't take very long then we'll go back to the hotel so you can rest for a few hours. I know you're trying to process all this and can see the tension in your shoulders. You have a headache, don't you?"

She nodded.

"When we're done for the day, I'll give you a massage. We'll order room service and spend the night alone in our room. It'll be quiet and peaceful. I think that's really what you need most right now."

Miranda smiled for what felt like the first time since she got the call at the restaurant three days ago. "Thank you. I know I should be reacting, but it's as if my emotional slate has been wiped clean when it comes to Drew. Do you think I'm a bad person because of that?"

Chase squeezed Miranda's hand. "No, honey. I'm no professional counsellor but I imagine that, with everything you dealt with as Drew's wife and how hard you've worked to overcome those effects, maybe it simply means you really have moved on with your life. Maybe you'll get to a point where you want to cry, maybe you won't, but neither possibility makes you a bad person in my eyes or Vic's or anyone else who truly knows you."

Miranda thought her mother would most likely disagree with Chase's opinion, but she really didn't want to open up that can of worms. She looked out the window. Here she was, back in her hometown. Maybe twenty minutes away from the house she was raised in, and yet Miranda had no desire to contact her parents. Did that make her a terrible daughter?

They drove in silence, following Mr Thomas' car back into the heart of downtown. Miranda let Chase worry about navigating the crazy streets, and was very glad to find that he wasn't easily rattled. They pulled into a parking garage and a few minutes later Miranda stepped into a large suite with a wall of glass facing Lake Michigan. She found herself looking out at the view rather than peeking around the obviously well-appointed office. Miranda had come to love Boston Harbour with all its rich culture and history, but there was something to be said about the blue expanse of water of her home town.

"Please Ms. Green, Dr Pruitte, have a seat."

Miranda and Chase both sat on a sofa along one wall and Mr Thomas retrieved a folder from his desk before sitting across from them. He opened the green file and looked down at the contents for a second.

"Now I could read this word for word, as sometimes families prefer to hear the actual words of their loved one, but I get the feeling that in your case that wouldn't be appreciated, am I correct?"

Miranda nodded. "Please just tell me what I need to know."

Mr Thomas picked up a pair of glasses on his desk. "Very well. The long and short is that Mr Harper left to you one hundred percent of his estate. Since you and Mr Harper were legally divorced at the time of his death, you will not be responsible for any of his incurred debts. However, Mr Harper did take out a whole life term policy shortly after your marriage, and according to my documentation you are listed as the beneficiary. I have a copy of Mr Harper's death certificate, and if you have the time, we can visit the insurance company's office immediately. They are conveniently located in the building."

Miranda didn't know what to say. She wasn't even quite sure what to think. The concept of Drew in essence giving her a gift was such a foreign concept that her mind had trouble processing the information. Still, her and Drew's relationship issues had nothing to do with Mr Thomas or the insurance company, so she simply nodded her head and Mr Thomas escorted them up to the eighteenth floor where Miranda, Chase and Mr Thomas were shown into the office of Mr Wynn who worked for Lakeland Term Life. Mr Thomas showed Mr Wynn Drew's death certificate and in short order they were all seated.

"Now, as a matter of protocol I must ask you a few questions. May I see some identification to verify that you are in fact Miranda Green formerly Harper, the true beneficiary listed on the policy?"

Miranda took her wallet out of her purse and removed her driver's licence then handed it over to Mr Wynn.

"Thank you. You needn't worry that this will be a complicated process. Mr Harper had a whole life insurance policy with us. In the event of his death, the beneficiary of the policy – that would be you – is the recipient of one hundred and fifty thousand dollars. You have two options in regards to the payout. We can do an electronic transfer for the lump sum or you can set up monthly instalments. There are no taxes on the benefit, so the decision is strictly based on whether or not you want a secured income or would rather receive the bequest all at once."

One hundred and fifty thousand dollars? Holy Shit!

"I...I...oh my God," she whispered.

"I'll give you a few moments to talk it over with your attorney and companion."

Miranda didn't bother to correct Mr Wynn assumption that Mr Thomas was her attorney. She watched him leave the office, speechless. She turned to Chase whose face showed no reflection of his thoughts. "What do I do?"

"What do you want to do, honey?"

"I have no idea. I feel almost guilty for even accepting it. I mean Drew's and my life together was over. I was *glad* it was over."

"And yet, even after the divorce Drew continued to pay on the policy and never changed the terms. We'll never know why, but he must have had his reasons."

"Well I can tell you that it wasn't out of guilt. Drew didn't know the meaning of the word. I'd wouldn't be surprised if he'd set up the payments to be deducted automatically and simply forgot about them. I can't even imagine what possessed him to set up the policy in the first place. I was nothing more to him than a convenience."

That sounded bitter even to her, but the words had escaped before she even realised they were about to. Miranda had been so focused on putting her daily life with Drew behind her, it seemed there were a few deeper emotions still churning inside her. She didn't want any part of her former marriage to touch the relationship she was building with Chase and Vic. Maybe she should talk to a professional.

"I'm sorry. That...that was—"

"Honest. It's okay, honey. God knows that I have a few uncharitable thoughts about Drew Harper rolling around in my head, and I didn't even know the man. He hurt you, and *that* is unacceptable."

Miranda took a steadying breath. "So what do I do now?"

"Ms Green, may I say something?" Mr Thomas said.

Miranda nodded.

"I can't begin to understand the intricacies of your marriage to my former client, but I would say take the money and use it as you best see fit."

Miranda waited to see what Chase had to say. She could practically see the threads of thoughts in his clear blue eyes, and was dying of curiosity to know what her man was thinking. Miranda had been in awe of Chase's mind practically from the moment they met. His skills as a doctor and surgeon were some of the best in his field, but more than that, Chase was also a wonderful person. He always treated the support staff with respect, he'd been able to let Miranda into the heart he'd already reserved for Vic, and it always made Miranda's heart go a little mushy to watch Chase play with Axel as though he were a little boy.

"I know that since leaving Drew, something that has been important to you is making your own decisions. And obviously we're talking about a lot of money here. So I need to ask, do you really want me to tell you what I think you should do, or do you want me to listen while you talk out your own ideas?"

Miranda smiled at Chase's earnest expression. Those had not been empty words, and that meant so much. Since regaining control of her life, she'd been very protective of her independence. The first couple of months after the divorce, Miranda had spent a great deal of time discovering exactly who she was at this point in her life, rather than whom Drew had moulded her into. When she went to the grocery store, she'd initially found herself automatically reaching for items she'd bought because Drew had expected to have them, and once she'd realised the habit, Miranda had spent several weeks tasting and experimenting with different foods to find out exactly what *she* liked.

Since Drew had kept her in the dark when it came to their finances, control over her accounts was extremely important to her. In the beginning, Miranda had obsessively checked the balance of her bank accounts. Chase and Vic had apparently picked up on her behaviours. She never argued with them if they offered to pick up the bill when they went out, but she made sure to offer to do the same whenever possible.

But Chase was right. This was *a lot* of money. More than Miranda had ever even imagined being within her control. It was a little daunting, and since she suspected Vic and Chase probably made at least three times what she did, she'd be stupid to turn down the opinion of someone who was more familiar with managing significant assets.

"I do want to hear your opinions, and I will definitely take your suggestions into consideration."

Chase smiled. "Okay then. I think you should take the lump sum. Take a portion out now to use what you need to gain immediate stability, and put the rest into a diversified investment fund so you have financial security in the future."

"Sounds reasonable, but I don't have any idea how to invest money. I wouldn't even know where to start. My idea of financial security is having a couple of hundred bucks in a savings account."

Chase put his hand on Miranda's knee. "Vic or I would be happy to introduce you to the guys we use or we can ask either of them for a recommendation if you want to work with someone different."

Miranda nodded and was about to lean in to kiss Chase when the office door opened and Mr Wynn walked back in. He came back over to the chair and sat.

"Have you made a decision?"

"Yes, I'll take the full payout."

"Very good. I believe that is a wise decision. While the monthly instalments are a good idea for some, as young as you are, you have an opportunity to invest the money for greater gains in the end. All we need is your bank information, and we'll get the electronic process started."

Miranda lifted her chequebook and pen out of her purse. She wrote 'void' in huge letters across the front of a cheque then handed it to Mr Wynn. "Will this work?"

Mr Wynn reached across and accepted the check. "Perfect. This should only take a few moments. We'll have some final paperwork for you to sign then you can be on your way."

"Thank you."

Mr Thomas stood and held out his hand. "I believe my presence is no longer required. I wish you the best of luck, Ms Green."

Miranda shook the attorney's hand, and after he left the room, she found herself leaning into Chase's side. His arm came around her and she snuggled in close.

Chase kissed Miranda's forehead and tightened his arm around her. "How's your headache?"

"It's a little better. I'm still liking the idea of a quiet night in the hotel room though."

"You wish is my command."

* * * *

Chase straddled Miranda's hips and kneaded his hands into her shoulders. Chase worked steadily on the smooth silky skin until the hard muscles beneath became pliant to his touch. They were both naked in bed and Chase tried to keep his awakening body from becoming obvious as he worked the muscles of Miranda's neck, shoulders and back.

"I've been thinking," Miranda said.

Chase smiled at the way her voice sounded with her face burrowed into the pillows of the bed. "You're not supposed to be thinking. You're supposed to be relaxing."

"I'd like to take a portion of the money and donate it to some foundation or something that supports victims of domestic violence." Miranda wiggled onto her back and looked up at Chase. "It took a long time for me to get up the nerve to leave him, and when I did, it was like the blinders came off and I'd been tossed into this huge world naked. I can't help but think about those men and women who are stuck in situations two or three times worse than I was. Where there's physical abuse or if they have children and they have to live everyday in fear that their spouse will hurt the kids if they don't protect them. Maybe even live knowing that the babies are also abused, but trapped in the vicious cycle with no idea how to find a way out. I know that part of that fear is the unknown. The *what if*. What if a life out there is worse than the life I live here? I knew I wasn't happy with Drew, but some part of me always accepted that unhappiness. I grew from not only complacently accepting his abuse to expecting it as my due. You hear someone tell you how worthless you are enough times, and you eventually believe it. If I can help just one person break out of that cycle, then I don't care if it takes all the money, it'll be worth it."

Chase's chest hurt at Miranda's words. He moved off to the side and pulled Miranda against his chest. Part of him thought he might be crushing her, but he couldn't help it. He needed her in his arms. He needed to know that she was there. Whole, healthy, happy. Listening to her talk about her life with Drew was always difficult, but Chase had forced himself to listen quietly as she slowly worked her way out of the darkness that had encapsulated her during her marriage. To hear her say she had actually come to believe the degrading words Drew had spewed at her made a tear come to his eye. His and Vic's Miranda was a beautiful, sexy, intelligent and loving woman. Every time Chase heard her laugh, his life became a little brighter.

It was amazing how she'd brought him and Vic closer together. Before, they'd been content to spend whatever time they chose to be together. Both recognised the love between them, but neither had been able to take that final leap and commit their lives to one another. However, now all Chase wanted to do was be with Vic and Miranda. He found himself searching out Miranda on the days he did surgery, even if she wasn't on his team. On days he spent in his office, he'd spend his lunch break on the phone with Vic or the two of them would sneak away for some quality time together. There were some perks to having your lovers work in the same hospital complex as you.

Chase speared his hand through her hair, dragging her head towards him as he forced her lips to meet his. He needed to show Miranda how desirable she was, how much he hungered for her touch, her taste. He needed to prove to her that she was everything to him and Vic. Once he'd got her attention, Chase backed off to place, sharp little kisses all over her lips. He nibbled and licked the already swelling flesh. Her soft lips begged for his touch with their simple existence. He scooted closer and came halfway over Miranda's body. Their lips melted together as Chase gathered her close. Their heads tilted and it became a battle to discover who would capitulate to the need for air first. Chase was determined that it wouldn't be him. Who needed air, when they had the taste of Miranda keeping them alive?

Miranda was busy with her own assault. Her busy little tongue licked at his before drawing back. Her chest arched against him, knowing Chase loved the feel of her soft breasts shoved against his hard body. His lips tugged at hers, sipping from them. Miranda's body may not have been virginal the first time he and Vic had made love to her, but in many ways her mind was, and Chase tasted the inexperience which sent his need raging. Eventually Miranda would recognise her own power, and God help him and Vic when she did.

Miranda's sweetness was something that called to Chase's soul. He craved her like a drug. Now that their relationship had moved to the stage where he could sample her kisses and body to his heart's content, Chase knew he'd become an addict in no time. His lips moved over hers and his tongue pressed its way inside. A whimper echoed from Miranda's throat and her hands gripped the thick strands of his hair, much as Chase loved Vic to do. She must have picked up on that kink of theirs. Miranda tasted of fresh fruit and hot summer nights. A rough growl left his throat as his lips slanted over hers and he jerked her to him.

Miranda's hard nipples pressed against his chest. The tips made of velvety flesh that Chase loved to roll around his mouth and flick with his tongue. He actually suspected he gained more pleasure from sucking Miranda's breasts than she did. His thorough research to date had exhibited that the full mounds weren't actually that sensitive, but every time he paid homage to Miranda's chest she would comb her fingers through his hair and smile down at him as though he were bestowing a wonderful gift. For that smile alone, Chase planned on continuing to beg for his treats for the rest of their lives.

Chase was so ready, so hard, so desperate to have Miranda's pussy surround him in a chamber of pleasure. Chase lifted his head to stare down at the woman he loved. Her dark was hair fanned out on the stark white pillow, her eyes were half lidded with arousal and her lips crept into a little smile that nearly took his breath away.

"You are so beautiful." His lips dipped to the hollow of her throat and he felt the moan vibrate against his kiss. His hand slid down her body, spending a few moments at her breasts. When he pinched one nipple hard, Miranda moaned and arched up into his hand. His eyes flew to her face, but all he saw was pleasure. He did it again and this time Miranda's sweet lips opened and her breathing increased. Maybe it just took a stronger touch? He knew that Miranda most likely hadn't been comfortable to say the words out loud, and the discovery made him smile. Now Chase had another tool to drive Miranda crazy.

He lowered his head and licked at the elongated peaks. His hand slid down her body, following the curves and soft swells he loved so much. When he reached the bare lips of her pussy, the liquid satin of her body's response coated his fingers. Chase slid his touch between the folds and followed the slit down to the opening of her vagina.

"Chase, please don't tease me."

"Not teasing, honey. Loving. I'm gonna love every inch of your body tonight. I'm going to throw everything in my arsenal at you to capture that amazing heart that beats in your chest."

Miranda cupped Chase's cheek. "But it's already yours. Yours and Vic's. I love you Chase Pruitte, as much as I love your partner. The two of you have taught me to smile again, and I'll be thankful for every second you want to keep me around."

Chase's spirit soared and he closed his eyes in thankful prayer. "Well then you'd better get comfortable because we plan to hold onto you for the rest of our lives."

His lips took hers again, his tongue plunging deep into her mouth as his finger rimmed the tight circle of her opening. Hot cream poured from Miranda's body, and when Chase pushed his finger inside, the inferno of plush tissue had him groaning. Miranda's legs spread, and Chase moved between them. He moved down and pressed her thighs wide, staring at the succulent flesh weeping for him. Chase lay on his stomach, and his stiff cock rocked against the mattress searching for something to ease the ache burning inside him. Chase stuck his tongue out and licked through the narrow cleft of her pussy. Miranda's cream coated his tongue, and Chase felt as though his would shatter from the pleasure of Miranda's taste.

He licked gently, lapping up everything she had to offer and when her hips rocked against him searching for a deeper touch, Chase lifted her ass up from the mattress and buried his mouth against her. Miranda cried out and twisted above him. Her hands clutched at his hair, the needy tugs ratcheted Chase's arousal higher. "God you taste so good. So sweet. I could spend hours down here loving you." Chase sucked her clit between his lips. His finger circled the fluttering entrance to her pussy then slid inside the flesh that griped him in a silken vice. He nibbled at her clit, the blood making the tiny bud so red it stood out against the peaches and cream tone of the rest of her skin.

Chase added another finger to Miranda's pussy and probed deep inside her. He pushed up against the back of her pelvic wall.

"Oh God!"

She came apart around him and Chase couldn't hold back another second. He rose up between her thighs and positioned himself at her entrance. He rubbed the head of his cock around her entrance and cursed as her hot juices coated the sensitive skin. Chase closed his eyes and wished beyond anything and everything in existence that he could bury himself in Miranda's body with nothing between them, but he and Vic had made a promise. Chase had stuck by that promise to the letter, and he knew he couldn't break it now. Not when he had everything he ever wanted within his grasp.

He reached over the side of the bed and lifted out the strand of condoms from his carry-on. At quickly as possible, he sheathed himself and flung Miranda's legs over his shoulders. He worked his way inside Miranda's tight pussy. He grimaced and his chest heaved at the feel of her folds separating. The tissues surrounding his dick still rippled from the force of her orgasm.

Chase used strong, steady thrusts as he worked his way inside. Tension filled his body as he fought the desire to ram home. Chase had slept with a fair number of women over the years, but none of them had ever called to his body or soul the way Miranda did.

"So perfect, honey. Nothing and nobody compares to being inside you. So fucking tight, so wet. You burn for me. For us." He jerked her against him and pierced her to the hilt.

"Chase," she moaned.

He tried to stay still till her muscles accommodated his invasion, but when Miranda started to rock her hips, his brain turned off and his body took over. He moved in and out. His cock slid through her channel, the movement eased by the cream flooding from Miranda's womb. She jerked in his arms, pleading him to go faster. His cock thrust inside her, at first slow and easy then fast, hard and deep, penetrating in long strokes till he brushed her cervix.

Her expression held him spellbound — suspended in pleasure as Chase plunged into her over and over. He came over her and his lips covered hers roughly. Miranda's hips rose and the new angle made Chase brush against her G-spot with every stroke. Her body tightened around him and he fucked her fiercely, long hard strokes that had Miranda screaming, and had Chase on the verge of an earth shattering orgasm. He plunged his tongue deep into her mouth as his chest rasped across her breasts. Chase's entire body was on fire, and only Miranda's sweetness could douse the flames.

He pulled her into his arms and buried his face in her hair. The silky dark curtain covered him. Her nails pierced his shoulders and her legs locked tight around his waist. Miranda's pussy convulsed around him, milking the seed from his balls. When her little teeth bit the tendon of his neck, semen rushed from his body in an explosion that had him shaking and bellowing out her name. The moment was perfection personified as Chase's soul filled with pleasure.

Chapter Eleven

Vic paced outside airport security. The screen showed that Chase and Miranda's plane had landed ten minutes ago, and he itched to have them back in his arms. He'd never been as disappointed as when he realised that it would be impossible to arrange the time off to go with them to Chicago, but at least Chase had been there to support Miranda. He'd talked to them several times over the last five days, but the sound of their voices over the phone was nothing compared to hearing them in person.

He looked over the crowed, smiling when he saw Chase's dark blond hair heading his direction. He couldn't see Miranda through the throng of people, but when his and Chase's gazes met, Vic was rewarded with one of Chase's million watt smiles and Chase bent over. Vic saw his mouth move, his eyes never left the sight of those firm lips, and inside he danced in anticipation of feeling them against his again.

Chase and Miranda had said that they had a surprise to share with him, and Vic had his own churning in his gut. Excitement and a touch of fear bubbled in anticipation at their reaction.

When Chase and Miranda made it past the checkpoint, Vic rushed them and scooped Miranda up into his arms. He lifted her high against him and kissed her hungrily. Chase's hand landed on his shoulder and squeezed. Vic leant back into the caress.

They made their way through the terminal and out to where Vic had parked. As soon as all the car doors were shut, Vic pulled Chase into his arms and took those firm lips under his command. God he wanted to eat Chase alive, to feel his lover beneath him, in front of him, riding him… Vic didn't care, but it'd been five long days since they'd made love and he was a bit desperate.

"We're going to my place. I have something I need to share with you both, you can tell me all about the surprise you've been keeping from me then we'll all spend the night making love till we collapse from exhaustion."

Vic saw Chase and Miranda share a little smile and his heart tugged in happiness that the trip had given them the opportunity to grow closer. Vic had an ulterior motive for wanting to go to his place. Since the collapse of a ceiling panel in the Fort Point tunnel a couple of weeks ago, killing a woman and injuring the family member who'd been driving, traffic in the city was twice as bad now as it had been before with the closure of the structure. Vic wanted to go to his place in Charlestown because he could avoid the major construction areas of the dig project.

Avoiding traffic completely wasn't realistic though, and when they came to a standstill on Washington, Vic caught a glimpse of Chase and Miranda snuggling in the back seat in his rear view mirror. The blare of a horn jerked his attention back to the road, but Vic found his way still blocked. He never understood why people insisted on honking in the midst of a traffic jam. It wasn't as though the annoying blare would magically make the cars move any faster.

He cruised his way along until the turn for the Charlestown Bridge came up and once free, it was only a few more minutes until they pulled up in front of his condo. "All right you two, enough canoodling. Come inside where we can all share the love."

All of them exchanged kisses and touches as they piled their way in his front door. There was a bark from his little back garden, and Miranda ran over to the patio doors. She greeted Axel by kneeling in the earth and wrapping her arms around his sturdy neck. Vic had loved having Axel spend the week with him. Miranda's dog had kept him company with both his lovers being gone, and they'd shared a couple of nights chilling out in front of the television together. When Miranda came back inside, Vic pulled her into his arms and backed her towards his living area. They tumbled onto the sofa and Vic luxuriated in the feel of Miranda's soft body beneath him. A large hand stroked the skin of his back beneath Vic's T-shirt and he arched up into Chase's caress.

"Vic...love? Talk first, make out later."

Vic lifted his head from Miranda's lips and mockingly growled at his partner. "Easy for you to say — you've had her all to yourself for almost a week, while I've only had Axel and my hand to keep me company."

Chase's head swooped down and captured Vic's lips in a blistering kiss. His toes curled in his shoes and his cock hardened against Miranda's stomach. Just as Vic's eyes were about to roll back up into his head from the pleasure, Chase pulled back.

"I promise we'll make it up to you." Chase smoothed his hand over the top of Vic's head.

Vic sat up and pulled Miranda into his lap. Chase sat next to them, pulling Miranda's legs over his quads and wrapping his arm around Vic's shoulders. "This is nice," he said.

"So who wants to go first," Miranda asked.

"You go ahead, princess."

Vic listened as Miranda told the story about Drew's final surprise. To say he was shocked would have been an understatement, but part of him also looked at the bequest as a restitution of sorts. He knew the money would make Miranda's life easier. She never said how much debt she'd incurred as part of the divorce, but Vic had got the impression that paying it down took a substantial portion of her weekly paycheque. When she told him that she wanted to donate part of the money to a domestic violence foundation, Vic gathered her close against his heart. "I love you more each and every day."

"So what's your news, love?" Chase asked.

Vic smiled. "I got a promotion."

"That's fantastic!" Chase and Miranda exclaimed.

"They made me director of the musculoskeletal imaging and intervention division."

"But I thought you specialised in nuclear radiology?" Miranda asked.

"I actually did fellowships in both nuclear medicine and musculoskeletal radiology. I really loved both aspects, but it just happened that I was offered an attendee position in nuclear first." Vic looked over at Chase. "Lately I've been feeling a little burnt out." He adjusted Miranda on his lap and ran his hand up and down her bare arm. "The last several months I've been talking to the other physicians in the department about making a change. I'd heard that the position had opened up and I put in for it, basically on a whim. When Carrington came to see me the other day, I figured he was about to laugh in my face, but instead he said the hospital had made a decision to hire from within house and out of all the applicants, I had the most experience and potential to run the division efficiently. They offered me the position."

Miranda wrapped her arms around Vic's neck and squeezed. "I'm so proud of you."

Chase tilted Vic's head over towards him and they shared a kiss. "Congratulations, love."

"That's not all." Vic took a deep breath. This could either go really well or really poorly. "I found us a house."

Both Miranda and Chase went completely still. He couldn't tell if it was a good still or a bad still. If they were simply surprised or furious. Had Vic gone too far? Was he being presumptuous in his assumptions that now that the three of them had committed to each other that it was time for kids and dogs everything he and Chase had talked about wanting someday? Vic and Chase were thirty-eight. He was ready to settle down, but maybe he had moved too fast. They'd only known Miranda for a few months. She was only thirty-four, and had just got out of a bad marriage. Maybe she didn't want to lock herself back in. Hell, maybe she didn't even want children.

"I'm sorry. It's too soon. Forget I said anything."

Vic put Miranda aside and got up off the sofa. He walked over to the patio doors, somehow finding a smile when Axel came up and tilted his head in that funny way that made Vic think the dog was actually thinking about you. He heard a soft whine through the glass, and placed his hand on the cool barrier. Axel went up on his hind legs and one of his paws landed opposite Vic's hand. His heart lurched at the thought of not being able to play with Axel in the big backyard he'd toured the other day.

"Vic?" Miranda asked, softly.

"Yeah."

"Come back over here, please?"

He turned and saw Chase's arms wrapped around Miranda. He felt as though he was going to his execution as he crossed the room. Their faces were unreadable, and that wasn't a good sign. Most of the time Vic had no trouble reading his lovers, but right now they were completely closed off to him. He sat at the end of the sofa and faced them.

"Will you tell us about the house?" Chase asked.

"You…you want to hear? I thought—"

"You mistook our shock for anger. We've never talked about when we'd move in together. Miranda and I have just walked in the door from what was a rather emotional trip, and you dropped a little bomb on our laps. Forgive us, love, if we seemed a little rattled."

Vic scooted closer to the two people who meant more to him than anything in the world. "No, no it was my fault. I've kept this little surprise inside me for almost three days, then blurted it out without any consideration or preparation." He took one hand of each of his lovers in his. "I guess the most important question we all should ask each other is 'Do we want to live together?'"

"I know that if I went and asked some psychologist about their opinion, he or she'd tell me that moving in with you would be a big mistake. That's it too soon after everything that happened with Drew, and that I'm probably using my love for the two of you as a crutch to avoid healing the wounds deep inside me. They may even question whether I truly love you? That somehow I'm misinterpreting the emotions of experiencing my first positive adult relationship."

Vic's shoulders fell and he nodded slowly. Miranda's words hurt, but he knew there would be those out there who wouldn't be shy about saying exactly that.

"But every day I spend with you, I step further away from the woman I was back in Chicago. When we're together you make me smile, you make me burn, you make me realise that I'm so much better than I ever gave myself credit for. I see the truth of your love in your eyes, and I can't think of a better way to start each and every day than looking into that light, knowing I make your life complete."

Vic's vision swam and he blinked away the emotions brought on by Miranda's words. He looked over at Chase—always his friend, and his lover off and on for more than a decade.

"You know I always wished for a someday. Now that we've found Miranda, I can't believe you'd think that desire would magically disappear."

Vic closed his eyes and said a quick silent prayer of thanks. When he opened them both his lovers had smiles on their faces, and Vic knew that presumptuous or not, he'd done the right thing after all.

* * * *

Chase moaned as Vic's tongue rimmed his hole. Miranda's lips met Chase's and their tongues slid together. He pushed his ass back, begging for more from Vic's talented tongue. The man always said Chase was the more oral of the two, but Vic could give a rim job that sent Chase's mind reeling.

Vic tongue speared his ass at the same moment Miranda's thrust into his mouth. He was being possessed by both of the people he loved, their puppet of pleasure. They could move him any way they wanted. Torture him with their kisses. Send him to the rafters as their hands stroked his body from head to toe, and Chase would love every second of it.

He heard the snap of the lid to the bottle of lube seconds before the cool gel hit his skin. Vic's fingers circled his pucker, while his mouth attached itself to Chase's neck. Miranda's hand encircled his cock right as Vic's finger slid inside him. Chase had difficulty concentrating, his attention flitting back and forth to the pleasure of Miranda's soft hand stroking his dick to Vic's fingers pumping in and out of his ass.

Chase opened his eyes to see Miranda watching him. The brown depths sparkled with passion, desire and love. Vic's demanding hands transmitted the deep emotional connection Chase had with his partner. But right at that moment Chase craved a different kind of connection.

"Please," he begged.

"Please what?" Vic whispered against Chase's ear.

He angled his head back towards Vic. "I need you inside me, I've missed you."

Vic fingers rubbed inside Chase, sliding over his gland. It was as if Vic had set off a sparkler inside him — a long, drawn out flare of light that burned brighter and hotter the longer Vic played with him. Chase's body trembled and Miranda soothed the vibrations with her hands and lips. She peppered Chase's chest with kisses, and when her tongue flicked over his nipple, Chase's hands threaded through the long, dark tresses he loved and held her to him.

Vic nuzzled Chase's neck, taking deep breaths. "You smell so fucking good, babe. I've missed you too. I've missed you both."

Vic sucked on the hollow beneath Chase's ear then nipped at the skin. His fingers stretched Chase's hole. Miranda's soft suction on his nipple nearly drove Chase insane. Chase moaned, "Oh yes." Miranda's warm tongue flicked against his nub, and if he didn't know better he would have sworn that there was a direct connection between the nerves of his nipple and his cock. Miranda's thumb collected the fluid leaking from his slit and rubbed it around the mushroom shaped crown. Chase's hips surged forward, which meant he pulled away from Vic's fingers. He was trapped between heaven and hell.

"More," whimpered, not caring how desperate or unmanly it made him sound.

"What kind of more?" Miranda whispered. "This kind?"

Miranda's hand slid beneath Chase's nuts and one finger traced the patch of skin back to Chase's entrance. With a little pressure she also pushed her way inside him.

"Oh Fuck!" Chase bore down to take more of his lovers inside him. They were both there, both inside, both touching the deepest part of him. Chase gripped the base of his cock to stave off the orgasm that threatened to rip through him.

"So gorgeous. So ours," Vic chanted. "Look at you all flushed and straining into our touch. You need something more, don't you babe? You need my cock inside you. You need Miranda's sweet pussy taking you to heaven."

"Yes! I want it." They didn't pull out and Chase felt Miranda's smaller finger bump his gland, working the kernel till sweat beaded on Chase's brow, and his voice became horse from pleading upon their mercy.

The second their fingers left him, Chase wrapped his arms around Miranda and rolled on top of her. Her legs automatically separated and lifted to rest high around his back. Before conscious thought prevailed, Chase roared out and buried himself deep inside her soaking passage.

Miranda's cry filled the air and her arms and legs tightened around Chase. His hips jerked back and slammed into her. Miranda would have sworn that her insides shook with the force of his thrust. But there was no pain, only mind exploding pleasure as her body had come to crave both Chase's and Vic's possession. She now understood the pleasure of sex, the ecstasy that could be experienced in a lover's arms. Chase grabbed the backs of her knees and held them straight-armed out to the sides. The muscles of her inner thighs stretched and Miranda was thankful for the yoga classes she'd been taking recently. Chase's knees came up and he crouched over her bent body, pounding his thick cock all the way in her with a force and speed that shook Miranda's small frame and made Chase bellow. Chase came over her and captured her mouth, taking ruthless possession with his tongue as he had with his cock. She rocked against him, echoing the movement of his tongue in her mouth. When he tried to pull back, Miranda dug her fingers into the long strands of hair at the back of his head and took charge of the kiss, exploring his mouth, the shape of his lips, feasting on the sexy male taste of him.

Chase managed to separate his mouth from Miranda's. His lips grazed her ear as he said hotly, "You burn me alive with your fire, honey. Your sweet pussy clenching my dick, your heart racing against mine. I love you. I love fucking you. Come for me, Miranda."

The control her men had over her body was unreal. All they had to do was whisper a few sexy words in her ear, and Miranda became a willing slave to their passions. Chase slid his hands under her butt, canted her hips up and slid back and forth across her clit. That was all it took to make her come, moaning harshly, convulsing in his arms. Her pussy pulsed around Chase's cock and her cum flooded from her body. The sounds of wet slapping skin filled the room.

"It's not enough, not near enough. Give it to me again, honey. Give us everything you have, everything you are."

Unbelievably Miranda found herself once again racing up the mountain and jumping off the precipice into bliss.

"Yes, love!"

Vic's hands gripped Chase's hips and held him prisoner. Chase fought against the restriction as Vic's cock nudged against his entrance. Chase relaxed and Vic's next push had him sliding halfway inside. Chase's heat surrounded his bare cock and Vic fell atop his lovers as his mind shorted out in pleasure for a moment. It was the first time he'd ever gone bare with a lover and to share the experience with both Chase and Miranda made Vic eternally thankful they'd waited for this moment.

"Sweet fucking Jesus," Chase groaned

"That's it, babe. Take it all. Take us both." Another push and Vic's cock slid all the way in.

Chase had stalled partially inside Miranda. Vic looked over Chase's shoulder and saw her dark eyes begging them for more.

"Move, Chase, our princess needs you." Vic ordered. He pulled back and then surged in. "Follow me."

Chase did. Vic set the pattern, and their cocks pumped slowly at first, their thrusts rhythmic, intentional, controlled.

"Harder," Miranda said from below them.

Vic picked up the pace and Chase followed. Vic fingers dug into the flesh of Chase's hips, driving Chase into Miranda. He'd become the ultimate puppet master. Vic grunted as his balls slapped Chase's and he took his lover deep and fast. The scent of Miranda's arousal filled the air and Vic knew before the night was out he'd be buried inside the woman he loved, feeling her soft wet walls cling and pulse around him. He couldn't wait to fill Miranda with his seed. The very thought of Miranda pregnant with his or Chase's child had him climbing higher and further than he'd ever gone. Each slam of his throbbing cock into the inferno of Chase's ass had Vic groaning.

"Fuck! Yes!" Vic shouted.

"Touch yourself, honey. Make yourself come all over me," Chase said roughly.

Vic saw Miranda's hand slither down her chest, but couldn't see when her fingers strummed the nub, making him growl.

"Not so delicately, honey. Make it count. Milk that clit. I want to feel you shatter around me again. I want to see your little body thrash as hot explosions rip through you. Give it to me, Miranda. Give it to us. Now!"

"You heard him, princess. See all these glorious muscles standing out? Chase is so close, so hard he probably aches. His ass is so tight around me. He wants to come. He wants to fill you to the brim with his cum."

"Oh...my... God!" Miranda cried.

"That's it, baby! That's it. Oh fuck, Vic...you should...I can't..."

"Let go, babe I've got you. I've got you both."

Chase's orgasm swamped him and Vic felt his chute ripple and clench down around his cock. Vic's hips pumped, his rhythm faltered then burst into a final series of rapid thrusts. He stiffened. It felt as though his body turned inside out, and his heart was about to explode from the cavity of his chest. He poured his soul into Chase as he slammed hot jets of cum into one of the two people who held his heart.

Epilogue

Two months later

Miranda flipped the switch for the master bedroom light and heard a twin set of gasps behind her.

"Holy toledo!" Jenna gasped then dashed into the bedroom. "I've never seen anything like it."

Miranda looked around the room she'd decorated with Vic and Chase. She'd been adamant that her lovers help her. She wanted her men to be as comfortable in this room as they were in the rest of the new house, since she planned on spending a lot of time in here over the years. The walls were painted a creamy slate blue, and the dark stained wood of the floor and mouldings set off the colour to perfection. Chase had found a massive sleigh bed, and all three of them had gone to find the perfect mattress. Blue curtains with gold accents hung from the bow windows that made up the tower, as Miranda called the concave feature in the front of the Victorian home built at the turn of the twentieth century that Vic had found for them in West Newton Hill.

Their bedroom had a fireplace with an elegantly carved wooden mantel, as did seven other rooms in the house, and was connected to a remodeled ensuite that had a massive shower and Jacuzzi tub all big enough for three. At first, Miranda had been a little nervous around the lavish accents. The floor, shower lining, bath and vanity tops were all white and grey marble. There was a small crystal chandelier that hung from the ceiling and the fixtures were all made from original Victorian glass. The entire bathroom exuded a luxury that was completely foreign to her. But, the rest of the house was warm and comfortable. In Miranda's opinion, the house was the perfect blend between modern conveniences and contemporary styling with a traditional flair. It spoke of traditions and family. Darkly stained hardwood blended with the cream coloured walls and soft fabrics of overstuffed furniture. Vic and Chase had taken over the study whose entire walls were comprised of carved wooden panels and windows lining the wall overlooking their side yard.

The yard was bigger than any Miranda had ever seen in her life. The kitchen and family room were all one big open space. The family room had two sets of French doors that opened up onto a covered porch, and a door leading out to the backyard from the kitchen served as the anchor to a large slate patio that now held a couple of extra large lounges and a fire pit.

"Okay, unless my counting skills are rusty I've added up fifteen rooms. How many square feet is that?"

"I think somewhere around fifty-six-hundred."

"Holy shit, girl!" Jenna exclaimed. "Damn, I should've hit on Dr Pruitt when I had the chance."

Miranda knew Jenna was kidding, but she felt her fingers clench in indignation that Jenna even joked about taking her men away from her. Not to mention she made a slightly veiled reference to Miranda's new home being a prize of some kind. This home was the realisation of Vic's and Chase's dream, and Miranda was the lucky woman who'd been granted the blessing of their love. They'd found her, fallen in love with her, made her fall in love with them and now the three of them had made a home together. They'd spent two months talking about and planning exactly how they wanted to decorate it. Which rooms would belong to the children they hoped to have, which rooms would be for guests. Vic and Chase had even built a home gym in the basement so the three of them could maintain their workouts as fall turned to winter, and a recreational room where all their friends could gather.

When she walked in the door from work, Miranda didn't enter a house, she entered a home. And, if she were honest, it was the first one she'd had in her life. So if she was a tad protective, it was only to be expected.

"Jenna, that was crass," Calleigh admonished.

Jenna blushed. "Sorry, it's just that this place is so cool. I'm a little jealous."

Miranda went over to Jenna and hugged her. "It's okay."

Miranda looked over at Calleigh who face scrunched up as she rubbed her protruding stomach. She hurried over and placed her hand over Calleigh's. "You okay?"

"Yeah, probably indigestion. Happens a lot now that I'm at thirty-six weeks."

"You're not going into labour are you? Any lower back pain?"

"No, no back pain. The other day my obstetrician said that I was dilated two centimetres, but she didn't expect anything to happen for at least another week."

"Have you talked to Kevin recently?"

Calleigh nodded and continued to rub her stomach. "He's in Baghdad. I told him I'd try and call when the boys arrive." Calleigh looked over at Miranda with tears in her eyes. "I wish he were here."

Miranda held Calleigh close. It was hard to see her friend so emotional. Over the past several months, they'd become close and while Miranda knew that Calleigh loved her husband it was hard to see the loneliness on her face. When Calleigh had asked Miranda to be her birthing coach, Miranda had tears of her own.

"I know, sweetie. But soon you'll have two beautiful little babies to lavish your love on and before you know it, Kevin will be home."

"But they keep saying that the bombing is getting worse over there. I was watching the news the other day and..." Calleigh sniffled and wiped at her eyes. "I heard that something like thirty two soldiers have died this month alone."

"Cal, you can't do that to yourself. You know right now your emotions are all over the place, if you do nothing but sit there was watch depressing news reports, you'll make yourself go crazy," Jenna said.

Calleigh sniffed again and a wavering smile crossed her lips. "Miranda, you think I could maybe use one of your four bathrooms for a moment?"

Miranda laughed and pointed towards the ensuite. "Right through there."

She kept her eye on Calleigh's back. She was so focused on her friend that she jumped when a pair of strong arms encircled her waist from behind.

"What has you so jumpy, honey?" Chase said.

"I'm a little worried about Calleigh. Maybe she should stay here with us. I don't think she should be alone right now. It's getting close to her due date and she's really emotionally fragile with Kevin being gone and —"

"Okay, princess." Vic said as he walked into the room. "Why don't we offer her the green room? The soft mint walls and cream drapes you picked out are very calming. Maybe it'll help soothe her."

Miranda held out her hand for Vic and he came over. She stood between her men, surrounded by their love and closed her eyes to inhale their mingling scent. Her body responded predictably as did Vic's and Chase's, as evidenced by the bulges pressing against her lower back and stomach. She heard Vic and Chase exchange a kiss over her head and smiled.

"Wow, that's hot," Jenna said from the far side of the room.

Miranda peeked out from between Vic and Chase — in truth she'd forgotten about Jenna's presence in their bedroom. Jenna looked back and forth from the bed to Miranda, Vic and Chase, then back again. Miranda giggled when she heard a low moan come from her friend.

"Miranda?"

She turned to see Calleigh standing right outside the bathroom door. Her lower lip was caught between her teeth and one finger twisted around a stand of honey blonde hair.

"What's wrong?"

"How long does it take you to get to work from here?"

"About twenty minutes. Why?"

"Cause I'm pretty sure my water just broke."

The room erupted. Vic and Chase went into doctor mode and rushed over to Calleigh's side. Miranda calmly walked over to her dresser and pulled out a pair of yoga pants. She walked over to Calleigh and with one hand up silenced the entire room.

She held out the pants. "Don't worry about any clean up in there, but do you need any help with yourself?"

Calleigh shook her head, took the pants and disappeared back into the bathroom.

"All right, gentlemen. Vic, go get your car, it'll be easier for Calleigh to get into than Chase's SUV or my Jeep. Jenna, call labour and delivery tell them that we're on the way and with whom. Chase, call Dr Sandborne and tell her that Calleigh's water has broken."

Everyone rushed from the room to do their chores and Miranda rolled her eyes. Her lovers and friend had acted more like a gaggle of geese than a group of highly trained medical professionals. She stepped up to the bathroom door and knocked softly. "They're all gone," she said through the panel.

Calleigh opened the door with a soft giggle. "Is it always like that with those two?"

"No, most of the time they're pretty quiet guys. So give me the scoop."

"I figure maybe five minutes apart, and the last one was around sixty seconds."

"To the hospital for you, madam. Let's go."

"What about my bag?"

"Give me your keys. I'll have Jenna pick it up on the way. It'll give her something useful to do."

"Thanks, Miranda."

"No, thank you, Calleigh. Accepting your friendship was one of the first steps I took in this new beginning that's given me a blessed life. That will always be something I cherish, and if you ever need anything all you have to do is say the word."

* * * *

Miranda lay in bed with Vic and Chase as dawn crept over the horizon. They'd just finished making love and she was warm and snuggled between the two men she loved.

"So Brandon and Michael are good names," Vic said.

"Yeah, and did you see Calleigh's face when her and Kevin's call was finally connected? I could hear his shout from across the room," Chase added.

Miranda still floated on a haze of pleasure. When they'd got home, the three of them had barely made it to the bedroom before they ravished each other. When Vic had slid deep inside Miranda's ass and Chase had filled her pussy to the brim, they'd taken her higher and made her come so hard she'd backed out for a second. The emotions of the night had been so overwhelming for all three of them that their orgasms had drained the last of their energy, and now she wanted nothing more than to sleep in their arms, secure in their love for her and each other.

"You know, princess. You looked pretty good with Brandon in your arms."

Miranda placed a kiss against Vic's chest. "As did you with Michael. You think Calleigh will let us come over every once in a while?"

Chase nuzzled Miranda's hair and his arm tightened around her. "I'm sure she will."

"Good, because I think the three of us could use the practice."

Chase and Vic stiffened against her. They rolled her onto her back and loomed over her.

"Why is that, honey?"

"Because I think it'd be nice to have some idea of what we're doing…seven months from now."

"You're… We're…" Vic stuttered.

"Pregnant?" Chase asked at the same time.

Miranda nodded, smiling. When two sets of pleasure-filled blue eyes stared down at her in wonder, she laughed and held out her arms. Chase and Vic crushed her to them, and Miranda knew that in her lovers' arms, she'd finally found the life she always dreamed of. A life with perfect balance.

About the Author

If you look up the word conundrum in the dictionary, there should be a photo of Trina Lane. Her personality is so multifaceted that her friends have spent countless hours scratching their heads in wonder. A scientist with a passion for history, music and photography she loves to travel and experience new places but is terminally shy around people she doesn't know.

Trina has been devouring romance novels since her tender teenage years, although only began writing two and half years ago. When her debut novel was met with resounding success, she said "Hey I can do that again". The rest as they say is history.

Her choices in reading and writing material are as diverse as her iTunes library, which contains music from Mozart to Metallica. Her one concession is all stories must have a happily ever after ending-did we mention she's incurably romantic?

She lives in Missouri with her loving and indulgent husband, and orange tabby cat–affectionately referred to as 'Houdini' for his stealthy escape attempts.

Trina Lane loves to hear from readers. You can find her contact information, website details and author profile page at http://www.total-e-bound.com.

Total-E-Bound Publishing

www.total-e-bound.com

Take a look at our exciting range of literagasmic™
erotic romance titles and discover pure quality
at Total-E-Bound.